The Long Way Back to You

Welcome to Redemption, Alaska

The Other Side of Goodbye
The Long Way Back to You

PRAISE FOR
The Long Way Back to You

"This was an anticipated sequel in the fantastic Redemption, Alaska series! McCahan perfectly balanced her second-chance love story with redemption and mystery. I hope we get to know more about these two in another sequel, as I wasn't ready to say goodbye to them yet!"

— The Literate Leprechaun, Goodreads

"Gritty page-turner ensures readers late nights or wee hours of the morning. Family baggage creates fallout when mixed with the emotional toll on adult children. The give and take for much-needed forgiveness weaves through the storyline and frozen landscape. Local, pesky wildlife sprinkles humor into the drama. Enjoy!"

—Kim, Goodreads

"*The Long Way Back to You* is a heart-warming romance about second chances, second chances, family dynamics, and family legacy."

—Allyson, Goodreads

"Second book in this Alaska series about second chances. Great characters that struggle with life and choices. Romance, faith and family relationships."

—Joni, Goodreads

WELCOME TO REDEMPTION, ALASKA

The Long Way Back to You

HEIDI MCCAHAN

The Long Way Back to You
Welcome to Redemption, Alaska - Book 2
Published by Sunrise Media Group LLC
Copyright © 2026 Heidi McCahan
Print ISBN:978-1-966463-21-4

All rights reserved. No part of this publication may be reproduced or transmitted in any form or by any means without written permission of the publisher.

This book is a work of fiction. Names, characters, places, and incidents are either products of the author's imagination or used fictitiously. Any similarity to actual people, organizations, and/or events is purely coincidental.

Scripture quotations taken from the (NASB®) New American Standard Bible®, Copyright © 1960, 1971, 1977, 1995, 2020 by The Lockman Foundation. Used by permission. All rights reserved. www.Lockman.org

Additional scriptures taken from the Holy Bible, New International Version®, NIV®. Copyright © 1973, 1978, 1984, 2011 by Biblica, Inc.™ Used by permission of Zondervan. All rights reserved worldwide. www.zondervan.com The "NIV" and "New International Version" are trademarks registered in the United States Patent and Trademark Office by Biblica, Inc.™

For more information about Heidi McCahan please access the author's website at the following address: HeidiMcCahan.com.

Published in the United States of America.
Cover Design: Sunrise Media Group LLC

For my family

One

THESE THRILL-SEEKERS WERE EITHER FEARLESS or fried.

Every time extreme skiers boarded his chopper, Luke McGuire had to remind himself that the resort needed the money. Because their quest for epic powder only made his job harder.

Luke gripped the cyclic control, the steady thrum of the chopper vibrating under his hands, and tried not to think about all the ways this trip could go sideways. Through the windshield, he surveyed the endless, jagged expanse of Alaska's Chugach Mountains. An unforgiving, steep wilderness cloaked in miles of pristine snow. The sun glinted off razor-sharp peaks, dazzling white against the brilliant blue sky, but he wasn't in the mood to appreciate the view.

"Yo, Captain Luke." One of the skiers' voices crackled through the headset. "Are you taking us to the secret backcountry location or what?"

The guy reeked of marijuana and sweat. His two friends weren't any better. Super rowdy with their crude jokes, and laughing like hyper middle schoolers instead of taking it seriously that they were minutes from hurling themselves down a near-vertical slope.

"Slow your roll, fellas," Luke said, leaning forward to gauge the best place to land. "If you want to ski, you'll stay put until our skids touch the snow."

His brother Ethan, riding in the copilot seat, shot him a look. "Relax. They're just pumped. It's going to be okay."

Luke huffed, his grip on the controls tightening. "I'm counting the minutes until we're on the ground."

"Don't you remember how it was when you were young and wild and free?"

"Hmm. I wasn't quite that free," Luke said.

In the back, one of the skiers let out a whoop and slapped his buddy's shoulder. "Bro, this is gonna be sick! Best heli-skiing in the world right here!"

Luke dragged his hand down his face. "We'll be on the ground in just a minute."

"You're such a buzzkill," the third guy grumbled.

Laughing, Ethan shook his head. Luke glared at him.

Ethan turned his laugh into a cough. "At least they paid up front. Right?"

Luke didn't respond. Instead, he focused on the controls, guiding the helicopter toward a plateau carved out like a cereal bowl between surrounding peaks. Tight landing, but he'd done it a hundred times before. His gut told him not to waste time finding a better spot.

"Hold on. We're coming in."

The skiers barely acknowledged him, too busy shouting at each other about who would drop first, how the powder looked "gnarly" and "wicked," and who was going to film what on their GoPro.

Luke ignored the noise and eased the skids onto the snow with a delicate bounce.

"All right, out," he said, flipping the switches to keep the rotor spinning at idle. "Grab your gear and stay clear. Got it?"

"Yeah, yeah, we got it. We're professionals, man," one of them said, laughing.

The trio spilled out onto the snow, still laughing and jostling each other as they pulled their skis and gear from the cargo rack.

"Hey, I'll pick you up at Lookout Point at three thirty," Ethan called, leaning out the door. "Don't be late."

"Chill, dude," one of the guys called back, waving a gloved hand. "We won't stand you up."

"Somehow I'm skeptical." Luke blew out a sharp breath, his patience fraying. "They seem like they kind of enjoy ignoring deadlines and itineraries."

Ethan slid the door closed. With a wave, Luke lifted the helicopter off the ridge. The skiers turned into specks below them.

"Man, stoned adrenaline junkies are not the way to go," Luke said, adjusting his headset.

"You say that, but these guys are keeping the lights on. No clients, no income. You know the math."

Luke gritted his teeth. "I know the math. I've seen the numbers. Doesn't mean I have to like it."

"Last time I checked, it's not like we've got a line of tourists waiting to book accommodation in March," Ethan said. "Not with Redemption still half-wrecked from the tidal wave."

"Don't remind me." Luke altered their heading, cutting around a fog bank drifting in off the bay. "Dad shouldn't have let those volunteers who came to clean up stay for free. It's killing us. We barely had enough money to fix the generator last month."

"Dad's tenderhearted these days. You know that. Ever since he got hurt..." Ethan's voice softened, tapering off as if he was unsure how much to say.

Well aware, thank you very much.

Luke swallowed back the snarky words. Ethan had spent twenty years saving lives—rescue swimmer, aviator, Coast Guard hero. Luke was proud of him. Really, he was. But sometimes, when he thought about everything his older brother had accomplished, it was hard to ignore the ache of what could have been.

Ethan had flown off to adventure and purpose, while Luke had stayed behind, trading his own dreams to keep the resort operating after the fire. Someone had to step up. And Luke didn't regret the choice. How could he? Family came first. But that didn't mean it was easy.

"To your point, that's why I booked as many extreme skiers as I could. But I'm regretting my decision. They're trashing the place and getting high. Did you see the mess that last group left? Beer cans everywhere, a hole in the drywall..."

Ethan exhaled, shaking his head. "Repeat after me: This is all temporary. We have to make it to May. Once the tourists show up, we'll be back on track."

"You think Dad's going to let people keep staying for free all summer?" Luke tightened his grip on the cyclic. Part of him felt bad about complaining. He didn't want to admit how much it worried him—how much Dad's generosity, while admirable, made him feel like they were teetering on the edge of a cliff.

"Hope not," Ethan said. "Are you planning to talk to him, or should I?"

Luke hesitated. "I'll try."

They fell into silence, the sound of the rotors filling the space between them. Below, mountains gave way to dense forests and half-frozen creeks that fed into the bay.

As they passed over a peninsula jutting out into the water, Luke spotted a house sitting alone, shingles missing from the roof and windows boarded up. The old Carlisle place.

That ache in his chest, the one he worked so hard to ignore, flared to life. Emma. He hadn't thought about her in months, but seeing her family's property brought it all back. Her laugh. Those gorgeous eyes. The freckles on the bridge of her nose.

Where was she now? Did she ever think about Redemption?

About him? He hadn't set foot near the place since she left town almost two decades ago. Redemption had chewed her up and spit her out, so she and her mother had fled. He couldn't blame them. Not really. But she'd left him behind and never looked back. And that part still stung.

He should've been over it by now. Should've let go of the hope that she might come back, that they could ever be what he'd once imagined. But some stubborn, irrational part of him still clung to the notion, like a splinter he couldn't dig out. And now, here he was, thirty-five years old, single, childless, and clinging to a failing business.

What a legacy.

"You okay?" Ethan's voice broke into his thoughts.

"Yeah. Just noticing the Carlisle place. It's a mess."

Ethan raised an eyebrow. "Didn't you, uh, have a thing for the girl? You're not still hung up on her, are you?"

"No," Luke said quickly. Too quickly. "It's just weird, you know? Feels like another lifetime. I don't understand why they're letting it fall into disrepair."

Ethan didn't push, thankfully.

The peace didn't last long though.

"Hey." Ethan leaned forward, pointing through the windshield. "Do you see that?"

A thin column of smoke curled up into the sky. It was coming from the direction of their resort. Luke's stomach dropped.

"That's us," Ethan said, his voice tight.

Luke adjusted the controls, bringing the helicopter around for a better view. "Maybe somebody's burning trash."

"That doesn't look like a trash fire," Ethan said grimly.

Squinting through the fog, Luke kept his eyes on the faint orange glow flickering through the trees.

The smoke was thicker now, black against the sky. That wasn't just a pile of burning debris—it was a cabin. One of their cabins.

"No," Luke muttered, his pulse racing. "Hang on. I'll have us on the ground in a minute."

Ethan grabbed the radio, already calling it in. "Redemption Base, this is Helo One. We've got a structure fire on the south side of the property. Repeat, structure fire. We'll need assistance."

Luke's mind spun, tamping down memories of the last time they'd battled a fire at the resort. He couldn't think about that. Not now.

But the same old fears pushed to the surface. No amount of repairs or blind faith seemed to be enough these days. A single thought echoed. Relentless. Unshakable.

How much longer could he hold this place together?

―

Boston's rush-hour traffic was about to ruin her Friday night.

Blasting his horn, the Uber driver pumped his brakes to avoid rear-ending a luxury SUV. Snow fell in thick wet flakes, forcing the windshield wipers to work overtime. Emma Carlisle tugged a black cocktail dress over her sports bra, then tipped sideways in the back seat when the car suddenly sped up. She smacked her elbow against the window, wincing as pain shot up her arm. The silky fabric snagged against her leggings, and the semi-sheer insets clung to her torso.

Ugh. This thing was so not her style. But her future mother-in-law had given her the designer dress and insisted it was perfect for tonight's celebration.

Sighing, Emma shimmied the fabric over her hips, then peeled off her leggings and stuffed them into her black knockoff Birkin handbag.

The driver glanced at her in the rearview mirror. "Everything okay back there?"

"Just fine," she said, struggling to free her curls from the keyhole closure at the nape of her neck. Oh brother. She untangled her hair with one hand and dug through her bag for her earrings with the other. Maybe staying late at the gym to help one of her favorite clients finish that last set of ten burpees had been a questionable choice.

The car jolted to a stop at another red light. Gritting her teeth, she glanced at the digital display on the dashboard. Seven minutes until Kendall's party. At this rate, she'd be lucky to make it before dessert.

Emma shivered. The sleeveless dress offered all the warmth of tissue paper, and her short suede boots, still stuffed in her bag, weren't going to help. She should've worn the emerald-green pantsuit—her style, her color, and her choice—but no. She'd caved. Again.

The bitter thought lingered as her phone buzzed against the seat beside her. Emma grabbed it, half expecting the usual check-in from her fiancé, Nathan. Instead, it was Abbie, one of her best friends from middle school. Emma tapped the screen to accept the call, then held the phone to her ear. "Hey, girl. What's up?"

"Don't panic," Abbie said. "But my bridesmaid's dress is back-ordered. Until July sixth."

"Oh. Wow. That's—"

"Less than a week before your wedding. I know." Abbie sighed. "I called three other stores, but they all said the same thing."

The car lurched forward, tires spinning on the snow-slicked street. Emma clutched the overhead handle.

"Emma? You there?"

"Yeah. Listen, um, don't stress. It's not a big deal." Emma forced a laugh. "I'm sure it will all work out."

Abbie paused. "Really? That's not what I expected you to say."

"Well, to be honest, that dress is the least of my worries. I stayed late helping a client hit a personal best. She just got divorced and wants a fresh start. Long story. Anyway, now I'm rushing to a party for Nathan's sister, Kendall. She made partner at her law firm."

"That's nice of you," Abbie said. "I'm looking forward to meeting Kendall at your shower in June."

"Yeah, that will be fun." Emma cradled her faux-diamond earrings in her palm. Frankly, the thought of her Alaska friends meeting her East Coast people made her palms sweat.

"I'm sorry about the dress. I'll keep you posted," Abbie said. "Are you sure you're okay?"

Emma hesitated. "Yeah, I'm fine. Why?"

"You don't sound like you. Oh, hang on." Abbie muffled the phone, but Emma still heard her welcoming kids as they got in the car. "School's out. Gotta run."

"I'll call you soon," Emma said. "We need to catch up."

"True. Love you."

"Love you too."

She ended the call as a new message popped up.

> Nathan
> Running late. Save me an appetizer?

She stared at the text. No apology. Just clinical efficiency. Typical.

"Almost there, miss," the driver said, slowing to turn onto the street leading to the Prescotts' neighborhood.

"Great." Emma fastened her earrings, slipped on her boots, then jammed everything else back into her bag. She used the selfie camera on her phone to check her makeup. Brushing a stray curl from her face, she practiced making a genuine smile. The reflection portrayed a woman she barely recognized—Nathan's polished, sophisticated fiancée.

Fake it till you make it, right?

A few minutes later, the Uber pulled up in front of the Prescott family's brownstone, its grand facade glowing against the dark, snowy night. She added a generous tip in the app for her ride. After all, she had changed in the back of his vehicle.

"Thank you. Have a great night." Emma closed the door of the car and draped her heavy bag over her arm. A gust of wind bit through the flimsy fabric of her dress as the Uber drove away. She slipped into her secondhand wool coat, then hurried toward the towering double doors. Her stiletto heels clicked against the salted sidewalk, and snow clung to her curls.

Squeezing her eyes shut, she drew a ragged breath. Only a couple of hours. Smile, make polite small talk, and celebrate Kendall. No problem.

She tapped the brass knocker, but when no one answered, she went inside. Warm air greeted her, along with muffled sounds of classical music and the hum of lively conversation. A uniformed staff person stationed nearby greeted her with a polite smile.

"Emma, darling." Sylvia Prescott's voice floated across the foyer like a silk ribbon, and she glided toward Emma wearing a gorgeous mauve gown that hugged her toned figure. Her tennis bracelet and matching teardrop earrings sparkled under the light from the chandelier. The sleek bun at the nape of her neck was so perfect, not a single hair dared to slip out of place.

"We were wondering if the weather had gotten the best of you." Sylvia's voice was smooth yet tinged with the kind of warmth that felt forced. Emma caught the subtle once-over her future mother-in-law gave her.

"Sorry I'm late." Emma shed her coat and resisted the urge to tug down the hem of her dress. "I stayed late to help a favorite client push through a challenging workout."

"Of course." Sylvia's smile faltered as her dark eyes lingered on Emma's bare legs. "You should've worn tights, dear. It's too cold to go without."

Emma blinked and glanced down at her bare legs. Tights? She wasn't five.

Before she could respond, Kendall Prescott appeared at Sylvia's side, her shoulder-length silky black hair reflecting the light and her aubergine pantsuit flowing as she moved. The deep V-neck and gauzy cape screamed power, and she wore the chic outfit effortlessly.

"Glad you made it," Kendall said, giving her a quick hug. "Thank you for coming."

"Wouldn't miss it." Emma hugged her back, then offered a bright smile. "That's a fabulous color on you. Oh, wait—" She fumbled in her bag and pulled out a small wrapped box. It was a charm bracelet from a local designer. A splurge she couldn't really afford, but she knew better than to arrive without a gift. "I brought something for you. Congratulations on making partner. That's a huge accomplishment."

"Oh, you didn't have to do that." Kendall added the gift to the pile on the glass console table nearby. "Thank you for thinking of me. We need to—"

"Honestly, these caterers are the worst." Frowning, Sylvia craned her neck and surveyed the formal living room. "They claim they're shorthanded this week, but the lack of adequately trained servers is untenable."

"I'd be glad to help," Emma said. "What's wrong?"

Kendall and Sylvia stared at her. An awkward silence stretched between them.

"That's so kind. Thank you, dear." Sylvia's brittle smile accompanied an obligatory pat on Emma's arm. "You're wonderful with people, and I know everyone here would love to see you. Put your things in the closet under the stairs, then check with the staff in the kitchen."

"Of course." She scooted past Sylvia and Kendall. Where was Nathan? He probably wouldn't be thrilled that she'd volunteered to sub in and serve appetizers, but nobody wanted Sylvia to be unhappy. And Kendall deserved to have a wonderful party.

Emma spotted him walking into the room. He looked incredible in a dark blue suit with a matching tie and crisp button-down shirt—monochromatic from head to toe. Grinning, he paused and spoke to a tall blonde woman wearing a trendy black cocktail dress and sky-high red heels. Courtney? Sydney? One of his classmates from back in med school. Emma hesitated, but he didn't notice her, and the weight of Sylvia's hawkish gaze propelled her into action.

After tucking her coat and bag out of sight in the closet, she went searching for further instructions. Emma found the caterers in the kitchen, where a frazzled woman handed over a tray of champagne flutes. The glasses wobbled as Emma adjusted the tray. She hadn't done this since college, when waiting tables had been her escape from mean-girl politics. Now, it felt like she was back in their crosshairs.

She stepped into the living room, where guests in tailored suits and glittering formal gowns circled the room, their laughter and chatter mingling with the string quartet's live performance.

Emma plastered on her best smile and began circulating.

"Champagne?" she offered to a group of older men huddled near the fireplace. One of them took a glass, barely acknowledging her presence, while the others continued their conversation about hedge funds. She moved on, approaching three women she recognized from the club.

One of the women waved her tray away, but another guest smiled warmly and took a flute. "Thanks, hon. You must be Emma, yes? The personal trainer and fiancée."

Emma nodded, her smile tightening. "That's me."

"Sylvia showed me the wedding invitations," the third woman said. "They're stunning. And just four months to go. Are you nervous?"

Before she could answer, Nathan appeared at her side. Relief swept through her.

"Hey," she said.

"Hey, you." He leaned in and kissed her temple, his hand resting low on her back. "You didn't have to do this."

She gave a half-hearted laugh. "I offered. Your mom mentioned that the caterers were short-staffed, and I figured..."

Nathan looked at her, his expression softening. "You don't need to prove anything to anyone, Emma. Least of all my mother."

"I know," she said, shrugging. "But it's your sister's big night."

He took the tray from her and set it on a table nearby. "You're more than enough. You always are." He kissed her again, this time letting his lips linger on hers.

Her pulse sped and she pressed her palm on his firm chest.

When he pulled away, his chocolate-brown eyes roamed her face. "As much as I'd like to keep kissing you, I think we'd better find our seats. Come on."

They made their way to the table, and just as Emma settled into her chair, a familiar voice called out from behind. "I thought that was you."

Emma turned and blinked. "Mom?"

Her mother, elegant in a silver sheath dress, stepped closer with a glass of champagne in hand. Her brown hair styled in a chignon, her lipstick, and her designer beaded clutch purse were all flawless.

"What are you doing here?" Emma gripped the wooden back of the upholstered chair. "I didn't know you were invited."

"Sylvia and I ended up playing in a pickleball tournament together last week. She insisted I attend. Said it would be lovely for the families to connect before the wedding." Her mother's smile didn't quite reach her green eyes. "I thought, why not?"

Emma forced a smile. "Right. Of course."

Nathan reached over and offered his hand. "Mrs. Wendel. It's good to see you again."

Her mother's face lit up. "Likewise, Nathan. And please, call me Pam."

Just then, Nathan's phone buzzed on the table. He glanced at the screen, frowning. "Sorry," he said. "I need to take this. It's about a patient. I'll be right back."

Emma watched him disappear into the hallway before turning back to her mother. "So . . . you and Sylvia are friends now?"

Mom chuckled. "Hardly. But we move in the same circles. And I do like to keep up appearances."

No kidding. Emma sipped her water, hoping the conversation would stall there.

But her mother leaned closer, lowering her voice. "Besides, you and I need to talk."

Uh-oh. Emma hesitated. "Everything okay?"

"Not really. I didn't want to tell you this way, but I got another notice from Redemption. I haven't paid the property taxes on our house."

Emma's mouth went dry. "What do you mean? As in you haven't paid this year's taxes yet or . . ."

Her mother sighed. "As in never."

Emma gasped. "Never? Why didn't you say something sooner?"

"I didn't think it would be an issue. But now there's talk of liens and legal action." Her mother shrugged, then took another sip of her champagne.

Emma's stomach twisted. Maybe she should've seen this coming. "You couldn't stand that house. Why have you hung on to the place all these years if you can't afford the taxes?"

Something unreadable flashed across Mom's face. "I never said I couldn't stand that house."

"Then why did we leave?"

Her mother huffed out a laugh. "After what your father did? And what happened between you and Luke?"

Emma's breath hitched. Luke. "He didn't—"

Mom held up her palm. "Don't, Emma. Don't romanticize it. Alaska ruined our family. Your father ruined us. And now he's exactly where he belongs. Thankfully, his parole was denied."

Emma squeezed her eyes shut. The words stung like lemon juice in a paper cut. No point in defending her father's behavior though. At least not to her mother. Instead, she drew a calming breath, then opened her eyes. "So you just . . . what? Let the place rot?"

Her mother drained the last of her champagne. "It's not my fault Redemption is grappling with mud and water damage and flooded houses. Somebody at town hall probably decided they had an axe to grind, and now they're coming after me for these stupid taxes."

Emma stared at her, stunned. "You're unbelievable."

"I'm realistic," her mother said. "And I'm not going back there. Not now. Not ever."

"Then I'll go," Emma said, the words tumbling out before she gave them much consideration. "I'll reach out to Gavin. He'll help me figure out what to do."

"Will he though?" Her mother smiled, but there was no warmth in it. "I think you need to just let it go, but if you decide you're going back, I won't stand in your way. And I'm not about to cancel my honeymoon."

"Honeymoon?"

"Egypt," she said, her smile widening as she reached for her cloth napkin. "It's a bucket-list destination. We've waited long enough since the wedding. Richard and I leave next week."

Richard. Right. Husband number three.

Emma massaged her aching forehead with her fingertips. What was happening? How could she possibly be responsible for that house? She leaned back so the server could set a kale, quinoa, and avocado salad topped with candied walnuts in front of her.

A text message from Nathan popped up on her phone.

> **Nathan**
> Sorry had to leave quickly.
> Patient coded.

"Oh no." Emma pressed her fingertips to her mouth. No point in texting him back. He wouldn't read the message anyway.

Mom glanced at her from across the table. "Everything okay, love?"

No. Not at all. Because somehow she'd have to explain to her fiancé that she was headed to Alaska to sell a house.

Two

EMMA CLIMBED THE STEEP WOODEN STEPS, clutching her white plastic basket filled with a small load of clean laundry. Scuffed floors creaked under her sneakers as she passed the old bronze-plated sconces draped in cobwebs. She gave the peeling floral wallpaper her usual grimace. The charm of the place had worn off somewhere around month three of paying way too much rent for too little space.

Brittney, who rented the room across the hall and worked at the same health club, trailed behind. "Are you sure you don't want to think about this? Maybe at least until Monday?"

Emma stopped in front of her bedroom door on the third floor. The hinges groaned as the door gave way. She slipped inside, her breath leaving visible puffs in the air as the cold hit her. She shivered and rubbed her hands together. Under the broad windows overlooking their South End neighborhood, her temperamental radiator knocked as if it were scolding her for expecting it to do its job.

"I'm already packed," she said over her shoulder. "Except for my favorite pajamas."

Emma set the basket on the floor, pulled the pajamas out, then rolled them up and tucked them into her suitcase.

Stifling a yawn, Brittney stopped in the doorway. Her platinum blonde hair was twisted into a messy bun, and she wore an oversized sweatshirt with leggings tucked into fuzzy socks. "That doesn't mean you have to go."

Emma nudged the basket across the floor and left it at the end of the narrow twin bed. She didn't have time to put the rest away. Besides, the towels could wait until she got back. "Britt, I bought the tickets. Cashed in my vacation to take time off at the club. This is happening."

Brittney folded her arms, concern tugging at the corners of her mouth. She skimmed the toe of her sock across the worn floorboards. "You told me once that you'd never go back to Redemption. You said the people there despised you."

Emma crossed to the bay window and adjusted the curtains to half open. Gray early morning light spilled in, catching the dust floating in the air. "Maybe they still do, but this isn't about them."

"Then what's it about? Because to me it looks like you're about to walk into a hornets' nest out of some weird sense of duty to a man who—no offense—destroyed your life."

Emma turned to face her. "He didn't destroy my life. He made awful choices, yes, but he's still my dad."

Brittney's pencil-thin brows scrunched together. "You haven't seen him in, what, fifteen years?"

"Eighteen, and I regret that. I was an angry, scared fifteen-year-old. And I had no choice but to let my mom drag me here and start over. I thought staying away would make it easier to forget, but it didn't." She coiled the cord on her phone charger, then slipped it into her bag. "I went back once, and to your point, people were not great. But I don't know. I just found out Dad's parole was denied again, and it hit me that he's not going to be here when I get married." Her throat tightened, and she swallowed hard against the ache that formed. "He's not going to walk me down the aisle, Britt. That's final. No more what-ifs or maybes."

Brittney's expression softened. "So you're going back for closure?"

"I'm going back to make things right," Emma said. "The least I can do is put the place on the market and pay the back taxes my mom owes. That house though—it's more than just walls and an oceanfront view. It was hot cocoa on the deck and watching the northern lights and eating waffles on Saturday mornings. The perfect childhood I somehow thought would last forever. I just need to go back one more time. To say goodbye."

Brittney leaned against the doorframe. "Can I ask you something?"

Emma nodded.

"What exactly did he do? I mean . . . to go to prison?"

Emma looked away. "He promised the people in Redemption that if they chipped in—kind of a small-town crowdfunding thing—he'd build a cannery. Something to help process the fish from the commercial fishing boats and keep business local. But the money disappeared."

Brittney blinked. "Disappeared?"

Emma's voice grew quieter. "There was a wire transfer. One he shouldn't have made. It broke a federal law, and he got a longer sentence because of it. He said it was a mistake. But in Redemption, people felt betrayed. They had trusted him. Some of them lost everything."

The silence stretched between them.

"So you're just . . . walking back into all that?"

"I'm not walking back into anything," Emma said, tipping her chin up. "I'm walking toward something. Toward the end of the whole mess. Then I can start my life with Nathan."

Brittney picked at the polish on her fingernail. "And you think just showing up will fix it?"

"No. I'm going to show up because I'm not that scared teenager anymore. I'm thirty-three years old, and I can face the past without letting it define me."

"What does Nathan think about all this?"

Emma turned and zipped up her suitcase. "He doesn't love the idea, but he gets it. Besides, he's swamped with his surgical patients, plus he's on call next weekend. He won't have time to miss me. I'll go, deal with the problem, then I'll come home. And we'll wrap up our plans and get married in July."

"Hmm. Okay. Well, I still think you're a little nuts."

Emma laughed. "Yeah, I can see that. I don't agree with much my mother says these days, but she's right about one thing."

"Oh? Enlighten me. Please."

"I need to let that place go."

Brittney studied her. "And you think going back will help you do that?"

"I hope so." Emma slid a bag with small souvenirs for Abbie's family into her purse, then glanced around her room one more time. "Wish me luck."

Brittney crossed the room and pulled her into a tight hug. "I'm not going to say good luck."

"All right." Emma pulled away. "Why not?"

"Because I hope you find more than that. I hope you find peace. And maybe some happiness you didn't expect."

Emma blinked a few times and nodded, her throat catching again. "Thank you. I'll keep you posted."

She stepped out into the hallway, tugging her suitcase behind her. The old floorboards creaked as she headed down the stairs and out the door to the light-rail station across the street. She tried to dismiss Brittney's doubts before they unpacked and took up residence in her head. Yeah, okay, this was unlike her, jetting off to the Last Frontier because her mother conveniently hadn't paid her taxes. But somebody had to go. Besides, it was just ten days. One last goodbye. That's all she needed.

These extreme skiers weren't worth the risk.

Luke stood by the back door in the resort's kitchen, arms crossed, staring through the glass at the blackened ruins of cabin six. Snowflakes fell in lazy spirals outside, and clouds hung low, clinging to the mountains.

"That's the third time this month we've had trouble and something's gone wrong with skiers." He turned and reached for the glass of water. His throat still hurt. Probably from battling the flames yesterday. Or the sour taste of his regrettable decisions.

His younger brother, Tate, leaned against the counter, putting a new bandage on a gashed knuckle he'd injured trying to knock the cabin door in with an axe handle. "Could've been worse. At least nobody was inside."

Ethan poured coffee with his usual calm demeanor, although the muscle in his jaw twitched. "Still don't know how it started. I've asked the volunteers who are staying in three of the cabins, but none of them saw or heard anything unusual."

"The volunteers weren't here," Luke said. "They were cleaning up in town."

Dad, seated in his wheelchair at the head of the table, ran a trembling hand down his ashen face. The lines around his eyes looked deeper than normal. "Still can't believe it happened. Again." He leaned his elbows on the rustic wooden farmhouse table. "I'll call the insurance company. It's the least I can do."

Mom set a mug in front of him and a handful of vitamins and supplements, then rubbed his shoulder. "Don't be too hard on yourself, Liam. This wasn't your fault."

"But it was my decision to comp all those workers that stayed here," he said, shaking his head. "Now we're stuck between a rock and a hard place."

Luke shot Ethan a meaningful look. Here's your opening, bro.

Ethan stirred creamer into his coffee. "You didn't let anything happen, Dad. You opened your doors when no one else could. After the tidal wave, we didn't have a choice. People came to help, and they needed a place to stay."

Oh, for the love. Really, Ethan?

"It wasn't sustainable," Luke said. His voice had an edge. He hated that he let the words slip out, but this time, he couldn't keep his mouth shut. "We lost a ton of income being gracious. Goodwill doesn't pay the bills. And now I've booked all these paying guests, and they nearly burned the place down."

Ethan stopped stirring, but he didn't look up. Dad's eyes flashed.

"You can't blame our guests, Luke," Mom said. "We don't know that it's their fault."

"Outsiders are trouble," Luke insisted. "These skiers and snowboarders don't care about anything but themselves. They're here for the thrill. They have zero respect for boundaries."

Mom gripped the back of the dining-room chair. "What are you saying?"

"I'm saying the gig is up. Time to change our ways, starting right now." Luke stormed out of the kitchen.

"Luke," Ethan called after him. "Take a breather."

He knew what he was doing, thank you. No breather necessary. He climbed the stairs two at a time, jaw clenched tight. He'd officially had it. The fire, the tension, the constant feeling that he was bailing water out of a sinking ship while his family clung to optimism like it was a flotation device. He'd cleaned up the mess after the first fire. Had to help pick up the pieces when their dad could no longer do it himself.

And maybe, if he was honest, he resented that.

As he reached the hallway outside the extreme skiers' guest

rooms, he passed a stack of duffel bags and outdoor gear leaning against a bench and kicked it over. The crash felt good. Then he turned and pounded on the first door.

"Up," he barked. "Pack your stuff. You're out in fifteen."

A muffled protest came from inside. He didn't wait. He went to the next room. Knocked harder.

"Let's go. Don't make me come back with a key. Shuttle leaves in fifteen."

Within minutes, he'd banged on all six doors and the hallway buzzed with groggy, grumbling skiers zipping up jackets and dragging out their equipment.

Tate appeared in the hallway, brow furrowed. "What are you doing, man?"

"These guys need to go."

"But they paid to stay through tomorrow."

"Too bad. They should've thought about that before they burned down a cabin. If we hustle, they can make the next flight to Anchorage. Then we're canceling all future reservations."

"What?" Ethan stood at the top of the stairs, hand on the railing. "You are not serious. We'll lose almost eight weeks of income."

Luke brushed past him and went back downstairs. "Better than another fire. Or worse."

He went behind the check-in desk and jabbed at the power button to turn on the computer. Tate and Ethan followed.

"You are not usually this impulsive," Tate said. "What's going on?"

"I'm exhausted," Luke said, pulling up the system that tracked the reservations. "I'm tired of cleaning up messes. Tired of scraping by. And I'm sick of watching this place become a liability. This is not who we are."

Mom appeared in the doorway, her face pale. "It's going to take some time to get the insurance money for that cabin, honey.

Your dad's on the phone with our agent now, but they don't move quickly. What do you plan to do for revenue?"

He didn't answer, because he didn't know.

"I'll be out in the Suburban. Tell these bozos to join me. I'll take them to the airport."

A few minutes later, he had five of the six irritated skiers and their gear jammed into the Suburban. But his mood had not improved. They were loud and hungover, still cracking jokes like they didn't have a care in the world. One of them muttered something about "five-star service," and another chuckled and asked if this counted as a surprise evacuation drill.

Luke gripped the steering wheel, knuckles white. If he opened his mouth, he might say something that provoked an argument.

He sat for a minute while they bickered about who had to buy a round of breakfast burritos from the restaurant inside the airport. His phone buzzed. He glanced down at the screen.

It was an email from the lodge manager in Petersburg again. The job was still open. Good benefits. Paid relocation. No fires. No skiers with ego issues. No family trauma.

Fewer emotional land mines.

He tapped the link, reread the description, and let his thumb hover over the Apply Now button.

But he didn't press it.

Instead, he shoved the phone into the cup holder and stared out the windshield. Wet flakes hit the glass in heavy silence, and the wipers smeared them away in slow, rhythmic strokes.

Tate helped the last guest load his skis into the back, then slammed the door.

"Here we go." Luke turned on a classic rock station, ignoring the protests from his passengers, and shifted into Drive.

Man, a fresh start in Petersburg was looking better by the minute.

Three

THE SMALL JET BANKED OVER THE RUGGED Alaskan coastline, then dipped lower, jostled by a pocket of turbulence. Emma's stomach roiled. She pressed her palm against her middle and focused on her breathing.

Inhale. Exhale. Only a few more minutes.

"You can do this," she whispered, then pressed her forehead against the cool glass. Beyond the plane's wing, thick fog parted to reveal jagged cliffs plunging into churning water. Snow blanketed the steep hillsides and coated the rocky outcroppings, stretching upward and clinging to razor-sharp peaks. Only the black rock face of the cliffs near the shoreline remained exposed, slick with mist from the crashing waves. Dense forests stood resilient, the tree branches heavy with clumps of snow.

Her pulse sped as the town of Redemption came into view. It looked much the way she remembered—a hodgepodge of colorful buildings and evergreen trees nestled between the stunning mountains and the fingerlike bay. Commercial fishing boats filled the marina, and plumes of smoke curled from a few chimneys. The airstrip appeared below, just a stretch of icy tarmac tucked between snow-covered mountains and a two-lane highway leading into town.

A middle-aged couple sitting nearby shot her furtive glances. She couldn't hear their whispers, but she sensed their unspoken judgment. Maybe they'd known her father. Would his sins always stain her name?

She shifted in her seat, concentrating on the blue-and-gray pattern imprinted on the upholstered wall in front of her. The plane touched down with a jolt, and she gripped both armrests, but the pilot handled the short runway with ease.

When the aircraft glided to a stop and the seat-belt sign flicked off, she waited for the other passengers to deplane first. Then she grabbed her purse and her small rolling suitcase from the overhead bin and walked toward the exit.

The flight attendant smiled. "Enjoy your stay."

"Thanks." Emma gave a polite nod and stepped out onto the airstairs. Snowflakes swirled around her, and the wind whipped her hair across her face. She pushed her curls from her eyes, then drew a deep breath. The air smelled of brine with a hint of diesel fuel. A scent she hadn't missed, but it still churned up a memory. One she wasn't ready to unpack.

Her boots wobbled on the metal steps as she descended. What had she been thinking, wearing heels? She pulled her coat tighter around her body. Juggling her roller bag and her purse, she got to the bottom and sidestepped a patch of ice.

The baggage handler zipped by her on his four-wheeler, towing a small cart. He grinned, offered a cheerful wave, then adjusted the hood on his parka. Snowflakes clung to her eyelashes and her coat as she followed the other passengers toward the modest two-story building.

The glass double doors parted with a soft whoosh, and Emma stepped inside the small terminal. Warm air hit her, and she welcomed the reprieve from the wet snow. She scanned the space, with its two rows of blue padded chairs, a low ceiling, and fluorescent lights that buzzed faintly overhead. To her left, a single attendant stood behind the check-in kiosk, scrolling through her tablet. Across the room, a hand-painted mural stretched along the far wall, vibrant despite the wear. Majestic Alaskan wildlife came to life across the scene—bald eagles soaring against a pale blue sky, grizzlies lumbering through pine forests, orcas rising from the surf. Quite the change from the hectic concourses she'd passed through in Seattle and Anchorage, but sort of comforting.

It was only a few steps to the makeshift security area marked by a metal barrier and a sign that read Authorized Personnel Only. The TSA presence was minimal, just two uniformed men standing beside a conveyor belt and X-ray machines, processing what looked to be a group of skiers and snowboarders. She passed between the waist-high stanchions and crossed over the worn rubber mats meant to catch snow and slush from arriving boots.

"Emma!"

She looked up in time to see Abbie barreling toward her, two little ones trailing behind.

"Hey," Emma laughed, arms open just in time to catch Abbie in a hug. "Oh my goodness, look at you."

Abbie had her light brown hair cut in a shoulder-length bob, and her eyes—the same honey color she remembered—sparkled as she smiled.

"I'm glad you made it," Abbie said. "This is the best spontaneous decision you've made in ages."

"Ha. Thank you. It's so good to see you." Emma bent down to greet the kids, her purse sliding from her shoulder. "Is this Jacob? And this must be Ava. Wow, you guys have grown."

Ava hid behind her mom's legs. Jacob offered a gap-toothed grin and a big wave.

"They're wild, but I love them," Abbie said, brushing Jacob's shock of blond hair from his eyes.

The warmth of someone staring at her heated Emma's skin. Before she could say anything, Abbie grinned. "Oh, look who's here. Luke McGuire. Hey, Luke! Come say hi."

Emma turned, her smile still in place.

Luke McGuire.

He stood about ten feet away, tall and broad-shouldered, his dark green jacket unzipped to reveal a blue-and-white-plaid button-down. Faded jeans fit him well, and he wore a pair of GORE-TEX hiking boots. The years had been good to him. Too good. His dark brown hair was longer than she remembered, curling slightly at the ends. And his cornflower-blue eyes locked with hers. For a second, he didn't move. And she didn't either.

Her stomach flipped. She scooped up her purse, then straightened.

"Emma." He moved closer. "I didn't know you were coming back."

"Yeah, me either," she said. "It all happened kind of fast."

His gaze dropped to her hand. "Wow. That's quite the ring."

She hesitated, glancing at the diamond solitaire. "Thanks. His name's Nathan. He couldn't make it on short notice."

"Too bad for him. He's a lucky guy."

Her heart thudded. She had no words.

Abbie cleared her throat, her gaze darting between them.

And just like that, Emma was fifteen again, standing on her parents' dock, arms wrapped around Luke's neck, the wind tangling her hair. He'd pulled her close and whispered, "I'd wait a thousand years for you, Em. You are it for me."

The memory vanished as quickly as it had resurfaced, replaced by the cold air blowing in as the front doors of the airport slid open.

"So," she said, "thanks for picking me up, Abbie."

"No problem," Abbie said. "I want—"

"Mama, Mama." Ava danced from one foot to the other. "I've gotta go potty. Now."

"Oh boy. Hang on one second, sweetie." Abbie turned back to Emma. "I'm still trying to figure out how to get you out to your house."

"Yeah, me too. I'll find a way to contact my cousin Gavin and hopefully come up with a plan to put that thing on the market."

Luke and Abbie exchanged a glance.

Uh-oh. Emma searched Luke's face. "What are you not telling me?"

"You're not going to sell that place anytime soon," Luke said.

"Excuse me?"

"Not with those sea lions camped out on your deck." Abbie gave an apologetic shrug. "I guess no one's mentioned those?"

Emma blinked. "Sea lions?"

Luke pulled his phone from his pocket. "You didn't see them when you flew in?"

She shook her head. "No, it was foggy and snowing. I couldn't see the house."

"They've taken over your property. Well, not the house—but most of the deck and what's left of the dock," Abbie said. "And rumor has it, the whole place smells like fish and, well, sea lions."

"Fish and sea lions," Emma repeated. "Sounds delightful." She pressed one hand to her cheek. "Welcome home, right?"

Luke held his phone screen to her. "Want to see a picture?"

Emma leaned closer. Massive sea lions—too many to count—had made her old home their colony. "No. Way. That's disgusting. Where'd you get that?"

"It was posted online. A few people have gone by in their boats and taken some videos too. Want to see more?"

"Um, that's a hard pass." Scrunching her nose, she held up her palm. "I had no idea."

Luke swiped his finger across the screen, then put his phone away. "Still want to sell it?"

She met his gaze. "More than ever."

"Mommy, Mommy." Jacob tugged on Abbie's sleeve. "I think Ava had an accident."

"Oh no. Oh—Ava girl." Abbie sighed. "Um, okay. Let's go out to the car. I have extra clothes out there. Emma, can you hang tight for a few minutes while I take care of this?"

"I can give you a ride," Luke said. "Where are you headed?"

"Hilltop B&B. Lainey's place."

"Got it. Come on."

"Oh. Luke, thank you," Abbie said, taking Jacob and Ava's hands. "Emma, I'm so glad you're here. I'll text you once I get the kids home, and we can grab dinner?"

"Perfect. Thanks." Emma waved. "See you later, kiddos."

She followed Luke outside into a gust of icy wind. Luke took her suitcase, then reached to open the Suburban's passenger door for her, and she climbed in. The cab smelled like leather and spearmint and more memories she wasn't ready to face. After he stowed her bag, he slid into the driver's seat and started the engine.

She snuck another glance, taking in his strong hands on the wheel and the profile she'd memorized once long ago. Why had she ever thought this would be easy?

⸺

Luke used to daydream about seeing Emma again.

Over the years he'd thought about what he'd say, how it would feel to stare into those stunning green eyes. He sure hadn't expected the whirlwind of emotions slugging him like a baseball bat to the chest. The second he'd spotted her hugging Abbie, the feelings he'd learned to stuff deep down bubbled right back to the surface.

And that massive engagement ring was tough to ignore. He gripped the steering wheel a little tighter as they pulled onto the highway, then stole another glance at her. She was trying too hard to look unbothered, staring out the window as if this was just another trip from the airport. As if Redemption wasn't the place that had built her.

"So," he said, breaking the silence. "What have you been up to?"

Oy. That sounded pathetic.

Emma shifted in her seat, then smoothed her palms over her dark-wash jeans. "After I left here, Mom and I lived with an elderly aunt in Connecticut. Then my mom's new husband paid for me to go to college. I didn't know what I wanted to do, so I majored in communications, then got a personal-trainer certification, and now I work at a club in Boston."

"A club? Like a gym?"

She gave a laugh, but it didn't quite sound like the Emma he remembered. "Not just any gym. It's a high-end fitness club, members only, lots of CEOs and Boston socialites."

"Wow, sounds fancy."

A pause stretched between them, just long enough for discomfort to creep in.

"I came back once, you know," she said softly. "Ten years ago. For Abbie's wedding."

His chest pinched. "I didn't know that."

"You weren't there."

"No." He raked his hand through his hair. "I didn't move back until after the fire at the resort. My dad got hurt. We needed someone to run the place."

She turned toward him, concern flickering in her expression. "Wait—hurt? Is he okay?"

He hesitated. "He's . . . partially paralyzed. Uses a wheelchair now."

Emma gasped. "Oh, Luke. I—I'm so sorry. I had no idea."

He nodded, staring straight ahead. "Yeah. It was rough. Changed everything."

"And you've been here ever since?"

"Yep. This is home."

For now.

Thoughts of the fire burning down the cabin and the wheelbarrows full of mud they'd shoveled out of every nook and cranny since the tidal wave hit spooled through his head. He wasn't about to mention the job opportunity in Petersburg. Not to her, and not to anyone.

A few minutes later, he drove up the hill and parked in front of an elegant Queen Anne–style two-story home.

"You've picked an awesome place to stay. Lainey's done a fantastic job turning this historical home into a bed and breakfast. Thankfully the damage from the tidal wave didn't impact the property up here."

"Looks beautiful," Emma said, then got out.

Luke climbed out of the vehicle, then pulled her suitcase out and set it on the ground. "I'll carry this up to the porch for you."

"You don't have to do that. I'm—"

Before she could reach the top, the front door creaked open and an older woman stepped out, holding a spray bottle and a rag.

"Well, well," the woman said. "Look who decided to show her face."

Emma froze. "Mrs. O'Brien?"

"Thought Redemption had standards about who we let back in." Mrs. O'Brien's piercing gray eyes narrowed. "Guess I was wrong."

Luke gave a small, strained laugh. "Easy, Mrs. O. Long day."

Mrs. O'Brien sniffed and stepped aside, jerking her thumb toward the door. "Lainey's not here, so she asked me to show you to your room. First door on the left at the top of the stairs. Evidently she thinks you're worthy of the turret."

Wow. Alrighty then.

As Mrs. O'Brien marched back inside, Luke leaned toward Emma. "She's... a little rough around the edges. Things are hard right now. A lot of folks are still reeling from the tidal wave."

Emma's gaze lingered on the open door. "Guess I'm not the only one carrying baggage."

"Nope," he said, managing a soft smile. "But Mrs. O's got a kind heart under all that bark. Somewhere."

She nodded, shoulders tight, lips pressed into a thin line.

Luke took the suitcase up the last step and set it beside the door. "You'll be okay?"

"I'll be fine."

He hesitated, then turned to go, but paused again. "Emma."

She looked up, eyes guarded.

"If you need anything... you know where to find me."

She nodded. "Yeah. Thanks."

Luke waited until she disappeared inside, the door shutting quietly behind her, before heading back to his Suburban. He exhaled hard and stared at the empty passenger seat.

The drive back to the resort was short, but his thoughts raced the whole way. By the time he pulled in, his head was a mess of old memories and what-ifs.

He parked, then tipped his head back and closed his eyes. A flash of curly hair burnished a coppery red by the sun, that yellow T-shirt, her laughter on the deck of her dad's boat. It all came back too fast, too vivid. She'd caught his attention, and he'd been a goner.

A knock on the window jolted him back to reality. He opened his eyes.

Ethan stood there, his gray knit beanie pulled low. "You alive in there?"

Luke pushed open the door and climbed out. "Yeah."

"Did you take those guys to the airport or just toss 'em off the end of the dock?"

"Dropped them at the airport." Luke's tone was flat. "Then ran into Emma Carlisle."

Ethan rubbed his fingertips along his jaw. "Emma Carlisle? Isn't she Caroline's friend? The one who—"

Shaking his head, Luke pocketed his keys and headed for the door. "Let's not go there."

Ethan followed him. "I thought she was getting married in Massachusetts or something."

Luke's steps faltered on the porch. "She is. Caroline's a bridesmaid."

"I'm guessing you're not thrilled about this?"

Luke refused to turn around. "Not even a little bit."

"Ouch. Sorry to hear that, man."

"Yeah. Me too." Luke ground out the words, then went inside. He'd help Emma if she asked. But he wasn't the kind of guy who flirted with someone else's fiancée, and he certainly wasn't a cheater.

He scanned the empty leather couches in front of the stone hearth. Since he'd booted all of their guests, he'd have to figure out a plan B to pay the bills. On top of taking care of the ongoing repairs. He dragged his hand down his face. Maybe he'd overreacted. About the skiers' behavior and Emma's arrival.

She'd said she was only here to put the house on the market. It wasn't like they'd spend a ton of time together. Then she'd go back to Boston and her fiancé, and he'd find a way to forget her. Again.

Four

EMMA SAT ON THE EDGE OF THE BED, PRESSING her palms into the mattress. It was firmer than she'd expected, though the queen-size felt luxurious compared to the cramped twin she slept on back in Boston. The remodeled room had wide-plank shiplap painted an inviting shade of beige, bronze-coated light fixtures, and at least four beautiful quilts draped over a rack by the door. Even though the snowstorm combined with the fading daylight made it difficult to see much beyond the trees outside, staying in a room with a turret made the grueling journey worth it.

She stood and crossed to the shelf tucked in the corner beside the windows. A small painting, maybe five by seven, sat propped on a delicate wooden easel. She traced her fingers along the edge of the canvas, its texture rough beneath her touch, and leaned in to look for the artist's signature. Her breath caught.

"Yes," she whispered. "I knew it."

Her mother had loved this artist's work. Sally Gibbons was a woman who had grown up on Prince William Sound and built a name for herself with stunning paintings of Alaskan landscapes.

Emma smiled, memories flooding in of her father gifting her

mother a framed watercolor one Christmas. It had hung in their living room for years, a small piece of beauty in an otherwise chaotic life. An unexpected lump formed in her throat.

What had happened to all of that art? Had it been left behind, collecting dust? Or worse—damaged? A chill skittered down her spine, and she wrapped her arms around herself. They had left so quickly, with only her backpack and a suitcase. So much had been abandoned.

She pulled out her phone, snapped a picture of the watercolor, and typed out a message to her mom.

> Emma
>
> Remember this? I'm staying at Lainey's B&B in Redemption, and this is on the shelf in my room. Whatever happened to all of Sally's work? You had notecards, watercolor paintings, and larger framed pieces. Just curious.

She attached the photo, then hit send.

A sharp knock at the door pulled her from her thoughts. She set her phone down and crossed the room. When she opened the door, Abbie stood on the other side.

"Good news," Abbie said with a half smile. "The kids are with Mark. Ready for dinner?"

Emma gave her a high five. "Absolutely. I ate my second breakfast in the Seattle airport, but that feels like a lifetime ago."

"I thought you'd probably need food and maybe some company. The options are limited right now. Since the tidal wave, some places haven't been able to reopen yet. Are you up for pizza? Or Italian? Dockside Pizza Company serves salads and chicken tortilla soup if that's more your vibe."

"Sounds perfect." Emma stifled a yawn. It had been a super-long day. She'd traveled for almost fourteen hours, including two layovers. But she couldn't pass up dinner with one of her childhood besties. She grabbed her purse, put on her coat, and followed Abbie down the long staircase, her fingers trailing over the gorgeous hand-carved wooden railing.

The front door banged shut, and they froze halfway down the staircase. Lainey stood inside, shedding her jacket, her cheeks splotchy and damp. She swiped at her face with the back of her hand, then yanked off her pink knit hat and ran her fingers through her short platinum blonde hair cropped in its signature pixie cut.

Without a word, she tossed her hat onto the console table, then plucked a pink gingham apron off the hook and layered it over her red sweater and stylish jeans.

"Uh-oh," Abbie whispered.

"Hey," Emma said, stepping down the last few stairs and hurrying toward her. "It's good to see you, Lainey. Are you okay?"

Lainey sniffed and forced a smile. "Emma. Wow. You're really here." Her voice wobbled as she pulled Emma into a warm embrace. "I'm so glad you made it."

"Me too." Emma squeezed her tight, then stepped away. "Thanks again for letting me crash in the turret room. It's gorgeous."

Lainey tipped her head to one side. "Of course. I wouldn't let you stay anywhere else. When it's not snowing, that room has the best light. How was your trip? Long, I bet."

"Only fourteen hours." Emma tacked on a smile. "Worth it, though, since I get to see both of you."

"Aww, that's sweet." Lainey headed toward the kitchen. "I'd invite you both to stay for dinner, but I've got to get muffins and coffee cake going. Double batch tonight."

"My goodness, that sounds like a lot," Abbie said.

Lainey opened a cabinet. "There are still crews of volunteers in town. Most of them are staying at Redemption Resort in the cabins. So a bunch of local small-business owners are teaming up to try to keep them fed while they finish cleaning up after the tidal wave."

The mention of Redemption Resort served up memories of Luke and his family. Emma conveniently squashed them and surveyed the kitchen. It must have been the formal dining room of the house when the original owners built it. Lainey had converted it into a bright, sprawling space with a soaring ceiling and whitewashed beams. Soft floral curtains framed the tall windows, and gleaming stainless-steel appliances were inlaid against custom cabinets. A massive island dominated the center of the room, topped with white quartz. The air held a faint scent of cinnamon and something floral—probably from the lotion or perfume Lainey used.

Lainey disappeared into the pantry, then returned with a mixing bowl in one hand and a huge plastic bin of flour in the other.

Abbie gently tugged Emma's elbow. "Come on, we should go. Lainey, do you want to come with us?"

"I wish I could, but you go on," Lainey said. "We'll catch up later."

"All right." Emma followed Abbie toward the front door.

Once they were outside, Abbie turned and said, "Lainey's stepdad, Gary—do you remember him?"

"Vaguely," Emma said.

"He's on disability. The only person in all of Prince William Sound to win his lawsuit against the oil company after the spill. Anyway . . . he makes life complicated."

"Sorry to hear that." The icy wind cut through Emma's jacket as they walked toward Abbie's Subaru Outback parked in the driveway. "Where's Lainey's mom? And her stepsister?"

"Lainey's mom divorced Gary and left him a couple years back. She moved to Idaho. Lainey sees her maybe once or twice a year. She does not like to come back to Redemption. And Scottie—Gary's daughter from his first marriage—is a camera operator, so she's usually filming on location or traveling to her next job. I can't remember the last time she came back to visit."

"Wow." Emma glanced back through the window, where she could see Lainey measuring ingredients into a large mixing bowl. "She always did carry more than her fair share."

She climbed into the passenger seat. Something crunched under her boot. "Oh no! I'm sorry," Emma said. "What did I step on?"

"No, I'm the one who should apologize," Abbie said. "We got takeout the other night, and one of the kids must have left their cup in here."

"Don't worry about it." Emma clicked her seat belt into place. "I'm relieved it wasn't something valuable."

"Here, I'll grab it." Abbie leaned over and plucked a smushed Styrofoam cup from the floor mat, then set it behind her seat. "Pretend you didn't see that."

"Your secret is safe with me."

Abbie started the engine, adjusted the defrost, then turned up the volume on the stereo.

"Do you know this song?"

Emma shook her head.

Abbie turned it down. "You're probably not into soundtracks from animated movies, are you?"

"Not really." Emma chuckled. "I don't have a lot of, uh, kids in my life. Not that I'm against them," she quickly amended. "I'd like to have three or maybe four of my own."

"Wow. Ambitious. I'm assuming your future husband is down with your plans?"

Emma hesitated. "Um, well, he's a surgeon. So, I guess? To be honest, planning this wedding has been all-consuming, and we haven't talked too much about kids."

Abbie shot her a look. "Emma Carlisle, are you telling me you don't know how many children your fiancé wants?"

"No, I mean, I'm pretty sure he loves kids." Wow, now she felt foolish. "We'll talk about it. Eventually. He's super busy."

Light snowflakes greeted Emma as she and Abbie stepped out of the car and into the parking lot of Dockside Pizza Company. The scent of garlic and melted cheese mingled with the salty tang of the harbor, where fishing boats bobbed in the dark water beyond the railing. Yellow light spilled from the restaurant's large front windows, and a group of five teenagers exited the one-level building.

Emma scooted out of the teenagers' way. "We had a lot of good times here back in the day, didn't we?"

"Sure did." Abbie smiled, then pulled open the heavy wooden door.

A blast of warmth hit her as Emma went inside, surveying the restaurant's well-worn charm. Wooden beams stretched across the ceiling, knots darkened and held together with industrial-looking bolts. Tonight, red-and-white checkered tablecloths and lanterns with candles inside adorned every crowded table.

A young woman stood inside the entrance, staring at her phone.

"Hey, Crystal," Abbie said. "What's going on?"

Crystal's curious gaze darted between Abbie and Emma. "Waiting on a to-go order. You?"

"Enjoying a girls' night out," Abbie said. "See you later."

The hostess was busy seating a couple near the back, so Emma and Abbie lingered near the small counter topped with a register and a basket of laminated menus. To their right, a long bar stretched the length of the room, its surface scarred with years of use. A man in a weathered flannel shirt and a baseball cap hunched over a pint of beer, his beefy hand clenched in a fist on the bar. He flicked a glance toward the television mounted overhead, where a local news segment played. The headline scrolling across the screen read: Carlisle Place Draws Controversy over Sea Lion Habitat.

The man snorted, lifting his glass. "Carlisle house is a lost cause," he muttered to the bartender. "Should let the sea lions keep it. At least they ain't runnin' off in the middle of the night leavin' folks high and dry."

Oh no. Heat singed Emma's cheeks. She turned toward the door. "Maybe we should go."

Abbie tugged on her sleeve. "Ignore him. He's always running his mouth."

The bartender, a petite woman with silver-streaked hair pulled into a braid, shot the man a warning look. "Watch what you say, Joe."

But Joe wasn't paying attention. He slid his beer closer. "Whole town got burned by that family once. No reason to think this time's any different."

Emma swallowed hard, her pulse thrumming. She forced her expression into something neutral as the hostess finally returned, then reached for two menus.

"Right this way," she said with a bright smile.

Abbie gave Emma a gentle nudge, and she followed her friend through the crowded dining area to a booth near the window.

Emma sat down, forcing herself to exhale. "Nice to know I still have fans around here."

Abbie winced. "Like I said, ignore him. Joe's bitter about a lot of things that have nothing to do with you."

Emma pressed her lips together, staring at the menu without really reading it. "Maybe. But that doesn't mean he's wrong."

Abbie leaned forward, her voice softer now. "Or maybe it just means you've got unfinished business here."

Emma didn't answer. Instead, she traced a finger over the edge of the laminated menu and tried to choose something to order.

Abbie leaned forward. "So, your old house . . . those sea lions . . . What are you going to do?"

"Yeah, I don't know. It's a problem."

"More than a problem, friend. They're federally protected. It's not going to be easy to shoo them away. Best-case scenario, you prove that you're actively using the property, and even then, it'll take permits, wildlife inspections, and time."

Emma groaned. "So I'm up a creek without a paddle?"

"I'm just saying it won't be easy."

Emma flipped the menu over, scanning the back side. "Well, I have to try. My mom hasn't paid the property taxes, so I want to make things right."

Abbie's expression softened. "I'm sorry that she's made this your problem."

Before she could remind Abbie that her mother was the queen of shirking responsibility, her phone buzzed inside her purse. Probably Nathan. She left it unanswered.

Abbie set her menu down. "You know, there's been two or three families who've rented the house over the years. Some people think they stole stuff when they moved out, and not everything was accounted for."

Emma huffed out a laugh. "Well, I wouldn't know. Mom and I only took two bags with us. We moved in with an elderly aunt in Connecticut, and then I was shipped off to boarding school. I don't speak to my ex-stepfather, and my dad's still in prison, at least for a few more years."

Abbie's eyes widened. "So those rumors are true. I'm really sorry, Emma. It sounds horrific. And even though it's been eighteen years . . ."

Emma swallowed hard. "You never really get over it."

"Well, just so you know, folks around here think there's more to your old house than feisty sea lions."

A knot tightened in Emma's stomach. She wasn't sure she wanted to know what Abbie meant. But given the way the guy at the bar had reacted to the news on TV, she wouldn't be able to ignore the scandal—or the gossip—for long. After all these years, was she really going to uncover another secret about her father?

There had to be a way to fix this.

On Monday morning, Luke stood on the gravel pad outside the resort's garage, massaging the ache forming in his forehead. His mother had convinced him they needed to accept new reservations because they desperately needed the income. Luke had agreed—as long as they didn't book any extreme skiers or snowboarders. Snowflakes drifted from a slate-gray sky. Not blizzard conditions. At least, not yet. But they'd finally groomed the trails behind the resort, and the weather was perfect for their four guests, a sweet family from Anchorage, who'd paid to rent snowmobiles. Except they only had two available to rent, and one wouldn't start. Luke sighed. He so did not want to offer a refund.

Hank, the one guy in Redemption who could repair almost anything, stood beside him, his breath visible in the cold air. Frowning, he scrolled through his phone with grease-streaked fingers. They had tinkered with everything they could think of. Fuel line. Spark plug. Battery. Still nothing.

"My best guess is still the fuel pump," Hank said. He paused and coughed.

"Hank, you need to get that cough checked out, my man." Luke clasped him gently on the shoulder. "Are you feeling okay?"

Hank nodded, then dabbed at his mouth with a red bandanna he'd yanked from his overalls pocket.

"Going to the clinic in a few minutes," he rasped. "Didn't want to leave you hanging."

"Hope they can help you out. I didn't realize you were coughing so much or I wouldn't have asked you to come take a look at this."

"No problem." Hank coughed one more time, his cheeks getting red, and he held up his phone. "You're gonna need some new filters too. These are worn out. Best price I've found is online from a place in Colorado. While you're at it, wouldn't hurt to order more spark plugs. Have you taken a look at the track?"

Luke tugged his knit hat down farther over his ears to ward off the chill. "Not yet. Scared of what I might find."

Hank smiled. "Now you know why you got such a great deal when you bought this beast."

Frowning, Luke resisted the urge to kick one of the rocks on the ground across the yard. "I almost had Tate and Ethan convinced we should lease two more from a dealer in Anchorage. But since I kicked out the rowdy skiers, that's probably not a wise move."

Hank's kind eyes crinkled at the corners. "Don't give up hope. You've got four guests right now. More customers will come back soon. It's all in God's timing."

"Yeah." Luke sighed. "Timing is everything, isn't it?"

His thoughts leaped from the broken-down snowmobile to Emma. Not that he planned to help her. No matter how many sea lions camped out on her old deck.

The resort's back door squeaked open, and they both turned. Luke's pulse sped as Emma strolled toward them. She wore dark gray jeans, expensive sneakers, and a silver puffy vest layered over a gray hooded sweatshirt.

"Hank, this is Emma Carlisle. Emma, this is Hank Milton."

Hank offered a friendly smile. "Hi, Emma. I used to help your dad out sometimes, fixing stuff around the house. That's a great piece of property you've got."

Emma's eyes widened. "Not so great at the moment, but thank you."

"Ah, yes. The sea lions." Hank shook his head. "Don't that beat all?"

Luke shoved his hands into his jacket pockets. "What brings you by?"

She looked from Hank to Luke. "Abbie told me I should talk to you about getting a closer look at my family's property."

Hank coughed again, then tipped his head toward the parking lot. "I'd better run. Nice to see you, Emma."

"Keep me posted, Hank," Luke said, shooting him a knowing look.

"You got it." Hank gave him a thumbs-up. "I'll text you the link for those parts. If you place that order, it should be here from Denver by next week."

"I'll let you know," Luke said.

Hank ambled slowly across the parking lot to his well-loved F-150 pickup truck.

"Snowmobile's out of commission, so I'm afraid I can't give you a ride today." Luke grinned, then gestured over his shoulder to the machine behind him, sitting on the garage's concrete floor.

"I'm going to need something a little faster," Emma said. "I don't have much time."

Oh. He studied her, measuring his words carefully. Did she really think she could just swoop in and resolve this in a few days? He kept his judgy commentary to himself. "My truck will get us to the dead end and we can hike in. The trail's still there."

Her smooth brow furrowed. "Is that my only option?"

"No, but it might be your best option. I can take you on a flyover in the chopper. Or I can call in a favor and borrow a friend's boat. It's got a small cabin and plenty of horsepower, but you'll need warmer clothes and rubber boots."

"If we take the boat, what will we do when we get out there?"

Luke pulled his phone from his pocket. "I'm not sure. To be honest, I don't know how you're going to get past those sea lions. I'm happy to help you figure it out though."

She offered a relieved smile. "I'm up for whatever you think is best."

Man, she looked beautiful. Sleek, polished. A far cry from the wild-haired girl who used to challenge him to races down to the dock. He tried to play cool because that ring on her hand was like a beacon, reminding him that she belonged to another.

He scrolled through his contacts. "Let me text Cal. Then we'll go inside and see if my mom has some rubber boots, gloves, and a parka with a hood that you can borrow."

"Sounds good. Thank you." Emma fished her phone from her pocket. "Abbie sent me a link to a story about a sea lion harassing people and their pets near the harbor in Ketchikan. I'll read that and see if there are any hot tips."

Luke nodded as his phone hummed with an incoming text. "That was fast." He scanned the message. "Cal says he's down at the dock right now, and if we can meet him there in about fifteen minutes, we can use the boat for the rest of the day."

"Sweet." She jammed her phone back into her pocket, then glanced at the mess he'd left in the garage beside the snowmobile. "Are you available now? I don't want to interrupt."

"I'm more than happy to set this project aside. Hank thinks we need to order new parts anyway."

Except a boat ride meant more time, more space for conversation, and for memories to creep in. Whether he wanted them to or not.

He gestured for her to enter the resort first. "How are things at Lainey's place?"

"The bed is sooo comfortable. I haven't slept that well in weeks. And I had dinner at Dockside Pizza with Abbie last night. It was almost like..."

"Old times?"

Emma nodded, then stepped inside.

He thought about pizzas shared in the back booth. Pitchers of soda they'd called "swamp water," where Emma persuaded the server to mix all of the fountain drinks together in one sugary, carbonated concoction. Her uncanny ability to hold the record for highest score on the vintage Ms. Pac-Man arcade game.

Thankfully, Mom stood at the desk in the resort, and her infectious smile put a stop to his stroll down memory lane.

"Guess what? I just booked a family of six. They want to stay for three nights next week and celebrate a milestone birthday."

"Wow, that's great," Luke said. "Maybe we'll have snowmobiles available by then."

"Hello, Emma," Mom said. "It's been a long time."

"Nice to see you again, Mrs. McGuire." Emma stood in front of the desk, glancing around. "The place looks great. Did you renovate?"

Luke winced. Oof. She hadn't been here to see the damage from the fire.

"Not because we wanted to." Mom's smile didn't quite reach her eyes. "We had to rebuild the lobby, the great room, and add some ADA-compliant facilities after the fire."

Two splotches of pink stained Emma's cheeks. "Oh. Right. Luke mentioned that. I-I'm sorry to hear that happened."

Oy. Not a trip down memory lane he wanted to take. Luke cleared his throat. "Mom, can you set Emma up with a pair of rubber boots, a water-resistant coat, and some gloves, please? We're going to borrow Cal's boat and zip out to her property."

Mom's eyebrows sailed upward. "That sounds like an adventure. Those sea lions are creating quite a stir, aren't they? What do you think you're going to do, Emma?"

"I have no idea." Emma sighed. "There doesn't seem to be an easy solution."

Luke left them to find more appropriate gear for Emma and went down the hall and into the storage room. He grabbed water, snacks, and a first aid kit. Cal would have life jackets on board, so no need to pack those. He shoved everything into an orange dry bag and returned to the front desk.

Emma stood near the door, waiting. She'd donned a navy-blue parka with a hood and traded in her fancy sneakers for a pair of his mother's knee-high black rubber boots.

"We'll be back soon." Luke waved to Mom. "Thanks for your help."

Mom smiled at him over the frames of the reading glasses perched on her nose. "Be safe, Luke."

"Always." He grinned, then tugged the door shut behind him.

Emma followed him out to his truck. He stowed the dry bag in the back, then climbed behind the wheel. She got in the passenger side and buckled her seat belt. The aroma of something floral wafted toward him. Lotion? Shampoo? It was different from anything he'd smelled before. How had he not noticed yesterday? Maybe he'd been too shocked. He'd waited nearly twenty years to get Emma riding shotgun beside him again. What would her fiancé say if he knew she'd ridden with him twice in twenty-four hours?

They rode down to the dock in silence. As he slowed for the blinking caution light at the main intersection, Luke stole another glance at Emma. She stared out the window. What did Redemption look like through her eyes? Cars came and went from the small downtown. A few people lingered outside the Copper Kettle coffee shop, hands wrapped around steaming cups, their breath curling in the cold air. A sandwich board near the entrance read: Hot Coffee & Warm Company Inside. The buildings along Main Street stood tall with their flat roofs and wide windows, some still showing signs of the recent disaster—cracked trim, plywood over broken glass, and the occasional boarded-up storefront.

Luke parked in one of the many empty spots near the harbor. He turned off the ignition, then glanced Emma's way. "Ready?"

She hesitated, one hand on the door handle. "As ready as I'm going to be."

They both climbed out of the truck. He pulled the bag from the cab, then followed Emma along the sidewalk overlooking the harbor. At high tide, the ramp was nearly level with the floating dock. The scent of brine and fish clung to the air, and the cries of gulls echoed across the water, competing with the occasional creak of a mooring line.

As they walked down the grated gangway, the dock shifted beneath them. Emma clutched the handrail and slowed down.

Cal waved from a nearby slip, where his twenty-five-foot cabin cruiser bobbed in the gray-green water. He had his baseball cap on backward, a hoodie slouched over his shoulders, worn jeans, and scuffed hiking boots.

"Hey, Cal." Luke bumped his friend's fist. "Thanks for helping us out."

"You need me to ride along or you got this?" Cal asked.

"I got it," Luke said. "Tate taught me well."

"I'm sure he did." Cal stuck out his hand, his nails black with grit. Emma didn't hesitate. She shook it.

"Hi. I'm Emma. It's nice to meet you, Cal."

"You as well. That's a cool piece of property you've got out there."

Emma winced. "That's what Hank just said. It used to be cool."

"Come on." Without thinking, Luke reached out, took her hand, and helped her step onto the boat's deck. "This is Eliza Jane. Welcome aboard."

Once they were settled and Luke had figured out the controls on the center console, Cal undid the lines and gave the boat a gentle shove off the dock.

"Text me when you're on your way back. I'll meet you here."

"Got it. Thanks again."

"No problem," Cal said. "I owed you."

The engines rumbled to life, the vibration humming beneath their feet as Luke eased out of the slip. Emma stood near the stern on the port side, hands stuffed in her pockets, her hair whipping across her face in the salty breeze. He steered them past the last row of slips and out of the harbor, the town shrinking behind them.

She braced against the shifting deck as they moved into open water.

The last time they took this route together, they were fifteen and seventeen, sneaking off in an old skiff for a covert adventure. The same salty wind had tangled in her hair then, but back in those days she laughed as she tried to steer, her hands layered over his on the throttle. Now she was quiet and guarded. He already knew she was different. He'd seen it the second she stepped back into town. Her Boston polish was a sharp contrast to Redemption's rough edges. But out here with nothing but the bay and old memories between them, the change seemed starker.

"You're quiet today," he said, keeping his tone easy.

She glanced over at him. "I'm just taking it all in."

And maybe deciding whether she regretted coming back. He looked away, then adjusted their speed, steering them along the rugged coastline. Salt spray kicked up over the bow, and he shivered as the icy wind cut through his jacket collar.

"Remember that cove up ahead? We camped there once and built the worst bonfire known to man."

A flicker of something crossed her face. Maybe a memory. "You did most of the work."

He huffed out a laugh. "Yeah, and you mocked the whole process. Said I didn't stack the driftwood right."

She almost smiled. Almost.

They cruised past the cove, but he wouldn't allow himself the luxury of a second look. Instead, he slowed down as they prepared to round the bend. Because once he passed the rocky outcropping on the right, her house and the sea lions would be in full view.

"Are you ready to see the house?"

She didn't answer, just stared out across the water. Probably lost in another memory.

"Emma?" He tried again. "Are you sure you still want to do this?"

She straightened. "I have to."

His chest pinched. Oh, how he wanted to protect her from the onslaught of hurt and grief she was about to encounter. Part of him wanted to whip Cal's boat around and head for home. But he couldn't shield her. It wasn't his role. Not anymore. As much as he wanted it to be.

Five

IT WAS WORSE THAN SHE'D EXPECTED.

She'd expected disrepair. She'd even braced for maybe a broken window or a sagging railing compliments of the sea lions, but nothing had prepared her for reality. Blinking back tears, Emma pressed her fingertips to her lips. A custom-built sprawling one-level with cedar siding, once stained a deep golden brown, had faded to a weary gray. Their house, perched at the water's edge over five miles down the coast from town, used to be so charming. Now it looked abandoned. Battered by time and neglect. Huge windows offering a breathtaking view of the bay and the mountains rising up out of the sea were clouded over. Two had been boarded up.

And her favorite, the wide deck where she and her parents had sat for hours, entertaining guests and watching the sun paint the sky shades of cotton-candy pink and orange, now hosted a colony of sea lions. Their hulking forms sprawled across the rocks, the deck, and parts of the dock, except for the half already submerged, one piling leaning at a precarious angle. Her father's boat was long gone, likely sold off after his schemes unraveled.

And that horrid smell.

Emma yanked the neckline of her hoodie up over her nose. The sagging dock and the porch barely holding together were bad enough, but the real problem? That awful stench. Ugh. A pungent mix of salt, fish, and something far more unpleasant wafted around her.

Luke let out a low whistle. "Can't unsmell that, can we?"

Shaking her head, Emma stepped to the far side of the boat, willing herself not to gag. "I didn't think it would be this bad."

One of the sea lions let out a sharp bark, shifting its massive body across the deck like it had a mortgage on the place. The boat rocked as Luke slowed down and they rode over their own wake. Emma widened her stance to keep her balance.

"Were you planning on reasoning with them, or should I drop anchor? What's your goal here, exactly?"

Emma blew out a half-sighed, half-frustrated laugh. "I have no idea what I'm doing."

"Hey, I get it," Luke said. "Frankly, that dock does not look safe, and I don't feel comfortable tying up here."

She glanced at him over her shoulder. "So going ashore isn't happening?"

Luke craned his neck, probably surveying another less conventional route.

Even if the dock had been sound, she couldn't go toe-to-toe with two-thousand-pound sea lions. The whole colony looked poised for a fight.

She forced herself to take a second look at the house. How sad. It was just a deserted shell. She hugged her arms to her chest and glared at the creatures sprawled across the dock. They barked at each other in a cacophony of irritation. One lifted its oily head, its black eyes locking with hers, as if daring her to set foot on her own property.

"Not the friendliest neighbors in the world, are they?"

She shot Luke a glare over her shoulder, but there was no real heat behind it. After all, he'd been a sweetheart, setting aside his own problems, borrowing a friend's boat, and driving her out here. Two more sea lions barked at the sky.

"I think that was sea lion for, 'You are not getting me out of here without an eviction notice,'" he said, his lips twitching.

"Not funny."

He shrugged. "It's a little funny."

Sighing, she turned away from him and pulled out her phone to take photos. No one had said a word to her yet about the unpaid property taxes. Or served her any official papers. But she still felt compelled to document her visit. Even though she'd much prefer to focus on the sweet memories she carried with her. This was the place where she'd learned to fish, where her mother had made pancakes on Saturday mornings, where she and Luke had spent an entire summer believing in forever.

Except forever had been a lie.

This dock was also where she last saw her father, gripping her arms, telling her she was being dramatic. Telling her Redemption wouldn't turn against them, that she'd be back. But his words had turned out to be empty promises. Fresh tears stung her eyes. She swallowed hard. The weight of Luke's gaze warmed her skin. She couldn't look at him. Instead, she held up her palm.

"I'm fine."

"I know you're strong, and I know you think you can do this, but we're going to have to come up with a plan B. These sea lions aren't going to leave on their own."

He wasn't wrong. Still, the only way out of this mess was through it. She just had to keep moving, keep breathing, keep reminding herself that somehow she'd find a way to fix up the house, sell it, pay the back taxes, then be on her way. Because this wasn't her life anymore. This house was not her home. Redemption wasn't her future. Her future was Nathan, Boston, life as Mrs. Prescott.

She tightened her grip on the railing as Luke maneuvered the boat around a broken piling. They put some distance between themselves and the sea lions, but she couldn't escape the memories that refused to sink beneath the surface. Or ignore the part of her that still ached for everything she'd lost.

Luke sped up, and water churned around the boat's stern.

"Where are you going?"

"I hate to say it, but your place looks much different up close than it does from my usual view in a chopper. Between the missing parts of the dock, broken pilings, and the twenty sea lions I've counted so far, getting to the house will be harder than I expected." Frowning, he tightened his grip on the throttle. "There's no way we can tie off and get past them."

"Are you going to turn around?"

Before Luke could answer, the wind picked up and cut through her layers like a sharp blade. He glanced at the sky. Clouds rolled overhead, purple and gray and bloated.

"This is a fast-moving storm," he said. "As much as I don't love the looks of this dock and broken pilings, we should wait for the weather to break. I don't feel comfortable maneuvering Cal's boat back to town in this."

"Really?" She scowled overhead. "It only takes twenty minutes to get back, right?"

"Doesn't matter." Luke killed the engine, then brushed past her. "Cal relies on this boat to make a living. I can't take any risks. We'll be safer if we hang here."

Rain speckled her face. The wind howled, sending sharp waves rocking against the hull.

"Got it."

"Come on, go inside. You'll be warmer."

He opened the door to the boat's cozy cabin. She stepped in, pulling the door shut while he went to the bow and chucked the anchor over the side. There was just enough space for a cushioned bench, a tiny kitchenette, and a Formica table. It smelled musty, but sitting here was much better than getting soaked out on deck.

Luke ducked in, and it felt tighter. Closer. He shook rain from his jacket, then took it off and hung it on a hook by the door. Water dripped from his hair, and he brushed it back. She looked away, pretending the sudden suffocating warmth in her chest was from the small heater blasting hot air.

He turned and opened a cupboard over the galley sink. "Cal texted me and said he left us a thermos with hot water and some instant coffee and hot cocoa."

"Wow. First-class service."

He shot her a grin. "Cal likes to keep his guests happy."

The boat rocked again, sending her off balance. Without thinking, she reached out and clutched his arm. His skin was warm, the muscles solid and familiar. Their eyes met. Rain hammered against the cabin roof, wind rattled the boat, and they rocked side to side—but somehow everything around her stilled. His muscles flexed slightly beneath her fingers, but he didn't pull away. She did though. Quickly. Too quickly. She backed up against the bench seat, snug against her lower legs, and flopped down.

"How long do you think the storm will last?"

He shrugged. "No idea."

"Super." She exhaled, rubbing her palms together. "Trapped on a boat. In a storm. With you."

He smirked as he pulled cocoa packets from the overhead cupboard. "Try to contain your excitement."

She pretended to be annoyed, but the truth was, Luke had never had to work very hard to make her laugh. His sense of humor and easygoing nature were two of the big reasons why, at fifteen, she'd harbored dreams of a future with him. But her father's choices had forced her to abandon everything she'd known. Everything she'd loved. After spending so many years away, she'd built a life that didn't really have anything to do with Alaska or Redemption. Those teenage dreams seemed silly now.

She retreated on the narrow bench, scooting closer to the window. Luke moved with ease in the cramped space. She tried not to stare. He tugged open a storage compartment beneath the small counter and pulled out two sturdy gray mugs with white logos she didn't recognize. Probably Cal's fishing charter service.

"Are you sure cocoa's okay? If you're not a fan of instant coffee, there's a couple of tea bags too."

"Cocoa sounds good, thanks."

Although to be honest, hot cocoa reminded her of the time spent with him on her porch, whispering about dreams too big for their little town.

A few minutes later, he handed her a steaming mug and settled across from her on the opposite bench.

"Sorry, all out of marshmallows."

"No worries." She wrapped her fingers around the mug, letting the heat sink in. "I still can't believe this has happened."

She meant the house, the storm, the sea lions, the way her chest felt like it had been hollowed out the second she saw those animals taking over. Luke stretched out his legs, crossing them at the ankles on the floor beside the table. His jaw was set, but his eyes were gorgeous, a shade of cornflower that reminded her of her favorite crayon from childhood.

"Yeah, I guess it's hard to know what to expect when you haven't been back in, what did you say, ten years?"

The accusation hovered there, just beneath the surface, sharp as a fishing hook. Emma looked away. The rain blurred the world outside the window, but she didn't need to see the house or the shoreline to remember.

"I had to leave," she said, her voice barely above a whisper. "My father was in prison, and my mother couldn't leave town fast enough. What else was I supposed to do?"

Luke slid his cocoa closer, watching her.

"Like I said, I came back once for Abbie's wedding." She forced a shrug, trying for indifference. "But that just confirmed what I already suspected."

His brows scrunched together. "What's that?"

"That the life we'd dreamed about was just a dream. None of it was going to happen."

The moment the words left her lips, she wanted to take them back. Luke's expression barely changed, but something in his eyes darkened.

"Just a dream, huh?"

Emma's chest squeezed. "I-I didn't mean—"

"Don't try to smooth it over, Emma." His voice was flat, but the wound was there, fresh and raw.

Guilt twisted her insides. "I was fifteen, Luke. I didn't have a choice."

His gaze burned into her. "But you had a choice when you turned eighteen. Or twenty-two. Or thirty."

She looked away. The silence between them stretched, thick with things she probably should've said a long time ago. She dragged her gaze to meet his. "I wanted to come back. You have to believe me. I begged my aunt and my mother to help me. Pitched three different scenarios, including living with Abbie. But they refused, so I stopped asking."

Hesitating, she glanced down at her cocoa, turning the mug in a slow circle. "And for the record, I looked for you at Abbie's wedding. Hoped that we'd reconnect. But you didn't come, and people said terrible things to me about my father, so—"

"So that's when you killed off any hope of us?"

His words landed like a slap. Sharp and unexpected. A cold knot tightened beneath her ribs. Heat flooded her face as she leaned forward, propping her elbows on the table. "You weren't here. And by the way, in all the years I've been away, you never once reached out. Never tried to visit me. I don't expect you to feel sorry for me, but my mother moved on and my dad went to prison. There's only so long a girl can wait, you know? Eventually Boston, well, it felt like I'd been granted a fresh start—a place where people weren't constantly telling me how awful my father was."

Luke took a sip of his cocoa, then set the cup down. "Does he know?"

She blinked, then met his gaze again. "What?"

"Your fiancé. Does he know what this place means to you, and what you left behind?"

She looked away. "He knows enough."

"Huh. Interesting."

Then he pushed to his feet, set his unfinished cocoa in the sink, and grabbed his coat from the hook near the door.

"We should get back," he said, his hand already on the doorknob. "I can probably get us through this."

Seriously? She stared after him as he left the cabin. She'd poured her heart out, defended herself, and all he wanted to know was what Nathan thought? Clutching her mug of unfinished cocoa, she stared out the window, speckled with a steady stream of raindrops. She hadn't come to Redemption to dredge up the past. But here they were, wading through it. Her heart pinched. Maybe Luke didn't want her apologies. Maybe he just wanted the years back. The ones she couldn't return.

Man, he owed Emma an apology.

Luke scrubbed his hand over his jaw, then slid his breakfast dishes into the dishwasher. He'd said too much yesterday. Or maybe not enough. Either way, the tone and the weight behind his words weren't okay. And he had no business behaving like he was the only one who'd had to deal with disappointment.

He'd been young when she left. Seventeen and thought he knew it all—so certain that he'd love her forever. And that she'd find her way back.

Except she hadn't.

She'd gone on with her life. Made choices that didn't include him. And somehow a twisted selfish part of him still expected her to apologize.

Oy.

"You've got to do better, McGuire," he whispered, grabbing his jacket and putting it on as he strode toward the front door.

Ethan stepped inside, stomping snow from his boots. "Good morning. Where you headed?"

Luke stepped behind the front desk and plucked his keys from the basket beside the computer. "Driving Emma out toward her old house. We tried to get closer with Cal's boat yesterday, but it didn't work out. Figured we'd try hiking in."

Ethan's eyebrows shot up. "You're hiking in? That's a commitment."

"She needs help."

Ethan's expression tightened as he leaned both elbows on the counter. "She needs a lot of things, Luke. You sure you want to be one of them?"

Warmth crept up Luke's neck. "It's not really your call, is it?"

Ethan's gaze didn't waver. "You're right. It's not. But I remember what it was like when she left. You were a mess."

"I was seventeen." Luke pocketed his phone and his keys. "Cut me some slack."

"Just don't let her wreck you again, all right?"

Luke managed a dry laugh. "Noted. Tell Tisha, Brody, and Sadie I said hey."

Outside, cold air nipped at him and fresh snow crunched under his boots. Blaming others who left Redemption when he'd chosen to come back wasn't right. Or fair. His resentment was on him. But it was easier to focus on Emma's leaving and not coming back than to admit the truth: Even though almost twenty years had passed, part of him still hoped she'd look at him and want what he wanted.

Even if she was engaged to someone else.

A few minutes later, Luke pulled up in front of the bed and breakfast. The familiar porch railings were strung with white lights, glowing softly in the morning fog. Before he could get out and knock, Emma emerged, her curls twisted into two neat braids. She wore a blue anorak, rubber boots, and a plaid button-down over skinny jeans.

"Hey." She climbed into the truck, then slammed the door.

"Good morning," he said, his voice steady though his chest felt tight. He gestured toward the plastic shopping bag she held. "What's that?"

"Lainey offered some snacks and water." She shook the bag lightly, her smile small but genuine.

"Cool." He took it from her and stashed it behind the seat.

"What's going on at the resort today?"

"Not much, sadly." He hesitated with one hand on the gearshift. "We're struggling."

"Sorry to hear that." She reached for her seat belt. "If you need to be doing other things today, please don't feel obligated to help me. I can find someone else."

"I'll make time."

She tossed him a look he couldn't quite read.

Oh brother. His mouth ran dry. Letting go of the gearshift, he raked his hand through his hair. "Emma, listen. About yesterday. I'm sorry."

She grew still. "For what?"

"For my bad attitude. For implying that you leaving was somehow your fault." He rubbed his clammy palms on his jeans. "I'm sorry that I didn't . . . try harder."

Tears welled, clinging to her lashes. She blinked them away. "I'm sorry too."

He looked away, his pulse hammering. Ethan was right. She had wrecked him when she'd left. Cleaved his heart wide open. And he couldn't go back there. Not again. He'd spent far too long dragging that hurt around.

He shifted into drive. "Let's see if the sea lions are in a better mood today."

The truck rumbled down the hill, cutting through town. Luke gestured toward the diner. "That's where Ethan's girlfriend, Tisha, works part-time. She has a cute little girl named Sadie, who loves to give my nephew Brody a run for his money. I'm guessing Ethan and Tisha will get married before long."

"Good for them," she said. "How's Tate?"

"High-strung and following all the rules, as usual. He's piloting tankers and cruise ships now."

Emma laughed, the sound warm and familiar. "That's fitting. Good for Safety Patrol."

Luke grinned. "Man, he hated that nickname. No wife and kids for him yet. Just a golden-doodle puppy that's more high-maintenance than he is."

"And your sisters?"

"Caroline's in Colorado. She's finishing her PA program. We're hoping she'll move back here and work at the clinic when she's done. Dr. Wallace says he wants to retire."

"I can't believe he's still seeing patients," Emma said.

Luke's hands tightened on the steering wheel.

"How's Megan?"

He hesitated. "Megan's . . . a situation. I don't want to get into it right now."

"What's the matter?" Emma turned toward him, her eyes searching his face.

"Emma, I really can't. It's not my story to tell."

Sunlight pierced through the clouds, reflecting off the hardware store's new metal roof. Luke fumbled in the console for his sunglasses, trying to ignore the knot in his chest.

"What about you, Luke?" Her voice was quiet now. "Are you seeing someone?"

He glanced over at her, holding her gaze a beat too long. "No."

The word echoed in the cab.

He wasn't about to get into his reasons for still being single. Because frankly, he'd tried to move on. Dated a sweet girl for a couple of years in Utah while he was in college. Majored in business and pretty much minored in how-to-get-over-Emma. But the girl had wanted a long-term relationship and Luke couldn't commit. Then he'd been interested in dating Tisha's younger sister Cami for a hot minute one summer. Back when he and Chase Binford had tried to launch a flightseeing business. He'd even visited her at Clemson when she'd gone back for fall semester.

But that relationship couldn't survive long-distance. Or fill the Emma-shaped hole in his heart.

Emma didn't say another word until he parked at the dead end of a gravel road known as Aurora Way. Moss-covered spruce trees loomed above them, their branches draped with moisture. Luke killed the ignition and turned to Emma. "If I remember correctly, it's not too bad a hike. Maybe half a mile."

Emma grabbed a water bottle and nodded. "Lead the way."

The forest carried the scent of damp earth and pine. It should've been peaceful, but Luke's thoughts churned. Memories of the two of them on this path—Emma's laughter, the way she used to race ahead just to make him chase her—crowded his mind.

Ahead, a fallen tree blocked the trail. Emma shoved her water bottle into her pocket and climbed onto the rough bark.

"Careful. It's—"

Emma squealed as her foot slipped and she tumbled over the tree, landing with a hard thud.

"Slippery," Luke said, rushing to her side. "Are you okay?"

She winced, cradling her wrist. "Yeah. Just... give me a second."

"Let me see." He crouched beside her, gently taking her arm. Her skin was soft, her wrist delicate in his hands. "No discoloration or swelling. You're lucky."

"I didn't need another thing to deal with," she whispered, her voice tight.

Luke sat back on his heels. "Think you can keep going?"

Her eyes flashed. "Do I have a choice?"

He stood and offered his hand. "We always have a choice."

She hesitated, then slipped her fingers into his. Their palms met and something passed between them. For a second, it was like nothing had changed.

But then she looked away, brushing dirt off her jacket. "Thanks."

Before he could respond, the sound of tires on gravel made them both turn. Through the trees he spotted a white truck pulling up at the trailhead. He squinted. Some kind of official seal marked the door.

Emma frowned. "Who's that?"

"Not sure. Maybe someone checking on the sea-lion situation."

Emma huffed out a breath. "Super."

Luke gestured for her to go first. "It can't hurt to hear what he has to say. We're not doing anything illegal. Besides, we might need help."

"All right." She pulled her water bottle from her pocket.

"Here, let me." Luke took it, twisted off the cap, then handed it back. When she'd finished taking a long drink, he tried to help her put the cap back on.

"I've got it." She tucked the bottle under her arm, then awkwardly twisted the cap into place with her left hand.

Luke shook his head. Still as stubborn as ever.

He let her lead the way back the way they'd come. A few minutes later, they emerged from the trees.

A young man in a brown Fish and Game jacket stepped out of the white pickup truck. He adjusted his brown knit cap, then lifted a hand in greeting. "Hey there. Are you folks dealing with the sea lions?"

"We're trying," Luke said. "I'm Luke McGuire. This is Emma Carlisle."

"Drake Foster." He pulled his phone from his pocket. "I'd like to take some notes, if you don't mind."

Emma shot Luke a worried glance.

Luke took a step closer, somehow feeling the need to protect her. "Notes about what?"

"I need to document that we spoke, that's all." Drake smiled, then looked down at his phone. "Don't panic. This isn't an investigation. You've done nothing wrong. Our records show we've reached out to you twice, Ms. Carlisle. Are you the homeowner?"

"The home belongs to my parents, but they're unavailable," Emma said, rubbing her wrist. "I guess that makes me the responsible party."

"Emma lives out of state," Luke added. "She doesn't have unlimited time or resources to deal with this. So what are her options at this point?"

Drake grimaced, then tucked his phone out of sight. "Depends on how much of a headache you're willing to deal with."

Luke glanced at Emma. She met his gaze, determination sparking in her eyes, even though she was clearly in pain.

He looked away. This wasn't his problem to solve. She had a life elsewhere. A man waiting for her in Boston. But that didn't change the fact that he still wanted to help her. Maybe more than he should.

Emma flexed and extended her wrist, then winced.

Poor thing. Her wrist probably wasn't broken and more than likely didn't even have a bad sprain. But this must all be so overwhelming.

He forced himself to focus on Drake, who'd launched into a long-winded explanation about why they couldn't force the sea lions out of their so-called natural habitat.

"As I'm sure you know, they are federally protected," Drake said. "I don't want to assume anything, but you've probably figured out by now that legally we can't chase them away."

"I was afraid you'd say that," Emma said, shifting her weight from one foot to the other.

Luke crossed his arms, then widened his stance. "Define legally."

Drake rocked back on his heels. "You could try some passive deterrents—something like an obnoxious noise that might drive them back into the water. But given how settled they seem, that might not do much. Your best bet is to wait them out."

"Wait them out?" Emma repeated, her brow furrowing.

"They'll move on eventually," Drake said with an easy shrug. "Might take a few weeks, might take a couple of months."

"A couple of months?" Her voice pitched higher. "I don't have that kind of time."

Drake cleared his throat. "Look, I'll check a few other options, maybe see if other officers have had success with relocation efforts. But for now? There's not much you can do except be patient."

Luke stifled a groan. "Do you have a business card? In case we have more questions?"

"Of course." Drake climbed into his truck, rummaged around in the center console, and returned with a card, which he handed to Luke. "My number and email address are on there. Reach out any time, and please keep me posted if the situation changes."

"Absolutely," Luke said. "Thanks for your time, Drake."

"You're welcome." Drake nodded to Emma. "Take care, Ms. Carlisle."

Emma waved, but her focus had already shifted. As Drake pulled away, she turned to Luke, who was rooting through his backpack.

"Come on," Luke said, straightening. He held up a small Bluetooth speaker. "I've got an idea."

"Really? What is it?"

"This speaker, and my phone with a playlist full of hot tunes I think sea lions will hate."

She couldn't help but laugh, shaking her head. "Seriously?"

"Come on. Trust me."

"All right." She nodded. "Let's try it."

They started back toward the trees, the path winding through towering spruce and cottonwood. Thick branches formed a canopy overhead, shielding them from the light drizzle.

This time, she let Luke help her over a fallen tree, her slender fingers cool, pressed against his.

Maybe he was getting in over his head—traipsing through the woods, meeting with Drake, and cooking up a grand plan to eradicate the sea lions.

Someone had to help her though. So he'd figure out how to get rid of those rascals. Then she'd go back to Boston. And he'd go on without her. Create his own fresh start in Petersburg or Sitka or maybe Seattle.

Six

THE LONGER SHE TREKKED BACK TO HER FAMily's old house, the more the memories came alive.

Emma followed Luke down a gentle incline, the trail lined with mossy rocks and gnarled roots. Just past the first bend, she reached out and touched a jagged boulder jutting from the hillside. She and her parents had always stopped here to rest, especially when they carried groceries and supplies.

Then came the fork in the trail—the place where veering left led to a rocky outcropping instead of the house. She stopped to check for the telltale markings carved into the bark of a massive tree.

She pointed. "Remember?"

Luke glanced at the tree where he'd carved their initials, then drawn a jagged heart around them. The letters and the heart were barely visible now. Two pink splotches formed on his cheeks. "Oh, I remember. Who could forget your dad's reaction? I thought he was going to push me off the end of the dock the next time he saw me."

"Ha." She nudged his shoulder with hers. "Turns out he had bigger problems than you dating his daughter."

Luke winced.

Uh-oh. Her insides twisted. "Sorry. That came out wrong."

"No, you're right," Luke said, staring through the trees toward the water. "He must've wrestled with a ton of guilt. I hate that he had such good intentions, wanting to build that cannery and all, but somehow his plans went off the rails."

Emma nodded. "I know it's hard to believe, but he had a big heart."

Luke turned, his expression filled with empathy. "He certainly loved you."

She swallowed past the tightness in her throat. "I know."

They walked in silence. Damp earth squished under their feet, and the rhythmic sound of waves lapping against the rocks filled the air, mingling with the rustle of the wind.

At fifteen, she'd walked this path feeling invincible, the whole world stretching out ahead of her. Now, the distance between her past and present felt insurmountable.

"You okay?" Luke's voice was quiet, but it broke through the web of memories.

Emma forced a nod. "This is a lot to process."

He didn't press her. He never had. Not when they were kids, and not now. It was one of the things she'd always liked about him.

Dangerous territory, thinking about what she liked about Luke.

Her breath hitched as the house came into view.

The back side of the spacious one-story home didn't look any better than the front. The sea lions hadn't budged, their massive bodies still draped across the deck in lazy defiance.

Emma covered her mouth with one hand, her other pressed against her chest. This place used to smell like pine, cedar, and sea spray. Before her dad had made a mess of everything, it had been a sanctuary. Now, it was nothing more than a neglected piece of property with a massive pest problem.

"I tried to warn you," Luke said, his words laced with empathy.

Emma wanted to tell him she didn't care—that she was fine—but the words wouldn't come. Because that was a lie. She did care. A stupid, hollow kind of caring that made her feel like the scared fifteen-year-old who had begged her mom to let her stay, only to be told she had no say in her own future. That leaving Redemption was her only option.

She turned away, blinking back tears. The past wasn't supposed to feel this raw. Not after all these years, not when she was engaged to someone else.

Nathan.

She drew in a ragged breath. Nathan offered her a future. A stable, secure, glorious future. The sooner she evicted the sea lions, fixed up the house, then sold it, the sooner she could get back to her life—and her man—in Boston.

Luke cleared his throat. "We don't have to do this today."

"Yes, we do," Emma said, more sharply than she intended.

But she couldn't snatch the words back. She needed to do this. To face what was left of her past and prove to herself that it didn't hold power over her anymore.

Even if, deep down, she wasn't sure that was true.

"You ever distracted a colony of sea lions before?" Luke set his backpack on the ground, then gestured to the mass of blubbery bodies sprawled across every flat surface they could find. At least on the side of the property facing the water. The animals grumbled and shifted, unbothered by their presence.

Cradling her aching wrist, she shot him a dry look. "Oh, sure. All the time. It was an elective in college. Sea Lion Eviction 101."

Luke grinned. "Good. Then you know that food might lure them away for a little while, but it'll just make them stay longer."

"I really don't care about their meal plans. I need to get in that house."

He nodded toward his backpack. "I've got a flare in here. We'll try noise first. If that doesn't work, we give 'em a little light show."

Emma stared at him. "Is that legal?"

"Drake didn't say it wasn't."

With a sigh, she took his speaker as he pulled up a playlist on his phone. A moment later, AC/DC's "Thunderstruck" blasted through the crisp morning air.

The sea lions lifted their heads, some of them startled, others looking downright irritated. A few snorted and shuffled in place, but none of them moved.

Luke turned the volume up. "Come on, guys. Get the hint."

Emma bounced on her toes. "Maybe something more annoying?" She grabbed the phone from his hand and scrolled until she landed on a banger. "Aha! 'Baby Shark'!"

The infamous children's song filled the air, and several sea lions let out distressed barks. One let out a deep, almost humanlike groan and flopped onto its side as if personally victimized. Another began moving toward the water.

Emma gasped. "It's working!"

Luke glanced at her, shaking his head. "Diabolical."

"Desperate times and all that. Right?"

Luke laughed as another sea lion flopped into the water. "Guess they do have taste."

Dancing to the beat, she tipped her head back and let out a loud whooping noise. Yeah, okay, so she probably looked and sounded ridiculous, but she'd try almost anything to get these beasts to move on. More sea lions shifted, some scooting toward the dock, others simply barking in protest.

Then a burst of red light streaked across the sky, fizzling over the water.

She turned around. "What was that?"

Grinning, Luke tucked a lighter back in his pocket. "Flare."

Several sea lions bolted for the water, flippers smacking against the dock. It was chaos. Emma whooped again, and more of the animals made a raucous, grumbling exit.

Her phone buzzed in her jacket pocket, and she fished it out, wincing as the motion tugged at her tender wrist. Nathan's name lit up the screen. She swiped to read the text.

> **Nathan**
> Everything okay? How's the house look?

She sighed, then tucked her phone away without replying. When she looked up, Luke was watching her, his expression unreadable.

"He worries," she said.

Luke lowered the volume on the music. "Understandable."

She hesitated. "He wants what's best for me."

A muscle in Luke's jaw twitched. "Does he know what that is?"

Before she could respond, a low buzzing sound squelched their conversation.

She whirled back around toward the water. "Is that—?"

"Uh-oh," Luke said. "We've got company."

A drone hovered a few yards away, its small camera lens locked onto them. Out in the water, a fishing boat bobbed not far from the end of the partially ruined dock. The men on board hooted with laughter as they held up their phones, clearly recording the whole spectacle.

Her stomach twisted. "Yikes. Hope our seal-lion eradication efforts don't go viral."

"Yeah." Luke dragged his palm down his face. "Drake might not be real impressed."

She studied him as he glanced toward the boat. Honestly, Fish and Game were the least of her worries. How in the world was she going to get this place cleaned up and on the market in the next six days?

Ethan liked to say that pie could solve almost any problem, a lesson he'd probably learned from Tisha and Sadie, but tonight Luke was not convinced.

"Did you guys save room for dessert?" Charlie, their server at Homestead Café, stopped beside their booth. "Tisha baked a fresh apple pie this afternoon."

"I'm still working on my fries," Luke said. "Thanks for checking in."

"No problem." Charlie glanced at Ethan and Tate. "Need refills on your pop?"

"I'm good," Ethan said. "Thanks."

Tate glanced up from his phone. "No, thank you."

"Let me know if you change your mind about the pie." Charlie smiled, then crossed to the L-shaped counter and chatted with two customers sitting on stools. The aroma of cinnamon and sugar mingled with the familiar scent of french fries and the half-eaten cheeseburger on Luke's plate.

Luke stared at the note he'd started on his phone. The words MORE CUSTOMERS served as the heading in bold capital letters, but he and his brothers had only come up with a bunch of half-formed ideas in a bulleted list. None of them were good enough to generate much income though.

At least not compared to the reservations he'd canceled, including six people tied to prepaid heli-flights. That was nearly ten grand in revenue. Gone. So now it was on him to replace what they'd lost.

Across the table, Ethan bit into his chicken sandwich. Tate sat beside him, his fries untouched as he scrolled through his phone, brow furrowed. Probably thought he'd find the perfect solution to their financial woes somewhere on the Internet.

Luke glanced around the dining area. Only five other customers in the whole place. Charlie stood behind the counter, tucking clean paper napkins into the stainless-steel dispenser. How did the Binfords plan to stay open with so few customers? Ethan might know since Tisha baked all the pies the café sold, but it wasn't really any of Luke's business.

"What about a spring-break promo for the resort?" Ethan dusted crumbs from his fingertips. "Easter and the public schools' spring break are at the same time this year. Something like...cozy winter getaways, hot cocoa by the fire—"

"That's not at all how people want to spend spring break," Tate said.

Ethan gave him the side eye. "Keyword cozy. Tisha tells me that's the vibe we're all going for these days."

"Nobody's going to drive to Redemption for the weekend if there's nothing to do," Tate said. "Most places aren't open, and the ones that are don't have much to offer."

A muscle in Ethan's jaw twitched. Luke dipped a fry into the ketchup. Man, Tate was such a negative Nellie sometimes.

"We're kind of dead in the water." Tate set his phone down and reached for his burger. "Speaking of water, I saw some drone footage. Was that you helping Emma out? The sea lions did not look happy when you cranked that music."

Luke finished chewing his french fry, then reached for his drink. "She doesn't know very many people here anymore, so I'm just trying to help. We spoke to somebody with Fish and Game, but his suggestions aren't effective, so we're trying whatever's legal at this point."

Tate narrowed his eyes. "Are you sure you want to put yourself in the middle of that? You know how people talk around here."

"So let them," Luke said. Gossip spread faster than the flu in Redemption. Emma had only been back for four days, and her name was on everyone's lips. And now, thanks to his efforts out at her family's property, evidently his name was mixed right in there with hers.

The bell above the door jingled, and they all looked over. Zeke Moeller walked in, his jacket unzipped and his boots leaving a trail of dirt across the linoleum floor. He'd been a year ahead of Luke and two years behind Ethan in school. Luke hadn't liked him very much back then, and, well, not much had changed. Zeke had that sort of self-satisfied air about him that rubbed Luke the wrong way.

Zeke headed straight for the counter and spoke to Charlie. She hesitated, frowning, then pulled out an order pad. His gaze slid to their booth. His annoying smirk morphed into a knowing smile. A prickle of unease crawled up Luke's spine.

"What do we have here?" Zeke called out, his baritone voice booming through the café. "McGuire boys, what is this, a family meeting? You're missing a few."

Luke exchanged a glance with Ethan. Zeke moved closer. Even his swagger made Luke want to punch something.

"Heard you've been spending a lot of time with the Carlisle girl. What's the deal with those sea lions?"

Luke stabbed at the ice in his drink with his straw. "We evicted a few."

Zeke chuckled. "Yeah, saw the video online. Seems like a waste of time to me, but hey, what do I know? Maybe that's your thing, rescuing people who don't belong here anymore."

Luke's stomach clenched. Heat crept up his neck. He stared at the note on his phone. The words fix snowmobile glared back at him.

"Let it go," Tate said quietly, an edge to his voice.

"Are you keeping busy, Zeke?" Ethan wiped his hands on a napkin. "Sorry to hear your son lost that last wrestling match. There's always next season, right?"

"You tell me." Zeke glared. "Bet you know a thing or two about losing state championships. Right, Coach?"

Luke silenced a groan. Ethan had set him up for that one.

"Zeke." Charlie pointed to the paper bag sitting on the counter. "Your order's ready."

Zeke offered them one last smug smile. Like an unwanted parting gift. "See you jokers around."

He paid Charlie at the register, grabbed his food, and then strode out, the bell jingling again as the door swung shut.

Tension lingered over the table. Heavy. Oppressive.

"That guy's always been a jerk," Ethan said. "Don't let him get to you."

"I'm not," Luke said. His tone betrayed him though. He rubbed his brow and blew out a long breath. "I don't get why everyone cares so much about the sea lions and the Carlisle place. I'm trying to help. That's it."

Tate pushed his food aside, then leaned on the table. "You're going out of your way, bro. Knight in shining armor and all that. That's probably not a good idea."

"Why not?"

Tate pinned him with a long look. "Seriously? She's engaged, right? To some rich doctor in Boston. And you—"

"Who said he was rich?" Luke swiped another fry through the ketchup. "And if he's so great, why isn't he here?"

"Don't know, but he is her fiancé," Tate said. "You helping her out like this—it's not just about knocking items off the to-do list or chasing sea lions back into the water. People are watching the videos, they see you together, and as you well know, this town is not over what the Carlisles did."

Luke shook his head. "She didn't ask me for anything. I offered. Was I supposed to walk away? Pretend I didn't know she'd probably struggle?"

Ethan looked thoughtful. "I get it. Tough to look away when someone is having a hard time. But why you? Like Tate said, she's got a fiancé, and I heard her mom married her third husband. Why can't they be the ones to step up?"

"They're not here," Luke shot back. "And she's not her dad. By the way, her mom hasn't paid the property taxes, so how about a little grace for Emma, who is just trying to clean up a mess she didn't make."

"That's fair." Tate nodded. "But remember that you don't owe her anything. Plus we've got a mess of our own."

Luke picked up his burger and took a bite, his mind spinning. His brothers had a point, although he wasn't about to admit it. Still, the idea of turning his back on Emma didn't sit right.

He finished chewing, then forced himself to focus. "Let's get back on track here. How are we gonna save this resort?"

"I finally got ahold of someone at the equipment-rental place in Anchorage. You're right, they have snowmobiles available, but he emailed me the terms for a six-week lease on four machines." Tate sighed and scrubbed his hand over his face. "The guy wants $1,200 a week for each machine plus we have to go get them."

Grimacing, Luke made a note in his phone. "That's a decent deal, but too steep for us."

"More than we can afford for sure," Ethan said. "Let's keep brainstorming. There's got to be something we can do between now and Memorial Day to fill the gap."

Luke tossed out some more ideas, but his thoughts kept drifting. To Emma. Her property. To Zeke's smug face. No matter what his brothers or Zeke said, the facts didn't change. Emma didn't deserve to be left on her own to deal with the sea lions plus the added pressure of cleaning up a house and a piece of land with a ton of baggage attached. And the resort didn't need to go under either. There had to be a way to help Emma and salvage the failing resort. Because he wasn't giving up. Not yet.

Seven

She was so done with those stupid sea lions.

Five days in, and she'd made zero progress getting past them. Wasn't there anyone in town who had an effective solution?

Emma stood in front of an A-frame building with its rough-hewn logs and bright white trim. Redemption's community library hadn't changed much in the last two decades. Dollops of white snow dotted the sidewalk, and jagged icicles marched along the roofline above the rectangular windows. The sculpture of a grizzly bear clutching a salmon in its mouth still stood near the front door.

Her phone hummed with an incoming text. She hesitated outside the entrance, shivering in the frigid morning air, then glanced at the screen. Nathan's message sent a spark of warmth zipping through her.

> Nathan
> I miss you, babe. Hope you're making progress. Annual fundraiser for pediatric hospital is March 18th this year. Can you get our tickets, please?

Oh no. She read the message again. His words sank in, and the warmth faded, replaced by an aching chill that curled around her ribs. She'd been so distracted with this trip and the house that she'd forgotten all about the fundraiser for the children's hospital. The Prescotts never missed it. Her fingers hovered over the keyboard. Would now be a good time to mention that at this point she probably wouldn't be back in Boston by March 18? Instead, she shoved her phone back into her bag. Maybe she'd come up with an acceptable way to evict the sea lions and get the house cleaned up and on the market in the next five days. Then she'd be back on track. On her way to Boston with time to spare.

She pushed open the heavy door and stepped inside. This place had been her refuge, especially in middle school. A quiet place to escape the chaos and arguments brewing at home. Books transported her to places where families didn't fall apart and life didn't always feel like a fight. The familiar scent of old paper wrapped around her like a warm embrace. She surveyed the sunken floor in the children's section, with a few beanbags and two comfy chairs arranged around rainbow-colored carpet squares. Taxidermied birds native to Alaska hung suspended on a mobile overhead. The place seemed smaller than she remembered, though maybe her sentimental memories had exaggerated it.

"Good morning, Emma."

The familiar voice stopped her mid-step. She turned to see Mrs. Manning standing near the front desk, a stack of books in her arms. Dressed in a cozy sweater, bell-bottom jeans, and sensible clogs, she hadn't changed much. Even her hair, more silver now than brown, was still coiled into a neat, no-nonsense bun at the nape of her neck.

"I was hoping you'd stop by."

"Mrs. Manning." Emma smiled. "Do you still work here?"

"Oh, heavens no. I retired three years ago," Mrs. Manning said, setting the books down. "But I volunteer when I can. Old habits die hard."

"I get that." Emma hesitated, shifting her purse strap higher on her shoulder. "I'm glad you're here because I need your help."

Mrs. Manning's kind blue eyes twinkled. "Looking for a compulsive read or trying to solve a mystery?"

"Some of both, maybe." Emma glanced toward the shelves. "I need to learn about sea lions, and so far the Internet's not doing me any favors."

Mrs. Manning's brows raised. "Ah, yes, I understand you need to serve an eviction notice."

"Ha." Emma shook her head. "You sound like Luke McGuire."

Mrs. Manning scrunched up her nose. "This probably isn't the best time for jokes, is it? Let's start back here." She led Emma to a section in the far corner, past a couple of tables with computers advertising free Internet service and resources for tax preparation.

"Let's see what we can find. Are you looking for regulations, statutes, or perhaps previous cases?"

"I guess all of the above." Emma sighed, rubbing her temple. "I've got to figure out how to get them off my property."

"I understand." Mrs. Manning paused, her forehead wrinkling as her fingers trailed along books shelved in the reference section. "I wonder if an online search would be more effective?"

"Maybe you have access to digital archives or something that I wouldn't know how to find. I'll take any advice you can give," Emma said. "Luke and I went out to the house twice. At least two dozen sea lions are sprawled across the dock, the deck, and the beach. You can hardly hear yourself think over all the noise they're making."

Mrs. Manning gave an empathetic nod. "That's quite the dilemma. What did Fish and Game have to say?"

"Told me to wait it out. Apparently, they'll leave eventually."

Mrs. Manning gave her a knowing look. "But you don't have time to wait."

"Exactly," Emma said, taking the magazine Mrs. Manning handed her. "I have a life in Boston, a job, a wedding to plan." She cut herself off, shaking her head. "Nathan—my fiancé—is going to get impatient if I have to stay longer than ten days. He doesn't understand why I can't just sign some papers or list the place and be done."

"Is there something else going on?" Mrs. Manning studied her. "What's stopping you from listing the house and then going back to Boston?"

"If I can't get past the sea lions and into the house, how will I stage everything? I imagine there's damage from the tidal wave. Or what if a previous renter trashed the place?" She followed Mrs. Manning as she walked to another shelf and plucked out a couple more magazines.

"Valid points. Sea lions are protected, you know. You can't just shoo them away."

"Oh, believe me, I know." Emma scanned a page about migration patterns. "That's why I need to figure out another solution. There has to be something I can do to speed this up."

Mrs. Manning slid some magazines and a hardcover book onto a table nearby. "And what happens if you can't?"

Emma stared down at the pictures of sleek bodies sunning themselves on rocky shores. "I don't know. I'll have to leave, I guess. I can't put my entire life on hold because a bunch of sea lions decided to move in. But my mother confessed recently that she hasn't paid the property taxes in quite some time, so I feel obligated to make that right. Or maybe part of me still clings to the good memories and isn't willing to let the place go. Sadly, at this point the house could slide off into the sea and I wouldn't be able to intervene."

Mrs. Manning hesitated, then offered a thoughtful smile. "I can't do anything about those sea lions or the unpaid taxes, but please know that we're happy to have you here for as long as you're willing to stay."

Emma's heart pinched. "Really?"

"Of course." Mrs. Manning clasped her hands together. "Not everyone associates your name with negativity, despite the local gossip that tries to make you believe otherwise."

Mrs. O'Brien's rude comments paired with Joe's criticism at the pizza place flitted through Emma's head. She brushed the hurtful words aside. Mostly because she respected Mrs. Manning too much to argue. "What else are you into these days? When you're not volunteering here."

"I love water aerobics, but since the tidal wave, we've struggled finding an instructor for the seniors' class. Our previous instructor left town, and we haven't found a replacement."

"I'm planning to be here for five more days. Maybe I could fill in one time?"

Mrs. Manning's eyes lit up. "Oh, we would love that."

"Don't get too excited. I wasn't much of a swimmer back in the day. Placed last in every event." Emma shivered at the memory. "But I'm happy to help if I can."

"You're probably the only one who remembers that." Mrs. Manning patted her arm. "Besides, don't you work at a fitness center now? I thought I heard that about you."

"Well, yes, but—"

"Then you're all set. We just need you to lead some exercises in the water. It's only an hour. These folks would love having someone young and energetic around."

Emma opened her mouth to protest again that she wasn't the best person to lead water aerobics, but Mrs. Manning tilted her head, giving her that same expectant look she used to give when Emma was in junior high and trying to avoid writing a paper.

"You were always a natural leader," Mrs. Manning said, her tone gentle but pointed. "And sometimes giving back is the best way to feel at home."

Emma swallowed hard. "This place hasn't been home for a long time."

"True, but that doesn't mean it couldn't be home again, right?"

Here in this library, with Mrs. Manning looking at her like she still saw something good in her, it didn't feel like such a far-fetched idea.

"Maybe." Emma sighed, then pulled out her phone. "Now, can you please help me figure out what I should search on the Internet to get some answers?"

"Yes, come with me."

Mrs. Manning led the way back to the front desk. As Emma trailed behind, her phone buzzed again. She fished it out and glanced at the screen.

> Brittney
> Hey, I haven't heard much from you. How are things? You're coming back, right? 😉

Emma's steps slowed. Based on the winky-face emoji, Brittney was likely just teasing. Still, her insides twisted. Five days wasn't long. She was running out of time. And options.

⚡

Man, he hadn't realized how much he needed a night out.

Luke chalked the tip of his cue stick, scanning the table as he tried to line up a shot. Cheers went up from the bar, distracting him, and he glanced across the crowded room. All three of the massive flat screens mounted on the opposite wall featured the same college basketball game: North Carolina versus Duke. Ever since a local kid had been recruited to play for Duke two years ago, Redemption had pulled hard for the team. He used to watch the games with Ethan, back before Tisha arrived. Not that he wasn't thrilled for his brother and his fresh start, but he did kind of miss bonding over college basketball.

He shoved the thoughts aside and zeroed in on the eight ball sitting near the corner pocket. One sweet shot and he could win.

His best friend, Justin, leaned against the end of the pool table, sipping his Coke and grinning—friendly but kind of competitive too.

"You're overthinking this," Justin teased. "Take the shot."

"I like to switch things up," Luke said. "Make you sweat a little. Besides, where else do you have to be tonight?"

Justin laughed and raised his tall plastic cup in the air. "If you must know, I've got to call Laurel at ten thirty."

"Wow, that's late."

"Dude, how old are you?"

"Thirty-five." Luke scowled. "Thanks for the reminder."

"I'm just messing with you," Justin said. "By the way, if you miss this shot, I'm cleaning up the table."

Luke didn't respond. He bent low over the cue stick, focusing a little harder than he needed to for a casual game of pool on a random Wednesday night. But to be honest, he didn't want to look at Justin right now. Not when everything about his friend's life seemed to be going in the right direction. He had certainty. A solid commitment. A plan. Things Luke had somehow misplaced along the way.

Stalling wouldn't change the outcome of this game though. He took the shot. The cue ball kissed the eight ball but not at all like he'd planned. It rolled wide.

Justin whooped and stepped forward, setting his drink on a nearby high-top table. "Whoa. You have lost your groove." He leaned on the table with easy confidence. Like a guy who knew he was going to win. "You used to wipe the floor with me at pool. What is going on?"

Luke shrugged and stepped back, propping his pool stick on the floor at his feet. "Isn't it obvious? I'm letting you win. If you're gonna take off for Wyoming soon, consider this a parting gift."

Justin paused mid-shot, pinning him with a look. "I haven't left yet, you know, and it's only for spring break. Laurel's taking vacation so we can hang out."

"Play it coy if you want, but I can tell you're a guy who is falling hard. You've pretty much already decided." He reached for his Coke and took a long sip.

Justin straightened, still holding his pool stick. He offered a sheepish grin. "Yeah, I mean, I guess I have." He hesitated. "You ever meet someone who makes you feel like maybe you've been looking at the world the wrong way? Like what you thought you wanted isn't really what you need?"

Luke's stomach sank. "Dude, you have no idea." He took another sip of his pop, the ice rattling against the red plastic. "So you're feeling pretty confident about Laurel, then?"

Justin's grin grew wider. "She's amazing. I've never met anyone like her. Wyoming feels like the right move, you know? I mean, I'll finish out the school year here teaching, but I could get a job there super easy, find a decent apartment, and start fresh."

Luke nodded. He didn't trust himself to speak. He wanted to be happy for Justin. Really, he did. But the thought of his best friend leaving Redemption left a hollow ache in his chest. He couldn't pretend it wasn't there. Justin had become a person who made this place feel less suffocating, less lonely.

Justin sank the eight ball with ease, then leaned on his stick again. Sympathy and curiosity flitted across his face. "What about you? You texted me about a job in Petersburg. Are you going to go for it or what?"

Luke set his cup aside. "I don't know. I thought about it. Started filling out the application, but it's hard, you know? I don't want to leave the resort or leave Redemption. This place has been my whole life."

Justin frowned, his gaze steady. "Has it though? I mean, yeah, you grew up here and moved back after college, but is that resort really yours? You have four siblings. Are you just holding on to it because it's what your family expects you to do?"

Luke winced. He turned away and grabbed the rack to set up for the next game. Mostly because he needed to give his hands something to do, not because he really wanted to keep playing.

"It's not that simple. I feel like if we sell it, we're just giving up. It's a piece of who we are."

Justin walked around the table, helped organize the balls, tucking them into the triangle. "Maybe it's time to give yourself permission to figure out who you are," he said. "I mean, I'm just saying. The Lord is sovereign over all things, so is He asking you to let go of something that you've been holding on to for too long? Maybe you don't even see that it's dragging you down."

Luke opened his mouth to protest but stopped short of mentioning how Emma's return had messed with his head. And his heart. Because it shouldn't matter. She belonged to Nathan. Before he could respond, his phone buzzed in his pocket. He pulled it out and saw a message from his mom.

> Mom
> Inspector dropped by. Says plumbing isn't up to code in cabins five and six. Can't rent them until it's fixed. Just thought you should know.

"Oh brother." Shaking his head, Luke put his phone away without answering.

Justin finished setting the rack, then stepped back. "Everything all right?"

"Just more stuff going sideways at the resort."

Justin raised an eyebrow.

Luke held up a palm. "I know what you're going to say, but it's my family's business."

"Exactly. Emphasis on family. Which means you don't have to fix everything on your own. I know you came back to help after your dad got hurt, which is awesome. But have you stayed here this long because it's safe? Because it's easy?"

Luke tightened his grip on the pool cue. "Well, that's the problem," he said. "It doesn't feel safe or easy anymore. It's full of memories of people who've left, people who've changed."

Justin smiled, but it carried a hint of sadness. "Redemption isn't going to stay the same. That tidal wave guaranteed that. Maybe it's time to stop waiting for things to go back to how they were."

A beat of silence hung between them. Luke stared at the table. "Maybe."

Justin let the cue rest against the table, then clapped a hand on Luke's shoulder. "You've got a lot going for you, probably more than you realize. I'm going to pray that you'll stop holding yourself back."

Luke leaned over the table, lined up his next shot, but he lost his focus. Justin's words lingered.

Maybe Justin was right. Maybe he'd wasted too much time putting his life on hold.

Eight

IF HER GOAL IN COMING HERE WAS TO SAY goodbye to the house so she could gain closure and move on with her life, then why couldn't she make herself go inside?

Cold wind whipped around her, carrying salt, sea spray, and a hint of snow.

"Do you smell that?" Emma turned to look at Luke. "I think it's going to snow."

Luke pressed his palms together and looked toward the sky. "Please, God, let it be so."

"You guys really need some, don't you?"

He nodded, weariness creasing the lines around his eyes. "A few feet. Six to twelve, really, if I'm being honest. One more wintery blast to bring in some customers that will get us through until May."

She smiled. "Maybe this is the beginning of a blizzard."

"Yikes." He frowned. "Let's get back to safety before we wish that upon ourselves, all right?"

"Fair enough."

She turned to face the house. It loomed ahead, looking just as battered by time and the relentless Alaskan elements as the last time they'd been out here three days ago. Sea lions still barked incessantly from the rocky outcropping, their presence a reminder of how the wildlife had slowly reclaimed the coast.

She glanced at Luke, who stood patiently beside her, his eyes fixed on the house.

"Are you sure about this?" He clutched the straps of the pack on his shoulders. "I can imagine it's tough dealing with the onslaught of memories."

She sighed, her breath visible in the cold air. "I have to get in there. I can't just let it go without saying goodbye. Besides, I can't list it in its current condition."

"Then let's get to it," Luke said.

She studied him. Part of her was surprised he hadn't tried persuading her not to sell it. Did coming out here dredge up memories of the past for him too?

Engaged to Nathan, remember?

She batted the reminder away. Her phone hummed with a text. She left the device in her pocket, ignoring it.

Together, they approached the back of the house. Thankfully, the sea lions weren't paying them any attention. Probably too busy preening, barking, and challenging each other over territory. Weeds and overgrown bushes flanked the back entrance. The door's six windowpanes were miraculously all still intact. The paint had chipped away from what had once been a vibrant shade of sea-glass green, her mother's favorite.

Luke pulled the key from his pocket. "I still can't believe Hank found this."

"Yeah, he seems to know a lot about this place."

"Hank's a humble guy, but I wouldn't be surprised if he helped with the construction."

She raised an eyebrow. "Really?"

Luke nodded.

"When he's feeling better, I'd like to ask him a few questions." Emma ran her hand along the siding beside the door. "Whoever built this knew what they were doing. I can't believe this place survived a tidal wave."

"That makes two of us."

Luke jammed the key into the lock and jiggled the knob until it clicked. He gently pushed the door open, a creaking sound echoing in the stillness. A musty smell wafted out—although it was nothing compared to the stench the sea lions had created. He motioned for her to go first.

"After you."

She hesitated, her heart pounding. Then she took a deep breath and stepped inside.

The pungent odor of mildew greeted her. The once-bright living room was dim, probably due to the grime-covered windows and the boards protecting at least two. What was left of the furniture lay covered in dust, and a stack of outdated hunting and fishing magazines, along with a water-damaged paperback, sat on the filthy coffee table. Her throat tightened.

"It's mostly empty," she whispered, taking in the dried mud clinging to the hardwood floors.

"The tidal wave likely ruined whatever was left," Luke said as he came in behind her and closed the door. "Can't beat that view though."

"True. My mom made sure we could see the water and mountains as much as possible." She walked farther into the room, pausing to rest her hand on the back of the upholstered sofa. "We were so happy here, Luke."

Luke nodded, tenderness in his gaze. He tucked his hands into his jacket pockets. "You had some good times here, didn't you?"

She nodded. "My dad told the best stories. My uncle too. I miss them."

"I wish I'd spent more time with your uncle Seth," Luke said. "He didn't come into town often."

"I didn't see him much. He had a terrible speech impediment and stuttered a lot. Sometimes he could only sing to get the words out. He really loved being in the gold mine the most."

Luke frowned. "Do you think your cousin Gavin might want the house?"

She shrugged. "Good question. My uncle had a cabin somewhere off the grid, but I'm not exactly sure where. And I'm still trying to get in touch with Gavin. I asked the radio station in Glennallen to send out a message. They said they would, but Gavin hasn't called me back yet."

"What happened to the gold mine?"

"I have no idea. My uncle never married Gavin's mom. I don't think we ever met her either."

"He kept things top secret, huh?"

She nodded. The weight of memories hung in the air as she turned toward the cased opening dividing the living room from the back hallway.

A floorboard creaked, louder than the others. She froze.

Luke, a step behind, tensed. "You hear that?"

She nodded, scanning the room. "The house is protesting. Probably not fond of those sea lions either."

"Understood. They've overstayed their welcome for sure."

"Oh my goodness, look." She pointed to the handwriting still legible on the cased opening. Her dad had measured her height year after year and marked it carefully with the date. The marks went all the way back to her second birthday and stopped just after she turned fifteen.

"Wow, that's impressive," Luke said. "I'm glad you can still see it."

"He used permanent marker. Made my mom so mad." She pulled out her phone and snapped a few photos of the lines and dates. Her throat tightened, and she tamped down the emotion. Part of her wanted to reach for Luke, to let him hold her. Comfort her. But she couldn't and she wouldn't. The tension between them was like a taut wire ready to snap.

"I don't know exactly where to begin," Luke said, breaking into her thoughts, "but let's start with the kitchen."

She nodded and led the way. Cabinet doors hung ajar, and the floor creaked beneath their feet. She opened the door to the pantry and dust billowed out, making her cough.

"Oh wow," she said, laughing. She waved her hand through the air.

Luke pointed to the floor. "Watch your step. These boards look weak."

Just as he said it, she stepped on a warped board and with a sudden crack, her foot plunged through.

"Emma!" Luke reached out, his hand clasping her elbow.

"Ow." She sucked air through her teeth, then pulled her foot free. The shattered floorboard revealed a gaping, dark hole into the crawl space.

"Are you okay?" He pulled her against him, his arms solid and sure.

"Yeah, I'm fine." She balanced on her right leg, then slowly rotated her left ankle in a circle.

"First your wrist and now your leg. Are you sure you're all right?"

Emma nodded, still clinging to him.

"Can you put weight on it?"

She put her foot on the floor, grimacing at the dull throb radiating from her ankle. "It's fine. A little sore."

He pulled his phone from his pocket and shined the flashlight into the hole.

Emma let go of him. "What do you think is in there?"

"Let's find out."

She pulled out her phone again, ready to take more photos. "That's a lot of mud."

"Nothing compared to what people had to deal with in town." He tested the board with his toes and then sank to his knees. "We've spent hours shoveling mud out of buildings and dealing with insurance claims from the flooding."

Emma shook her head. "That sounds awful."

"It's frustrating for sure," Luke said. "Especially for the people who might have to cut their losses and leave town because insurance won't cover their claims."

Before she could respond, he pulled a glove from his pocket, put it on, then scraped at the mud.

"What are you doing?"

"Your foot must've connected with something." Grunting, he clawed at the mud with his hand. "Otherwise, you would have sunk up to your knee or hip, right?"

"Good point." She leaned closer. "What do you think it is?"

"It's some kind of metal box like they used to keep ammunition in back in the day." He exposed the handle, then tugged, but it wouldn't come free. Frowning, he sat back on his heels. "I wish I'd brought a shovel."

"Maybe there's something in the utility closet. Hang on."

She went down the hall to the laundry room. The washer and dryer were gone. Weird. Too bad they didn't have any electricity, because extra lighting would really help right now. But Hank had already warned them that somebody had swiped the generator.

She opened the closet where they used to keep the broom. Sure enough, a broom, a dustpan, and a few gardening tools still sat on the floor.

Perfect. She grabbed the spade and carried it back to Luke. "Not a shovel, but it might work."

"Oh, awesome. Thanks." He took it and dug and dug and dug,

scraping away the dried, caked-on mud until he'd revealed a cube-shaped army-green box with old-fashioned buckles.

Emma's pulse thundered in her ears. "Whoa. This is wild!"

Luke set the spade down, then crouched lower, reached in, and tugged with both hands. The box didn't budge. He tugged again and it came loose, knocking him off balance. "Heavier than I thought," he said, chest heaving.

She crouched beside him and ran her hand over the dented metal. The hinges looked rusted but both latches were intact.

Luke glanced at her. "Why don't you open it? This house, this discovery—it's yours."

"All right." She scooted closer, scraped away more mud, then slowly undid one clasp and then the other. The lid creaked as she lifted it. The scent of damp earth and metal wafted up. Inside, nestled in layers of frayed burlap, sat a substantial amount of gold nuggets. Some as small as marbles. Others golf-ball size. Raw, gleaming, heavy chunks of gold.

Emma gasped, then clapped her hand to her mouth.

Luke's wide-eyed gaze found hers. "Oh my," he whispered.

With trembling fingers, she reached down and picked up one of the nuggets. Dirt still clung to the pock marks, and its craggy edges felt rough against her fingertips. "Is this real?"

"If it's not, then why did someone bury it?" Luke shined his phone's flashlight on the rest of the gold. "Do you think your uncle stashed it here?"

"Maybe, but why?"

"Emergency supply?" Luke said with a grin. "This is probably worth a fortune. Last time I checked, gold was sitting at almost three thousand dollars an ounce."

What? She shot him a look. "You're joking."

"I wouldn't tease you about the value of gold."

She stared into the mud-filled crawl space, mentally calculating the potential payout of their discovery. Was this one box of many?

Not that it mattered. She couldn't even be one hundred percent sure any of this legitimately belonged to her. And if it did? She rubbed at the tightness pressing against her sternum.

"There's got to be thousands of dollars in here. This has the potential to change your life, Emma."

"Or at the very least, pay the property taxes." She let out a shaky laugh. "Buried treasure. In my childhood home. Sounds like something from a movie."

Luke gave a slow smile. "Plot twist."

She let herself bask in his smile. Just for a minute.

Then his expression grew serious, and his eyes roamed her face. He reached up and tucked an errant curl behind her ear. "This gives you options that maybe you didn't know you had."

Her breath hitched. Part of her yearned to lean into his touch.

Luke pulled away. "I just want you to be happy."

Everything stopped, the past and present colliding as they knelt there on her old kitchen floor. "Who says I'm not?"

Doubt flashed in his eyes. "Call it a hunch."

Right. She stood, brushing mud and dust from her knees. "So what do we do now? Do you think there's more?"

He shone the light back down into the hole. "I have no idea. Maybe."

Raucous barking filled the air, startling her. "What in the world? What makes them do that?"

"Who knows?" He stood, skirted around the hole, then scrubbed at the kitchen window with the cuff of his jacket's sleeve. "Wow, it's finally snowing. We need to go."

She gestured to the metal box at her feet. "We're taking that with us, right?"

Luke turned away from the window. "I can carry it if you want me to."

"I don't want to leave it here." She looked around at the

abandoned place she'd once called home. "Obviously no one's been by in a long time, but if word gets out . . ."

He met her gaze, his eyes fierce. Protective. "I'm not going to tell anyone what we found."

"Thank you," she said. "But where will we put it? And if Hank had a house key, maybe other people do too? Who was the last renter living here before the tidal wave?"

"Whoa." Luke held up both palms. "Take a breath. One thing at a time."

She grimaced. "I know, I know. I'm sorry. But it's not every day a girl stumbles across thousands of dollars in gold nuggets stashed in her old kitchen."

"I understand." Luke gestured to the hole in the floor. "I don't know who else has a key, and it's not likely that I can patch that hole in the next five minutes. We really do need to get going. There's no water and no electricity, so as much as I love your company, getting stranded out here is not a good idea."

Flustered, she tipped her head toward the door. "Let's take it with us."

"You sure?"

She nodded. "I'm sure. You're right. We'd better go. Does the resort have a safe?"

He nodded.

"Then let's stash it there for now."

They carefully spread the haul between their backpacks, tucked the empty box back in the hole, then jammed the floorboard into place. As they made their way back toward the door, she couldn't stop thinking about what he'd said.

Because he was right. Finding a buried treasure could completely change her life.

His truck coughed, sputtered, and died.

Luke exhaled, then gripped the steering wheel until his knuckles turned white. Of all the times for his reliable truck to turn traitorous, it had to be now—when he was stranded in a snowstorm with his high school girlfriend. Somehow his heart had missed the memo that she wore another man's ring, because he couldn't overlook the sparks igniting between them.

He jabbed at the button again, but the engine didn't even try this time. Only a pathetic click, then silence.

"Uh-oh." Emma combed her fingers through her auburn curls, letting them cascade down the shoulders of her borrowed parka. He gritted his teeth, then looked away. Tucking her hair behind her ear had been a dumb move. A reckless mistake he couldn't afford to make again.

"Timing's not great, is it?" He managed to keep his tone light as he let his head fall against the headrest.

Emma let out a short laugh.

Outside, snow swirled around the truck, the flakes fat and slow, the kind that would stick. At least there was that. The resort needed every single inch. Because they were barely hanging on. And fighting the unpredictable weather wasn't the only issue. He harbored a sneaking suspicion that many tourists avoided Redemption in favor of something fancier than his family-run operation.

But frankly, the potential upswing in snow-seeking tourists wasn't the first thing on his mind right now. Not with Emma sitting so close, her body still carrying the warmth from their hike, her fragrance—something light and familiar—filling the cab.

Emma rubbed her palms together. "Does your phone work out here?"

"Yeah. Barely." He pulled out his phone and scrolled to his brother Ethan's name. He hesitated for half a second before tapping the call icon.

Ethan picked up on the second ring. "Hey, check it out. It's finally snowing."

"Yep, it's coming down out here."

"Dude, why don't you sound excited? This is awesome!"

Luke glanced at Emma. Her eyebrows sailed upward. He looked away. "My truck won't start. I need a tow or a jump or . . . something."

Silence, then a slow, knowing chuckle. "Let me guess, you're out at the end of Aurora Way."

Luke closed his eyes. Please, no lecture. Not right now. "Can you come help us?"

"Us?"

Luke swallowed back a frustrated sigh. "Just send someone, Ethan."

"On my way."

Luke ended the call and dropped his phone in his lap, then raked his hand through his hair. The wind picked up outside, howling around them. He reached behind Emma's seat and grabbed a thick plaid blanket with a sherpa backing. "Need this?"

"Sure, thank you." She shifted in her seat and spread the blanket across her lap. "Are we stuck here for a bit?"

"Ethan says he's on his way."

"I'm thankful you have family close by who can help out," she said.

Nodding, Luke tried to ignore the way her voice curled around him. They'd already spent more time together than they should have. Long enough to unearth a fortune in gold hidden beneath the floorboards of her childhood home. Long enough to dance around the reality of her engagement. Long enough for him to brush a stray lock of hair from her eyes and vow he'd keep her secret.

Sitting there together in her old kitchen, it had felt like nothing had changed. Except everything had. He flexed his fingers against his jeans, his pulse still thrumming. He should say something. Anything. He had to steer the conversation somewhere safe that didn't involve the past. Or the way she looked at him as if she wasn't entirely sure she'd made the right choice building a life in Boston.

"You sure you're warm enough?"

She smiled. "Yeah. Are you?"

He almost laughed. He was anything but cold.

She rubbed her hands along her arms and stared out the window. "I can't believe we found all that gold."

"Me either." He had questions. So many questions. But they weren't his to ask. Why hadn't her father ever told her about the gold? What was she going to do with it? Her parents had divorced and her father was in prison, and her uncle was deceased. As far as he knew, she was an only child. So that meant she had decisions to make. But the biggest question of all was why did she still look at him like that if she wanted to marry Nathan?

"Thanks, by the way," she said softly. "For everything."

He met her gaze, and once again something electric passed between them. Oh, how he wanted to reach for her. Just once. To see if her fingers still fit perfectly laced with his. Instead, he shoved his hands into his coat pockets.

"Anytime," he said, his voice rough.

The minutes passed, thick with unsaid words. The kind of charged silence that only existed between two people with a complicated history. He had no business wanting her like this. No business remembering the way she used to tuck her feet under his legs when they sat on the sofa watching movies, or the way she dropped her head against his shoulder when she laughed, her whole body rippling with happiness.

She wasn't his to remember.

His phone buzzed and he snatched it up like it was a lifeline.

> **Ethan**
> Almost there. Had to drop Brody off at a friend's house.

Luke typed back a quick "thanks" and set the phone down again. Another gust of wind shook the truck, and he glanced at Emma. "Are you sure you're okay? Do you need some water or a snack?"

Her slow smile sent a spike of something warm and delicious arcing around his heart. "I'm fine, Luke. Honest."

He nodded and forced himself to look away. His truck might've been dead but the spark between him and Emma sure wasn't. And that was a problem. A big one. Because now in addition to a boatload of memories, they had something else tying them together.

A secret.

And secrets usually got dragged into the light at the worst possible time. Pinching the back of his neck with his palm, Luke blew out a long breath. Ethan's words echoed in his head.

But I remember what it was like when she left. You were a mess ... Just don't let her wreck you again.

Yeah, well, he'd been wrecked before. Told himself he'd gotten over her. That he'd be fine. But now, sitting here in the truck, breathing the same air and guarding a shared secret—he felt it. That pull. An invisible, magnetic tug.

And if he wasn't careful, he'd have to walk through heartache. Again.

Nine

ONE HOUR OF WATER AEROBICS. THE PERFECT escape from worrying about the sea lions, the gold, and the fact that she was supposed to be on a plane back to Boston in two days.

Emma pushed through the women's locker-room door and out onto the deck of Redemption High School's pool. The pungent smell of chlorine welcomed her, and a playful slosh of water lapped at the pool's gutters. A dozen older adults and senior citizens already stood in the shallow end. Their bright-colored one-piece swimsuits and turquoise-blue floaty belts made them look almost welcoming.

Her flip-flops slapped against the damp tile as she walked to the two-tier silver bleachers closest to the end of the pool.

"Hey, everyone. I'm Emma, and I'll be filling in as an instructor for your class. It's my first time back in this pool in a very long time." She offered a wobbly smile. "So go easy on me, okay?"

A couple of people chuckled. The tension lodged between her shoulder blades relaxed a smidge.

"I hope you do a better job than the last girl who subbed," somebody grumbled.

Her smile faltered. Okay, so maybe one grumpy lady was to be expected.

"Olive, that was not necessary," Mrs. Manning chided from the front row of the group. "Emma has graciously offered to step in and help us out. We all need the exercise and the social time, so let's be kind."

"Her family wasn't kind to mine," the silver-haired woman shot back. "In fact, I wouldn't mind getting a refund on the money I donated for that cannery your dad never built."

"Okay, that's enough," Mrs. Manning said. "If you can't be kind, then maybe this isn't the class for you."

"You're not in charge of that." Olive glared up at Emma. "By the way, you're late. We need to get started."

Warmth flushed Emma's skin, and she shot Mrs. Manning a pleading glance.

"We do like our routines around here," Mrs. Manning said. "How would you like us to begin?"

Emma left her striped towel on the bleacher, slipped off her flip-flops, and unzipped her yellow terry-cloth cover-up. Then she slid into the pool, gasping at the cold water. "Let's start with some warm-ups," she said, her teeth chattering. "How about we march in place?"

She demonstrated the motion, letting the water wash over her extremities. "Like this."

All twelve of them complied.

"You're off to a great start," she called out, her voice echoing off the high ceilings. "Keep it moving."

She surveyed her attendees. A white-haired woman in a bright magenta swimsuit smiled back at her.

"Nice work."

The woman waved. At least somebody was happy she was here. Make that two somebodies, as Mrs. Manning set a great example for her peers and marched in place.

"All right, what's your favorite exercise? What do you typically do?"

"Isn't that your job to decide?" Olive's blue eyes flashed with disdain.

Oh boy. Emma glanced at the other ladies. "I can think of five or six exercises. I was hoping to start with something that you enjoyed. What's your favorite?"

Olive tipped her chin up. "Leg lifts."

"Perfect. Let's start with fifteen reps."

"Oh, I prefer twelve." Olive scooted closer to the pool's wall. "With support."

"Great, you can do twelve. Use the wall as much as you need to. Everyone else? Let's try for fifteen. Three sets. Let's go."

Her pulse climbed, her breathing increased, and she finally stopped shivering. Snide comments melted away as the women completed their reps. It felt good to encourage people and lead a group exercise class again. By the end, she was exhausted but exhilarated. As the ladies made their way over to the ladder and slowly climbed out of the pool, she wrapped up in her towel.

"That was great, honey. Thank you," the white-haired woman who had smiled at her said. She leaned in. "Don't let Olive get you down. She's rarely happy."

Emma pressed her fingers over her lips, stifling a laugh.

Mrs. Manning climbed out of the pool last. "That was exceptional, Emma. Thank you, darling. I'm really proud of you. I'll talk to the activities director at the senior center. Maybe this can be a regular thing."

Emma reached for her cover-up and pushed her feet into her flip-flops. "I'm afraid that's not possible, Mrs. Manning. I'm supposed to go back to Boston on Monday."

"Well, make all the plans you want, but those sea lions might have a way of prolonging your visit."

Hope not. She kept that part to herself and headed for the

locker room. After a hot shower, Emma layered on her warmest pair of sweatpants, a T-shirt, a hoodie, and a vest. She put on her socks and sneakers, then headed through the wide corridor leading to the exit. The lingering smell of popcorn and the hum of the bright vending machines brought back memories of her first year—and the only year—she got to spend at this school. Her heart pinched as she passed the trophy case, where a photo of Luke and his teammates hoisting a trophy from some basketball tournament caused her to slow her steps. There were quite a few McGuires in photos hoisting trophies. It was nice to see that Luke had had a good life here, but selfishly, she couldn't help but wonder what it would have been like if she'd been here cheering him on, going to dances, and—

Her phone chimed from the depths of her bag. Digging through it, she pulled it out to see Nathan's name glowing on the screen. She swiped to take the call.

"Hey, sweetie, how's it going?"

"You sound tired," he said, without bothering to greet her.

"Yeah, well, haven't slept much lately," she said, forcing a smile even though he couldn't see it.

"Join the club," he said. "My cross to bear as a surgeon, I suppose."

Emma pushed the door to the parking lot open, the cold air nibbling at her cheeks.

"Are you wrapping things up with the house?" Nathan asked, yawning.

She glanced toward the car she'd borrowed from Lainey, illuminated under a parking lot light. A gentle snowfall had started, each flake landing like a soft kiss on her jacket. She smiled. Luke would be thrilled; maybe this incoming snowstorm would add another few inches to yesterday's and the McGuires would get another boost in customers.

"Emma, you there?"

"Sorry. Got distracted."

"I'll say. You've been harder to reach lately."

She sidestepped his thinly veiled criticism. "I'm going to have to stay here a little longer."

Silence stretched between them.

"Nathan?"

"You said ten days. Today is day eight."

"I know, but things are complicated. The house needs to be put on the market, but there's damage from the tidal wave to deal with. My mom hasn't paid the property taxes in years, and yesterday we found something significant."

"We? Who's we?"

Nathan's tone made her wince.

"Um, an old friend. Luke. He's helping me figure out how to access the house since the dock is unusable and the deck is overrun with obnoxious sea lions."

"I don't like you having old friends who also happen to be male."

Seriously?

She clicked the key fob, unlocked the door, and climbed into the driver's seat. Tossing her bag onto the passenger side, she exhaled. "You don't have anything to worry about. Besides, if it weren't for him, I wouldn't have been able to move the thousands of dollars in gold nuggets we found stashed under the floorboards."

"You're kidding."

"True story. I don't know how much it's worth yet, but—"

"Then liquidate it." He cut in. "That solves everything, doesn't it? Pay the taxes, sell the house, and get back here in time for the gala."

Her stomach dropped. "I'm not going to be able to come to the gala. Sorry. I'll make it up to you next year though."

"Excuse me?"

"I need more time here. To figure out if the gold is even mine. It could belong to my cousin Gavin. And I can't list the house as is."

Nathan muttered an obscenity. "We agreed the gala was important. My colleagues will be there, not to mention the donors. And fundraising for the children's hospital is my mother's passion project. It's not just another party."

She started the car, then rested her forehead on the steering wheel. "I didn't plan any of this, Nathan. You're acting like I caused all these issues, when in reality—"

"When in reality, no one forced you to hop on a plane last-minute and shirk all your responsibilities here. Now you're telling me that you're caught up in some small-town drama and you have to stick around and play gold miner with your old friend Luke?"

"That's not fair." She squeezed the words past the emotion tightening her throat. "I'm trying to do the right thing."

"Really?" Nathan scoffed. "If you want to do the right thing, then get on the plane Monday and come home."

"But—"

"I've got to prep for a surgical consult. Call me when you're thinking clearly."

He hung up before she could respond.

She stared at the phone in her hand, blinking back tears. For the first time since she'd said yes to marrying him, an ugly thought crept in. Uninvited. Unwelcome.

What if Nathan wasn't the man she thought he was?

She set the phone down, cranked the defroster, then cleared the windshield with the wipers.

A classic country song played on the radio, and she sang along as she drove through town. Lights glowed softly behind frosted windows, and snowflakes drifted through the air. Something about Redemption in the snow gave her all the feels—a stark contrast to Boston, where everyone was rushing, always going, going, going. Here, the snow blanketed the town in a quiet stillness that felt almost magical.

A few minutes later, she turned up the hill toward Lainey's

house, her headlights catching the light dusting of snow on the driveway. Abbie's car was parked in front of the house. When Emma pushed open the front door, she was greeted by the sound of laughter and the savory aroma of melted cheese.

In the kitchen, Lainey and Abbie hovered over a massive platter of nachos piled high with tomatoes, lettuce, olives, and seasoned ground meat.

"Hey," Abbie said, waving a chip in greeting. "How was class?"

"Oh boy," Emma said, setting her bag down. "Some of the ladies were a little feisty, but overall, I think it went well."

Lainey laughed as she grabbed a can of pop from the fridge. "Feisty seniors, huh? That's a workout in itself. Want some pop? Pairs perfectly with salty, crunchy carbohydrates."

"Sure." Emma took the can and smiled as they carried the platter into the family room. Wrapped in oversized blankets, the three of them settled onto the couch with plates of nachos, and Lainey queued up a show she'd been raving about for weeks.

"If this show doesn't win every award, I swear I'm gonna riot," Lainey declared.

Abbie rolled her eyes. "You said that about the last show, and it got canceled after one season."

"Details," Lainey said, plucking a chip from her plate. "Emma, back me up. Doesn't this sound amazing? It's got everything we could want: Mystery, romance, and a ridiculously hot detective."

"I'm in. Let's watch." Emma smiled, letting their chatter wash over her. Unlike Nathan, who always chose documentaries or sports, Lainey and Abbie actually wanted her opinion. She settled deeper into the couch, the warmth of the blanket and the cheesy nachos filling a void she hadn't realized existed.

Midway through the first episode, Lainey paused the show and turned to Emma. "Oh! We almost forgot—we need to talk about the Easter egg hunt."

"What about it?" Emma asked, halfway through a chip.

"Redemption Community Church is hosting it," Abbie said. "We almost canceled because of the tidal wave and all, but decided we could still make it happen, and it's going to be amazing. We need your help stuffing eggs and wrangling toddlers."

Emma picked at the edge of her blanket. "That's in, what . . . seven days?"

"Yep," Lainey said. "You're extending your stay, right?"

Emma nodded.

Grinning, Abbie and Lainey exchanged looks.

"I can't believe I just agreed to help with a church event," Emma said.

"No pressure." Abbie nudged her. "Because it's not about church, really. It's about the kids and showing up. They'll love it. And honestly, it's just fun."

The thought of jumping back into anything resembling church made her chest tighten. She'd become a believer years ago at a sports camp, but Nathan had convinced her that church wasn't an essential part of their lives. And she'd been fine with that. Because brunches and lazy Sundays had been more appealing than sermons.

Emma reached for her drink. "Nathan's not thrilled that I'm staying longer. He was hoping I'd be back in time for that gala thing at the children's hospital."

Lainey tilted her head. "Is he okay with you being here at all?"

Emma sighed. "He's just stressed. The hospital's demanding, and the gala is a big deal for his department."

Abbie's brows furrowed. "Is he good for you?"

Emma rubbed at the tightness in her chest. "Yeah. I mean, yes. Of course. He's just . . . driven. And super smart. He works hard, and we're building a life together."

"But?"

Lainey's voice didn't carry a single ounce of judgment. Still, that one word made Emma look away. She picked at her half-eaten nachos. "He doesn't get what this place means, or maybe what it once meant. And he made it clear that he doesn't like me spending time with old friends."

Abbie's eyes narrowed. "Seriously? Does he know I'm one of your bridesmaids?"

"I didn't mean you." Warmth heated her skin. "I . . . mentioned that Luke was helping me, and that didn't go over well."

Something flitted across Abbie's features. "Ah. I wondered about that."

"Extending my stay has nothing to do with Luke," Emma said. "Looking back, I've always regretted the way our family left town. And even though it's not my fault, I hate how my mom let my dad rot in prison without ever paying back what we lost. So this time, I can't walk away from Redemption knowing that we owe money. I have to make things right."

Silence blanketed the room.

"I wish you'd stay," Lainey said. "Not just to deal with the house or help with the Easter egg hunt, but permanently. Redemption hasn't been the same since you left. You belong here, Em."

Emma looked up, her eyes burning. Before she could respond, her phone buzzed on the coffee table. Nathan's name lit up the screen. Her stomach twisted. Then slowly she reached over and turned the phone face down.

"By the way, since you're helping with the egg hunt, it's only fair that we help you with your house." Lainey reached for her phone. "Let me check my calendar and let's pick a day that works."

Emma hesitated. "I don't think you know what you're getting into."

"You're right." Lainey glanced up, smiling. "I probably don't. That's why I'm recruiting help. Many hands make light work. We'll all come out. It will be fun."

Abbie tilted her head toward the kitchen. "More nachos?"

"Absolutely." As Emma stood, something stirred inside her. Maybe it was the snow falling outside or the friends she hadn't realized she desperately needed, but for the first time in a long while, Emma felt a spark of belonging.

⁓

Luke stood at the resort's front desk and scrolled through the rest of March and the first week of April's calendar. Six new bookings. Better than nothing, but nowhere near enough to replace the income lost when he'd booted the skiers.

He clicked out of the database, then rubbed his eyes. A new job posting for a position as a pilot in Hearts Bay had landed in his inbox this morning. Great benefits, competitive salary, and a modest housing allowance. The kind of job he used to dream about. He hadn't applied. But he hadn't deleted the email either. Not yet.

Exhaling, he closed the laptop. The click echoed in the quiet room. Crossing to the worn leather sofa by the fire, he caught the scent of pine from the candle Mom had lit earlier, before she and Dad left to go to a friend's house for dinner. The fragrance mingled with garlic from the leftover pizza—comforting smells that clashed with the tension hovering in the room. Tate and Ethan sat across from him on the opposite couch, flames crackling in the fireplace, casting long shadows across their faces.

Tate ran a hand through his tousled hair. "Here's my unpopular opinion: I think we need to sell. If we put the place on the market mid-May, we'll probably have an offer quickly. We've hemorrhaged money for far too long. Selling is the smart move."

Smart? The word scraped something raw in Luke. He clenched his fists in his lap, forcing himself to stay calm. "Do you honestly believe throwing away our family legacy is smart? This is our history. We can't just give up. Our grandparents didn't give up when they fell on hard times."

"Whoa. Take a breath." Ethan leaned his elbows on his knees, his brows scrunched together. "It's not just about the legacy. It's about survival too. We can't keep pouring money into something that's failing. Are you willing to drain your savings to keep this place afloat? Or ask Mom and Dad to postpone retirement?"

Luke stared at the fire. *Am I?*

The jobs in Petersburg and Hearts Bay looked tempting. A steady paycheck. Fewer complications. Peace. But he hadn't told his brothers about the opportunities. Not yet. Maybe not ever. Because admitting he'd considered walking away too would make him a hypocrite. And expose the part of him that was scared he was failing.

"There are still ways to pivot," he insisted, grasping for hope. "We could invest in marketing. Attract summer tourists. Glacier hikes, fishing, kayaking, wellness retreats—"

Tate snorted. "Wellness retreats? Here?"

Luke gave him a flat look. "Why not? People pay thousands to unplug in the middle of nowhere. Sea kayaking tours worked pretty well back in the day. We've got beauty, space, and potential."

"Potential doesn't pay the bills." Tate shook his head. "I admire your optimism, but we are light years away from charters and summer camps."

"Oh, a summer camp." Luke pretended to make a note in his phone. "That's brilliant. Glad you thought of it."

Tate shot him an icy glare. "Don't be cheeky."

"Don't be a buzzkill."

"Boys." Ethan squashed their drama with a fierce glare of his own. "Let's keep this civil, shall we?"

"Even if we decide we want to diversify what we offer our customers, they're not going to come to a run-down lodge in the middle of nowhere," Tate said. "So we're looking at a substantial renovation. With what money?"

"Do you still believe we should just sell this 'run-down lodge'?" Luke quoted the air with his fingers. "Instead, why don't we make it more appealing? You both sound like you've already given up. You're walking away from our family's dreams."

"Like I've said before, dreams don't pay the bills," Tate said. "We're not kids anymore. We have to be realistic. If we put it on the market as is, we can list for three hundred seventy-five thousand dollars."

Luke rubbed his hands on his jeans, determined to ease the sting of Tate's words. "I keep thinking about guests who came year after year, cross-country skiing through fresh powder on the trails, laughing when they traipsed inside, completely exhausted. And thanking Mom profusely for her cranberry-orange scones. Those things mattered. They still matter."

Ethan rubbed his fingers along his jaw. "We have to think about the future. You really want to anchor yourself to this place forever?"

Luke hesitated. Frankly, he didn't have a solid answer. He had almost applied for that job in Petersburg. Now he had a second option to consider in Hearts Bay. But since Emma had shown up, his plans and his heart were tangled.

Wow, he was a fool. A complete fool for letting himself hope again. For letting his heart crack wide open.

How did one man make the same mistake twice?

Ethan shifted on the couch, glancing toward the fireplace. "I understand why you think selling the resort feels like abandonment. But there's something to be said for being practical. Maybe it's time to move on."

Move on. Luke's stomach twisted. "Look, I know you and Tisha are planning for the future and your family, but I don't understand how you can make up your mind so quickly. What if I don't want to sell? What if Caroline and Megan want to fight for this place?"

Tate let out a humorless laugh. "If Caroline moves back, she's going to be incredibly busy working as a PA, and Megan—" He trailed off, shaking his head. "She's a hot mess. We can't rely on her for much of anything."

Silence thickened the air between them. Adrenaline surged through Luke's veins. He glanced out the window, watching snowflakes swirl in the glow of the yard lights. His thoughts drifted to Emma, but he pushed them aside for about the fifteenth time that day and stared at his brothers. "I get it, I really do. But I'm not going to stand by and watch you sell the resort without at least trying to make it work. We owe it to ourselves, to our family, to give it one last shot."

Tate shook his head. "And what if it fails? What then? We can't keep chasing our tails."

"It won't fail if we believe in our plan," Luke shot back. "We need to get the snowmobiles running, we need to invest in repairing and rebuilding the cabin, and we need to get some plans rolling. Do a trek for summer tourists, put in a zipline, partner with other businesses in town to offer a package deal. But bottom line, I'm not ready to give up."

Ethan leaned forward, his expression unreadable. "And what if you're wrong? What if you're just holding on to a dream that's already dead?"

Luke met Ethan's gaze. "Then at least I'll know I tried. No regrets. I'm fighting for what I believe in."

Tate and Ethan exchanged glances. Luke studied them. He could see the flicker of doubt in their expressions, but he couldn't ignore the surge of hope. A wild notion that maybe, just maybe, they could find a way forward together.

"How about we decide after Easter?" Luke said. "Pray about it. Make lists of pros and cons. Do some research. If we can't come to an agreement about how to turn things around in the next two weeks, then I'll agree to talk to Mom and Dad about selling."

Silence stretched out again. He had found the chink in their proverbial armor and pressed on it. He had to keep pushing forward. Not just for the resort, but for his family. And maybe for himself too.

"Fine," Tate said. "Two weeks. But if nothing changes, we have to have a serious conversation—with Mom and Dad included—about selling."

"Deal." Luke reached out and shook his brothers' hands, but dread coiled in his gut. Despite Justin's pep talk at the pool table, he wasn't truly ready to let go. Not of this resort. Not of his dreams. And certainly not of his second chance with a woman he'd never stopped loving.

Ten

SHE COULDN'T PUT THIS OFF ANY LONGER.
Emma closed the door to her bedroom at Lainey's place, then crossed the room to the window. Outside, fresh snow coated the grass, weighed down the evergreen trees' branches, and covered two vehicles parked on the side of the road. She slipped out of her jacket and hung it on the coatrack beside the full-length mirror, then pulled her phone from the pocket.

Lord, please help me. I don't want to call her. She's going to brush me off and I hate that. Give me patience. And the right words.

It wasn't much of a prayer. But at least she was honest. After this morning's sermon at church about talking to God throughout the day, maybe a few scattered sentences here and there were enough to rebuild her frayed connection with the Lord. She wasn't entirely sure He was listening. Or that He even wanted to hear from her. But praying couldn't hurt.

Blowing out a wobbly breath, she scrolled to her mother's name in her contacts. She had to tell her about the gold. Still, she stared at the number, her thumb hovering over the call button.

The memories of their last interaction at Kendall's party, plus the lack of any calls or messages from her mother since she'd traveled to Alaska, had left her wounded. Surely discovering gold would thaw her mother's frigid attitude toward anything related to the property. Sometimes a girl needed her mom to help her navigate hard things.

She tapped the icon, then gnawed on her fingernail as the phone rang once, twice, three times. Maybe it would go to voicemail and she wouldn't have to have this conversation today. Then the call connected. Emma's stomach clenched.

"Emma," her mother's voice came through. Clipped. Preoccupied. "This isn't a good time. I'm trying to pack. We leave for Cairo early tomorrow morning."

"Well, hey, Mom," Emma said, trying to keep her tone light. "I'm sure you're busy, but I need to talk to you. It's important."

There was a pause long enough for Emma to envision her mom examining her well-manicured fingers or striding across her bedroom to the massive walk-in closet.

"What is it? Are you still in Alaska? Because I thought we agreed you'd handle whatever—"

"Agreed? No, you basically told me I had to handle it because you wanted nothing to do with anything connected to Redemption." So much for keeping things light. She sank onto the edge of the bed. "Given that you used to live in the house, I thought you might be interested to know that I found something substantial."

"Like jewelry? Money? Top-shelf liquor?" Her mother sighed. "You know what? Forget I asked because I don't have time for this. Do you think I should pack scarves? They're just not a good look for me, but Richard says the light in Egypt can be positively unforgiving in photos—not to mention the heat and the sand."

"Mom." Emma closed her eyes and pinched the bridge of her nose. "Can you focus for two minutes, please?"

"Fine." Another sigh. "What do you want me to do?"

"Did you hear me? I found something hidden in the house. I'm assuming it's something Dad put there."

"Please don't tell me you found weapons or drugs or anything illicit, because the statute of limitations on that surely has expired by now."

"Mom, it's gold," Emma said, keeping her voice low. "A lot of it. Hidden under the floorboards."

A beat of silence dropped. Had the call disconnected?

"Gold? Now isn't that interesting!"

Emma stifled a groan. That shift in tone, the sudden intrigue—it stung. She'd spent so long feeling like an afterthought, and the second money was involved, her mother was suddenly engaged.

"Sure is," Emma said. "I don't know how much yet. I didn't weigh it, but it's enough to fill a good-sized box. I thought you might want to know."

Her mother laughed, airy and dismissive. "This sounds like a scheme. Knowing your dad, it's probably not even real. He is in prison for fraud, after all."

Emma gritted her teeth. "I'm well aware."

"Are we talking nuggets? Flakes? Coins?"

"Nuggets. And it's real. I've held it, touched it. Not just a small amount, either."

Another pause. Then a thoughtful hum. "Well, that is quite the find. But what does this have to do with me?"

"Nothing, I guess, if you don't want to claim ownership. I'm happy to sell it and use the money to pay the property taxes."

In the background, hangers squeaked across a metal bar. "Don't sell the gold. Not yet. You'll need to make sure you get the best price per ounce."

Ah, so she was interested. Emma rubbed her forehead with her fingertips. "I'm already prolonging my stay here to deal with some issues with the house. I can't keep changing my flight back to Boston though."

"Of course not. You're getting married in July, remember?" Her mother's voice softened, but it felt practiced, distant. "That house and your father are both ancient history. I've turned a new page. Richard makes me deliriously happy."

"Glad to hear it." Emma blinked back tears. "You might have moved on, Mom, but I didn't have a choice. Nobody asked me what I wanted to do. I was fifteen, and unlike you, I didn't have the luxury of starting over with a new husband in a new state."

"Oh, here we go." Her mom sighed again, that defensive edge creeping in. "I rescued you, Emma, from absolute despair. Do you know how humiliating that was for me, begging my aunt to take us in? Then raising you alone, dealing with your father's deception and his arrest. It was all a horrific nightmare. I did what I had to do."

Did you? Emma pressed her lips tight to keep back the words burning on her tongue. There was no point in rehashing details that would only get twisted.

"I thought you might want to know about the gold because I thought it might make up for some of what we lost. Maybe—I don't know—I guess I was foolish to think this would serve as a bookend to a really dark time."

Her mother didn't answer. Emma heard the faint rustle of fabric. Mom was probably holding a scarf up beside her face in the full-length mirror, trying to decide which color looked best.

"So what are you planning to do next?"

"I don't know," Emma admitted. "It's in a safe place for now, but it's not just mine, is it?"

"Well, if it was in the house, then technically it is ours. We need to be smart about this, Emma. Now that I think about it, I need you to get the gold appraised and probably retain a lawyer."

Appraised? A lawyer? Emma stood and started to pace. This was not how she thought this conversation would go. "Wait. I'm so confused. You just said you didn't want anything to do with the house. Now that I've found gold, you do?"

"Oh, when you say it like that, you make it sound tawdry." Another light laugh. "You did say this changes things, right? It's not just about that old house anymore. This is about our future."

The future.

Why had she been so dumb to think the gold would bring them closer? Would bridge the chasm that had grown canyon-sized between them over the years?

"You know what? I'll figure it out. You're right. This is my responsibility."

"Now don't be hasty, darling. Let me finish my trip to Egypt, and when I get back, we'll talk about this properly. Richard can help us sort this out. He's very good with money."

"I'm sure he is," Emma said. "Have a great trip."

"Thanks, darling. Don't do anything rash, okay?"

"Don't you worry, Mom," Emma said, and then ended the call.

She sat back down on the bed and stared at her phone. Outside, wind howled around the house. The gold might be safely tucked away at the resort, but worry crept in, its icy fingers slithering around her heart and squeezing tight.

Her mother's words had uncovered something she wasn't prepared for.

Not just her mom's greed. That was familiar. But a deeper fear. Maybe her father hadn't been the only one with secrets.

She mentally replayed the way her mother had said, "He's in prison for fraud . . . retain a lawyer . . ."

Why?

She opened the notes app on her phone and made a short list: get gold appraised, ask Luke about a lawyer, ask Dad what really happened.

She stared at the words on the screen. That was the problem. She didn't know if she could ask. Not only because she hadn't spoken to her father in several years, but because he might not tell her the truth.

Or worse... what if he did?

~

He had to see Hank because that guy always had the right answer.

Snow crunched under Luke's boots as he approached the modest two-story home tucked away on two acres east of town. A ribbon of smoke curled from the chimney. Pink and orange streaks crisscrossed the late afternoon sky as the sun dipped behind the mountains. Fresh snow blanketed the Miltons' yard, and two chickadees perched on the barren branch of a willow tree near the corner of the house.

The aroma of his mom's homemade chicken soup wafted from the insulated bag he carried. His stomach growled, but this food wasn't for him. He'd brought dinner rolls and a container of oatmeal chocolate chip cookies. A meal was the least he could do for Hank and his wife after all they'd done at the resort.

Hank had been a fixture in his life for as long as Luke could remember. A steady presence, fixing broken pipes, shoveling snow, and keeping the old buildings running smoothly. Above all, Hank had always doled out the best advice. There was no way Luke would stand by and let pneumonia take Hank down. Somehow, he felt responsible for checking in on him. As he approached the door, he spotted Hank in the recliner through the window, soft yellow light glowing through the panes. He knocked softly.

The door creaked open, and Hank's wife, Willa, stood on the other side, her white hair pinned into a neat bun, her brown eyes crinkling at the corners as she smiled.

"Luke, what a wonderful surprise. Come on in."

"Sorry to bother you," Luke said. "My family and I wanted to bring you a meal."

"Perfect timing." Willa closed the door behind him. "I was just telling Hank I needed to come up with something for dinner."

Luke balanced the bag in both hands and toed off his shoes. The cozy living room smelled faintly of woodsmoke and menthol vapor rub. Hank had a thick blanket draped over him. The color hadn't returned to his cheeks yet. He looked like he'd lost some weight too.

"Luke." His voice was raspy but still carried that trademark warmth. "What brings you by?"

"You," Luke said, padding over in his socks. "I brought you some of my mom's chicken noodle soup, dinner rolls, and oatmeal chocolate chip cookies." He slid the insulated bag onto the counter that separated the living room from the kitchen. "I'm happy to shovel your driveway if you need it."

Hank waved him off. "Thank you for the food. Sounds delicious. You don't have to do the driveway. Our neighbors already offered." He pulled his beefy hand out from under the blanket and pointed to the worn couch. "Have a seat."

"I don't want to intrude," Luke said. "You need your rest, right?"

Willa took the disposable containers out of the bag and carried them over to the counter beside the stove. "You tell your mom thank you so much."

"Of course," Luke said. "It's the least we could do. You all have done so much for us over the years. It's time we return the favor."

"Nonsense," Willa said. "Hank has loved every minute working for your family."

She joined Luke on the couch. "You know, I've been hearing rumors that you all are thinking of selling. Is that true?"

Wow, that news traveled fast. Frowning, Luke nodded. "It's true. We're talking about it."

Hank coughed—a crackling sound that made Luke wince.

"Hey, big guy, I thought you were getting that taken care of."

Willa glanced at Hank, her brow pinched. "Believe it or not, this is an improvement. He's resting and taking his antibiotics like the doctor said. We have a follow-up chest X-ray next week that should give us more information."

Hank reached for his cup on the side table and took a sip from the straw.

"Hank, I got those parts for the snowmobile. I'm hoping I can get that thing up and running."

"I'm sure you can." Hank pressed a button on the side of his chair, elevating the back of the recliner, his eyes twinkling. "Don't forget to replace the spark plugs."

"Got it." Luke pulled out his phone and made a quick note as a reminder. "Say, do you know anything about Gavin Carlisle?"

"Oh, we haven't seen him in ages," Willa said. "But isn't the Carlisle girl back in town?"

Luke nodded. "Emma. She's Gavin's cousin and she wants to sell the house, but first of all, those sea lions are taking their dear sweet time leaving, and she'd like to speak with Gavin. There's some, uh"—he hesitated—"some personal items in the house, and she doesn't feel right not reaching out."

Hank's gaze sharpened. "Gavin and his dad, Seth, never came around that often. Even when Emma's folks were still here. Well, you probably know that gold miners turn up when they need something—food, a shower, human interaction. So back to the resort . . . Are you gonna sell?"

"I don't know. I don't want to, but some of my siblings are ready to move on."

Willa leaned over and patted his hand. "Then maybe it's time. Life has a way of happening whether we like the circumstances or not."

"I know you like to be in control, buddy, but sometimes you

have to let go and trust that God knows the path forward," Hank said.

Luke swallowed hard and rubbed at the tightness in his chest. Funny thing. Hank and Justin sounded almost alike. He respected Hank so much, but the idea of surrendering? Well, let's just say he wasn't a fan.

"I know you're right, but I still feel like I need to fight for what I want." Luke sighed. "I can't just sit back and let my family sell something that's been a part of us for generations."

Hank's expression softened. "Fighting is good, but don't forget to listen too. God has a plan, and it's a good one. Even if it doesn't align with your own desires. You're a good man, Luke." He paused, his breathing labored. "Remember that it's okay to seek guidance."

He wasn't wrong. Luke rubbed his forehead with his fingertips. The business was on shaky ground, and his relationship with Emma was getting more complicated.

"I appreciate your kindness, Hank, and your advice."

Willa glanced at Luke, her eyes twinkling. "You're doing a wonderful thing trying to help that sweet girl figure out what to do about those sea lions. Nobody asked for my opinion, but I bet they'll move along once the salmon start running."

"You think so?" Luke studied her. "Why?"

"Oh, my dad used to say that sea lions are the salmon's biggest threat." Willa shrugged. "Sea lions love a good salmon dinner just like the rest of us."

"Huh. Who knew?" Luke stood. "Listen, I won't keep you guys. If you don't need me to shovel your driveway, I'll be on my way."

"We're all good," Hank said. "Thanks again for coming by. And remember, trust the Lord. Each step you take is part of His plan. You're not alone."

Luke took a deep breath, allowing the warmth of Hank's wisdom to seep in. But warmth didn't make decisions any easier.

"Thanks, Hank. Get well, okay? I need you."

The older man smiled. "I'll do my best. Willa's taking good care of me. Can't wait to see where God takes you, son."

Luke collected the insulated bag, then pulled on his boots and stepped outside. Man, he didn't like facing the unknown. Didn't like being in limbo. And yet, that was exactly where he was. Willa's comment about sea lions and salmon stuck with him as he headed for his truck. Salmon didn't usually show up until mid-May. If Willa was right and the fish drew the sea lions back into the water, that would be a long time for Emma to stick around.

He couldn't help but smile.

Not that he'd complain.

Eleven

So much for their last-minute egg-stuffing plans.

Emma sat at the long table in the dining room of the McGuires' resort, slipping small pieces of candy and toys into colorful plastic eggs. She should've had help, but Lainey had rushed off when her stepdad fell and needed to be checked out at the ER. And Abbie had texted earlier that her daughter and her husband had come down with a stomach bug. Thankfully, a few other families in town had agreed to help, so she only had to prep twelve dozen.

Alone. Well, mostly alone. She glanced around the room. The place was like a time capsule with wood-paneled walls and a taxidermied bear and a moose holding court. Wagon-wheel style chandeliers and lanterns with candles in the center of each table added to the rustic charm. The long rectangular tables stretched out around her. Sturdy wood bore the scars of generations of skiers and hikers who'd dined here.

Luke moved methodically through the quiet room, carrying a tub of antibacterial wipes and cleaning every chair. His flannel sleeves were rolled up, revealing muscular forearms and a faint grease smear—probably from trying to fix the snowmobile again.

He looked over and met her gaze. "How's it going?"

"I feel like I've filled a thousand of these things." She snapped another egg shut, then leaned back and stretched, rubbing her aching wrist. She'd grabbed a splint from the drugstore, and the pain had subsided, but maybe opening and closing the eggs had irritated her injury.

"As soon as I'm finished cleaning up, I'll help you." Luke tossed a wipe into the trash can nearby. "I only have about ten more chairs to go."

"Cool." She reached for another plastic egg from the pile on the table. "Your mom wanted to add stickers or temporary tattoos or something. Any idea where those are?"

"Oh, right. I almost forgot." Luke set the container of wipes on the table, then nudged a chair out of his way. "Let me go check the cabinet in the office."

He paused beside her, offering a half smile, the kind that had always made her heart do a little flip. "You're not going to sneak out of here and leave me with a pile of empty eggs, are you?"

She laughed. "Tempting suggestion, but no. I'm sticking around until the last egg is filled."

Luke's expression grew serious as his eyes held hers. "Good to know."

She quickly looked away as her phone lit up with a new notification. Her stomach tightened when she saw Nathan's name.

Nathan
Call me. We need to talk.

Sighing, she squeezed her eyes shut. Harmless words, but something about the phrasing made her scalp prickle. She could interpret his subtext. Nathan didn't like to be kept waiting.

"Everything okay?" Luke's voice pulled her back. She opened her eyes. He stood a few feet away, his brow furrowed.

"Yeah," she said, locking the screen and flipping the phone face down. "Just Nathan, checking in."

Luke glared at the phone, then gave a small nod.

The silence stretched between them, no longer as easy as it had been a few minutes ago. She tried to focus on her project, but Nathan's text hovered, demanding her attention. It was only a matter of time before he followed up with a call. And right on cue, her phone buzzed again. Emma glanced at it, vibrating on the table.

"It's him," she said, more to herself than to Luke.

"You can take it," Luke said. "I'll give you some space and go look for the stickers."

"I'll step outside for a few minutes." She grabbed her coat and her phone, then headed for the door, her boots echoing against the wooden floor. The cold air hit her as she stepped onto the porch. Silhouettes of evergreen trees stood like soldiers, their tips pointing toward a velvety night sky dotted with millions of stars.

She swiped her finger across the screen, then pressed the phone to her ear. "Hey, Nathan."

"Finally," he said, clearly annoyed. "I was starting to think you'd forgotten about me."

She winced. "Sorry, I've been busy."

"I figured as much." He paused. In the background she heard the muffled voice of a woman speaking on the intercom. Was he still at work? She pulled her phone away from her ear and checked the time. It was after one in the morning on the East Coast. Weird.

"I know this trip is important to you, but it's been over a week. You left your job, and you still haven't told me when you're coming back. We have things to do."

"Nathan, I—"

"Let me finish," he snapped. "Please. We have plans to finalize.

My mother's waiting on you to go over the seating chart next week. If you keep dragging your feet—"

"I'm not dragging my feet," she said.

"Okay, then you're distracted. My mother and I are concerned that you're going to drop the ball and then this wedding will be a disaster."

"What?" She barked out a laugh. "Why?"

"Because you're more worried about sea lions than our wedding. Those animals aren't a legitimate crisis. Or your responsibility. You don't need to play hero in a town that doesn't even want you there."

She flinched.

"I had Kendall look into it," he continued. "She says if you own the house, then no one has any legal recourse against you. The town council probably just wants those seals gone."

Her scalp prickled. "Huh. I didn't realize Kendall was so well-versed in real-estate law. Isn't she more focused on intellectual property? Also, it's sea lions, not seals, and what about the property taxes? Is Kendall going to pay that bill?"

"We're trying to help you, Emma. A little gratitude would be nice."

"And I'm trying to do the right thing. This isn't about being a hero. My family is still responsible for that house, and I can't pretend we don't owe money."

Nathan sighed. "I'm sure you can work out a payment plan or something."

Oh brother. Was he always this patronizing? How had she not noticed before now? Sharp words caught in her throat. Instead of popping off, images from the last several days spooled through her head. Okay, sure, there had been wary glances, and the occasional snide comment from Joe and Olive. But there had been tentative smiles, and Abbie and Lainey had been quick to welcome her back. And Luke had been there when she needed him, even when he had a failing business to save.

"What's this really about?" Nathan's tone shifted. "The gold you found? Because I already checked, and our family's financial adviser can help you sell it. I want you to come home. You're supposed to be building a life with me. That's what matters. Not dredging up the past in some hick town."

Her chest tightened. She couldn't breathe. What could she say to that? He wasn't entirely wrong.

"Emma, did you hear me?"

She blinked back tears. "I heard you."

"I just want what's best. You know that, right? I'm trying to keep us on track."

"I like it here, Nathan. And I never got to say goodbye and have closure. I need this."

"I understand. But you can't fix what your dad did. Besides, you weren't involved—you were a high school kid. So say your goodbyes and come home."

She curled her fingers into a fist in her pocket. Her throat ached with rising emotion. "I'll call you later this week," she said, her voice barely above a whisper.

"Don't take too long."

"Good night, Nathan."

"Good night."

The line went dead, and Emma let out a shaky breath, then stared at the phone in her hand. Nathan was partly right. She needed to close the door to this town and her past. It was time to get on with her future.

The door creaked open behind her, and Luke stepped out. "Found them." He held up a thick mailing envelope. "Dinosaurs, emojis, butterflies, and lots of crosses and John three-sixteen tattoos. It's an odd mix, but it works."

She laughed, blinking back her tears. "Perfect."

He leaned against the railing and studied her. "You okay?"

"Not really."

His brow furrowed. "Want to talk about it?"

She hesitated, then forced a wobbly smile. "It's just wedding stuff."

The envelope crinkled as he held it against his chest, his breath visible in the cold air. "Not that wedding planning is my area of expertise, but if you need someone to vent to, I'm here."

She swallowed hard. Her insides quaked, and for a hot second, the unvarnished truth nearly spilled out. Oh, how she wanted to tell him everything. The nagging doubts, the pressure, all the times when Nathan's words made her feel small. But instead, she met Luke's gaze, surprised by his unselfish offer. No judgment. No pressure. Just kindness.

Something shifted.

Her breath caught as she looked at him. Really looked at him. Maybe it was the way he dropped what he was doing to help her. Or the quiet strength he emitted as he stood there, waiting.

Old feelings stirred. Nathan represented stability. Security.

But Luke . . . he made her feel as if a long-dormant part of her might finally be waking up. Her pulse sped. She looked away. Maybe Nathan was right. Maybe she needed to leave before she wrecked the future she had been so certain she wanted.

⁓

He had to get his mind off Emma, along with his terrible longing for her to stick around.

The tiny closet under the stairs that doubled as their office and supply closet was quiet, except for the heat blasting from the metal vent nearby and the occasional creak of the wood floor. Luke pulled open a cluttered drawer in the desk and dug around for a spare printer cartridge.

"I know there's one in here," he mumbled, more to distract himself than anything else.

He found the box and opened it, but even as he focused on the mundane task, his mind kept drifting back to Emma. To how tired she looked. To the unshed tears glistening in her eyes a few minutes ago when she'd ended her call with Nathan. It wasn't his business, not really. But that didn't stop the tightness in his chest, the burning frustration that clawed at his ribs. He couldn't exactly blame the guy—if he were Nathan, he'd probably want her home too. Want things back the way they were.

The door squeaked as Emma nudged it open, and the air shifted, the temperature in the room seeming to climb a degree as she stepped inside.

"Why are you hiding in here?" She leaned against the doorway, arching one brow. "You offered to help stuff plastic Easter eggs, remember?"

"Busted." He forced a quick smile, then slid the cartridge into place with a click. "I was just trying to fix the printer so my mom would have one less thing to deal with."

"That's sweet of you." She hesitated. Turned to leave and then turned back. "I didn't mean to brush you off out there. Thank you for checking on me."

He faced her and crossed his arms over his chest. "I wasn't eavesdropping, but I'd be lying if I said I wasn't concerned. You looked like you needed someone."

She hesitated, and for a second, he saw a flash of the girl he used to know. The one who laughed with her whole heart, who used to look at him like he was the center of her universe. But now, there was something else in her eyes. Something guarded. Defensive.

She let out a soft breath. "You've always been very kind."

Kind. Right. His fingers curled around the edge of the desk as he leaned against it. "Not always."

She blinked. "What are you referring to?"

His skin buzzed, adrenaline pulsing through him, fortifying

him with a shot of courage. "Do you ever think about that night? The last night you were here, before your parents made you leave."

Her lips parted slightly as she fidgeted with the hem of her long sweater.

"Luke, I—"

"I fought for you, Emma." Roughness crept into his voice, the words slipping out before he could overthink them. "I tried to convince your dad that you didn't have to go, that you didn't want to go."

Her eyes flared, guilt swimming in those deep green depths. "I know," she whispered. "I was there, remember?"

A dry laugh escaped him. "Yeah. And I got hit in the face for it."

Her expression softened.

He reached up, brushing his fingers over the faint scar on his jaw. "I was an idiot, taking a swing at your dad like that. Falling and smacking my face is exactly what I deserved."

She took a step closer, and before he could lean away, her fingers grazed the scar—a light touch, barely there, but it sent a current zipping through him, rooting him in place.

"I'm sorry," she said. "I tried to—"

"Don't." He caught her wrist, his grip gentle. He let his thumb brush against her delicate skin before forcing himself to let go. "I'm not telling you this because I blame you. You didn't have a choice. What happened wasn't your fault."

Her hand fell to her side, but she didn't move away. If anything, she was closer now. Her gaze roamed his face, lingering like she was memorizing every line and angle.

"I didn't want to leave you, Luke. Please, you've got to believe me."

His chest tightened. His arms ached to pull her against him, to tell her she didn't have to leave now, that she didn't have to marry someone who made her cry. But he wouldn't—because as of now, she wasn't his to keep.

"Why are you here, Emma?"

Surprise flashed in her eyes. Then she stepped back, arms tightly folded. "Because my mom hasn't paid her property taxes, so I want to make that right. And because I want closure."

He didn't break eye contact. "Closure so you can move on and marry Nathan?"

Her chin tipped up. "He's my fiancé. He's what I want."

Luke swallowed hard. Her words stung. "If you say so."

"I do," she whispered.

Silence fell between them. He longed to grab her hand, to beg her to stay—but then she took another step back.

"I should go," she said. "I'll get Lainey to come by and help me finish up with the eggs."

He nodded, hands still gripping the edge of the desk to keep from reaching for her.

"Yeah, you should go. We've got people coming to your house tomorrow to help clean up. It's going to be a busy day."

She nodded, then looked back at him one last time from the doorway.

"Thank you."

"For what?"

"For always fighting for me."

He smiled, a little sad, a little resigned. "You're welcome."

A ghost of a smile flickered across her face before she slipped out the door.

He collapsed into the worn leather chair, scrubbing his hands over his face. He'd thought he could handle this. Thought he could help her, stay neutral, and be her friend.

Except he was falling for her all over again. And this time, he knew exactly what it would cost him.

Pulling his phone from his pocket, he opened the latest email from the lodge on Prince of Wales Island. The owner had offered two potential times for a job interview later this week. Luke hesitated, his heart kicking against his ribs. Then he replied to the email and requested the second option. He could leave. Take a new job. Start over.

But what if she stayed? What if he left too soon and missed his chance?

Twelve

WHY HAD SHE LET LAINEY ORGANIZE A clean-up day?

"This is so not a good idea." Emma pulled on her thick, heavy gloves and glanced at the animals still lounging on her property. "What if the sea lions attack someone? Or what if they wreck any progress we make?"

The wind whipped around her, tugging at her jacket, and she tucked a stray curl behind her ear. She and Luke stood behind her house, their backpacks at their feet. The dumb sea lions barked and lounged on the dock, clearly put out that she'd had the audacity to show up again.

Luke turned to face her, his hands tucked into the pockets of his green puffy vest. His faded jeans emphasized his lean, athletic build, and his gray hoodie hugged his broad shoulders. Even his navy-blue knit hat framed his face in a way that softened his sharp jawline. She let her eyes linger on that scar. The one she'd touched without thinking last night in the resort's office. The memory sent a shiver through her.

"Sea lions are going to do what they want, unfortunately. If you need to make the house halfway livable so you can sell it, then you're going to have to let people help you clean up the place," he said.

"I know. You're right. But we can't tell anyone about the gold." She dug in her backpack for a knit hat. "I'm not ready for word to get out. Especially since my mother owes those taxes."

Luke's eyes softened, and he stepped closer, his warm, steady presence grounding her. "Nobody's asking you to do things you aren't ready for. But you can't do this by yourself. I'll do as much as I can, you know that . . ." His voice trailed off as he gestured toward the house. "This is more work than two people can handle. You need Lainey, Abbie, Mark, and Tate. And they want to help."

Emma sighed. "I'm just nervous. And maybe a little overwhelmed. I thought this would be easier. That I'd be on a plane back to Boston by now." Her voice was sharper than she intended, but she couldn't help it. Between the gold he'd helped her stash at the resort and her conversation with Nathan last night, followed by that tense interaction with Luke, her nerves were frayed.

Luke tilted his head. "Is that really what you want?"

She met his gaze but couldn't answer. Not truthfully, anyway. Not after last night. Because the pull she felt toward him and toward Redemption was getting harder to ignore. But there was Nathan. And the life she'd promised herself. How could she forget that?

The sound of distant voices carried through the trees, interrupting her thoughts. Laughter, shouted instructions, and the occasional bark of a dog grew louder. She glanced past Luke, and out on the water, the steady hum of a boat engine grew louder.

"That's Cal," Luke said, following her gaze. "He's convinced he can find a way to dock safely without disturbing your tenants."

"Ha." Emma glared at the sea lions as they shifted, barking and slamming their bodies against the battered wood on the dock, clearly irritated by the noise. "He's brave."

"Or stubborn." Smiling, Luke waved toward the boat. "He might end up beaching the boat around the point if the sea lions won't give him space."

Emma nodded absently, her anxiety bubbling up again. This had all been Lainey's idea, of course. Lainey, with her relentless optimism and her uncanny ability to rope people into her plans.

"We'll all come out," Lainey had said, her tone breezy. "We'll help you get the place cleaned up. It'll be fun."

Fun. That wasn't exactly the word she'd use. The thought of old friends sweeping through her past made her feel exposed. Especially Tate, who looked at her like she was a puzzle he needed to solve. Unlike Luke, who had that disarming charm and that easy smile that made her want to trust him.

Luke reached out now and placed a hand on her shoulder, his touch firm but tender. Her breath hitched as he met her gaze, his eyes steady and full of something she couldn't quite name—something she wasn't sure she deserved.

"It's going to be all right," he said. "We're going to get the repairs squared away, and you'll have this listed in no time."

Emma swallowed hard, her throat tight. "I know."

Luke's smile was small but genuine. "Good."

One by one, the group emerged from the trees, a strange little parade of reunited friends armed with tools and supplies. Lainey led the way, the faux-fur pom-pom on top of her pink knit hat bobbing as she waved. Abbie and her husband, Mark, followed close behind, lugging a cooler between them. Tate appeared next, a duffel bag slung over one shoulder and a puppy with golden brown hair trotting at his heels. Mrs. McGuire and Ethan brought up the rear, their strides purposeful.

"Hey, Emma!" Lainey's voice rang out, bright and warm.

Emma couldn't help but smile. "Hi."

Luke stepped forward. "As you can see, there's plenty to do:

basic deep cleaning, maintenance projects, and it goes without saying—watch out for the sea lions."

Mrs. McGuire clapped her hands together. "Well, let's get started. Where do you want us to begin?"

Emma hesitated. But then she caught Lainey's eye. There was something steady in her friend's gaze. A spark of reassurance. Emma took a deep breath.

"The inside is pretty much a disaster," she admitted. "And the exterior has issues as well. I'd love to take down the damaged railings and get those boards off the windows so we can see if they are all still intact."

"Let's do this," Tate said with a nod.

For the next few hours, the place buzzed with activity. People scrubbed, hauled debris, and repaired damage, their laughter and easy camaraderie filling the space. Emma floated between tasks, still feeling a little out of place but also . . . lighter, somehow.

As the group gathered outside for a lunch of sandwiches and chips, Mrs. McGuire smiled at Emma. "This place has potential," she said. "Good bones."

Emma blinked, caught off guard by the compliment. "Yeah," she said. "Too bad there are so many terrible memories."

A hush fell over the group. Emma winced, warmth crawling up her neck. "Sorry," she said quickly.

Luke leaned forward. "You don't have to be sorry. You've carried a huge burden on your own for a long time, but now you don't have to anymore."

Emma looked down at her sandwich, her throat tight. His words chipped away at the wall she'd kept around her heart. She wasn't ready to let it fall though. Not yet.

"You don't owe us anything," Mrs. McGuire said. "We're helping because we care."

Emma wanted to argue, to tell them they didn't understand.

But when she looked up and met Luke's eyes, something inside her shifted.

"Thank you," she said. "All of you."

Lainey beamed. "That's what friends are for."

Friends. The word settled around Emma like a warm blanket. For the first time in years, she felt like maybe—just maybe—she might've repaired the cracks in her relationship with Lainey. And Abbie too.

But just as she started to believe it, Mark leaned forward, his brow furrowed.

"So," he said, his brown eyes gleaming. "Is it true? About the buried treasure?"

Emma froze, her heart pounding in her chest.

—

Luke grew still. Mark's question hung in the air, bringing the easy lunchtime conversation to a screeching halt.

He didn't need to look at Emma to know all of the blood had drained from her face. He could sense it.

"Yeah, I've heard rumors about a treasure or something out here too." Abbie pulled a package of cookies from the cooler. "What's the scoop?"

Luke cleared his throat, forcing an easy smile. "You know how rumors are." He unwrapped the brownie his mom had packed, peeling the Saran Wrap back and stuffing it inside his empty chip bag. "People love to let their imaginations run wild. I think it's a stretch to call this place a treasure trove."

Mark frowned, tipping his baseball cap back as he scratched his head. "I don't know. This house, old as it is? And with everything Emma's dad was involved in, seems like the kind of place where somebody might stash something good."

Luke's chest tightened. He had to shut this down.

"Well, if there's any treasure here, it's probably buried under a mountain of mud and sea-lion poop."

Lainey, bless her, picked up on his vibe and jumped in. "And if there was gold, I'd be the first to demand a cut." She winked.

Laughter rippled through the group.

"You and me both," Luke said. He pushed to his feet, polished off his brownie, then dusted off his pants and stretched. Act casual. Play it cool. He grabbed his work gloves off the ground.

"All right, everybody. I don't want to be bossy, but break's over. We've got a lot to do before the sun sets and it gets too dark to hike back to the trail. Mark, how about you help Cal haul that junk from the old garden down to his boat?"

Abbie gave Mark a nudge. "Come on, Indiana Jones. Let's hop to it. We can do this."

The group dispersed slowly, chatting as they cleaned up their lunch.

"Remember, if you need to use the bathroom, the porta-potties up at the trailhead are your only option," Luke called out. "Plumbing here does not function."

A few people groaned. Cal headed toward the garden. Lainey and Mrs. McGuire gathered up the trash and shoved everything into the five-gallon bucket lined with a garbage bag.

Emma, however, didn't budge. She sat on her stump, hands clenched around her gloves.

Luke sank beside her and lowered his voice. "You okay?"

She nodded, but the tension in her jaw hinted that the conversation had gotten to her.

"Walk with me," he said.

She didn't move. Her gaze flicked toward Tate.

"Hey, Tate, is it okay if Emma and I take Sailor for a little stroll?"

Tate glanced up from tying a knot in the garbage bag. "Sure." He picked up a bottle of water and tossed it toward Luke. "Can you give him some more water, please?"

Luke caught the water bottle. "Sure."

"There's a plastic bowl sitting on the ground near where he's tethered," Tate said.

"Got it." Luke stood and offered Emma a hand. She hesitated again before slipping her fingers into his. His grip tightened as he helped her up, her warmth sinking into his skin. Too much. Too good. He let go quickly, but his pulse thrummed as they walked toward the tree line, picking their way around driftwood and rocks.

Sailor saw them coming and lunged, barking, his pink tongue lolling.

"I knew this was a mistake, bringing people out here," she said.

"Hey," he said, "don't stress. Their curiosity will blow over."

She shook her head, fidgeting with the zipper on her jacket. "No, it won't, and I should have been more careful. I told you—"

"Emma." He kept his voice steady. "Listen to me. Nobody knows about the gold. Just you and me and whoever was clever enough to stash it there. Mark's just being nosy. You decide what happens here, okay? Nobody else."

She looked away. "I'm just . . . I don't want people to think I'm like my dad. The last thing I want is for them to believe I'm taking advantage of their kindness, because I'm not."

Luke's chest ached. "Oh, Emma . . ." She was so vulnerable.

He reached out and brushed a smudge of dirt from her cheek. His hand lingered longer than it should have. And for a crazy moment, he let himself imagine what it would be like to kiss her. To claim her. To make her his.

But then reality crashed back in.

Sailor leaped in the air, barking at a bird, and Emma's engagement ring flashed in the light. A sharp reminder. She had a life—and a man—waiting for her back in Boston.

He had no business interfering.

Luke dropped his hand and shoved it into his pocket.

"You're not your dad," he said. "And anyone who spends five minutes with you can see that."

She pressed both hands on top of her hat. "Sometimes it feels like I'll never escape it. His mistakes, his reputation . . . it's all connected. No matter what I do, his long con is like my shadow. That's why I didn't want to come back here."

Luke crouched, untying Sailor's leash. Man, he hated that she felt this way. Hated that she still carried the weight of her father's sins on her shoulders.

"You ever wonder if it was really all him? I mean, he took the fall, sure. But . . ." Luke stood up, keeping an eye on Sailor as he sniffed under a nearby rock.

Emma's brows squeezed together. "But what?"

Maybe he shouldn't have said anything. "Seems like maybe there's more to the story, that's all."

She glanced over her shoulder toward the water.

"This is your house and your property, so you get to choose how this turns out. Not everyone in Redemption will cheer you on, but there are a few of us in your corner. Focus on the positive, okay?"

Her gaze slid back to meet his. Something like hope flashed in her beautiful eyes.

"Do you mean it when you say that you're in my corner?"

"Of course. I wouldn't say it if I didn't."

The air between them hummed with unspoken words. For the second time in about two minutes, he wondered what it would feel like to close the distance, to hold her, to tell her how proud he was of her strength. Her resilience.

Sailor barked, then Emma laughed as the puppy jumped up and planted both of his front paws on her jeans.

The wind picked up, blowing across the water and swirling around them as they trailed Sailor across the rocks and gritty sand. Oh, how he wanted to promise her that everything would be okay. Tomorrow he'd help her get the gold appraised. Not because he cared about what it was worth. But because she needed answers. And he'd do whatever it took to make sure she got them.

Thirteen

THE NEXT MORNING, EMMA WOKE TO THE SOUND of raised voices downstairs. She blinked and checked the phone on her nightstand: 8:15 a.m.

Two notifications lit the screen. One from Brittney. One from social media.

Yawning, she tapped Brittney's message first.

> **Brittney**
> You need to come back ASAP. Martin just went on paternity leave, and with you gone we are down two people. If you don't get back this week, they're already talking about bringing in someone new. I'll try to stall them, but I don't have much leverage. Please come back. I'm serious.

Uh-oh. Emma sat up straighter and leaned against the headboard. Well, she had been rather bold, expecting to leave work for ten days. Now that she'd stretched that into almost two weeks, it wasn't a surprise that the manager might consider replacing her.

"But I just need a little more time," she whispered.

Without responding, she swiped to the next notification. A tagged post from the gala back in Boston popped up. The fundraiser she was supposed to attend with Nathan. The one she'd bailed on to stay in Redemption longer.

Her thumb froze mid-scroll as she took a closer look at the photo. Nathan stood in a black suit, his arm draped around a stunning woman in a form-fitting purple dress. Courtney. The doctor Emma had met briefly at last year's gala, and the woman who'd shown up at Kendall's party and spoken to Nathan a few weeks back. Tall. Confident. Elegant.

Everything Emma wasn't.

Nathan and Courtney weren't kissing, but they didn't have to be. Courtney leaned into him like she belonged there. His hand rested in the curve of her waist. Sort of like he'd pulled her close before. They both sported wide smiles, their cheeks flushed in the soft lighting of the venue's ballroom.

This was the kind of photo you framed. Or posted with a caption like when things just feel right.

An ache climbed the back of her throat, and her eyes burned with unshed tears. Was this some kind of punishment for telling him no? For extending her stay? How could he do this?

Her hands shook as she tapped out a text.

> Emma
> Saw your photo with Courtney.
> You owe me an explanation.

Shoving back the covers, she swung her legs over the edge of the bed and crossed the room. She had to talk to Lainey about this.

When she pulled the door open, the voices downstairs grew even louder, bouncing off the walls. One of them was definitely Lainey, and the other a man. Older, with a raspy voice that hinted that he wasn't unfamiliar with confrontation.

She turned back, quickly used the bathroom, then pulled on jeans and a hoodie and pushed her feet into her slippers. She stepped out into the hallway, wincing as the argument grew more heated.

"Gary, for the love, you can't keep doing this." Lainey's voice carried a sharpness Emma hadn't heard from her before.

Emma padded down the steep staircase and skipped the loose step at the bottom that would warn of her arrival. Then she leaned against the wall just out of sight.

"I don't need a lecture from you," the man—must have been Gary—shot back, wheezing. "You think you know everything just because you run your own business? If it weren't for me, you wouldn't have this—"

"Don't you dare finish that sentence." Lainey cut him off, her voice icy. "You're spending your disability checks on junk again, aren't you? I have access to your account. You think I don't know? You think I don't notice? What are you into right now—vintage knives? Old VHS tapes of The Dukes of Hazzard?"

"I don't have to explain myself to you." Something heavy slammed onto the table, hard. "Can't you stop pretending you care about what I spend my money on, for crying out loud? Last time I checked, it was mine, and I suffered for every dollar."

Emma inched closer, then leaned around the corner. Lainey, usually composed and cheerful, stood in the kitchen with her hands planted on her hips, her face flushed. A pale, wiry man, probably in his sixties, sat at the kitchen table, a portable oxygen tank resting at his feet. His chest rose and fell with effort, his posture defiant.

"You don't need to spend your money on all that stuff," Lainey said. "You're the only one who got that settlement check from the oil spill, remember? The rest of us have to scrape and claw just to get by these days, and you sit back and blow it on nonsense while . . ."

She broke off, pressing her lips into a thin line, shaking her head.

"I'm not the villain here," Gary said. "You think I asked for this? For any of it? You think I want to spend my life"—he wheezed, pausing before continuing—"hooked up to this dumb thing?" He gestured at the tank. "That oil spill ruined me. Ruined my life. It ruined my marriage."

"I don't want to hear it," Lainey said, her voice rising. "My mother tried so hard to save you, but even she had her limits. How nice for you that you don't have to work. But that's the whole point, isn't it? You could use that money to, I don't know, make your life better, help people out, but instead, you're blowing it on things you don't need. And then you complain to me when somebody says something nasty to you in the grocery store."

Emma's throat tightened. She knew what it was like to have life unravel. Knew the shame of carrying a last name people spat like a curse.

"Hey, is everything okay in here?" Her voice was tentative as she stepped into the kitchen before things escalated further.

Gary and Lainey both turned to her, their faces a mixture of surprise and irritation.

"Sorry," Emma said, holding up both hands. "I heard voices, and I thought maybe—" She trailed off, feeling ridiculous now. What did she think? That she could just breeze in here and mediate this? She was Lainey's guest, not a referee.

Lainey ran a hand through her short, spiky blonde hair. "It's fine."

"Doesn't look fine." Emma pushed her hands into the front pocket of her hoodie. "Anything I can do to help?"

Lainey sighed, rubbing her temples. "Do you remember Gary? Gary Sheridan. My stepfather."

"Of course." Emma crossed the kitchen and shook his hand. "Nice to see you again. I'm Emma Carlisle."

Gary shot her a curious glance. "Huh. Carlisle. Sounds familiar. You used to live here. Good friends with Abbie too."

"That's right," Emma said. "I moved after ninth grade."

Gary nodded, his brows drawing together. "Your dad—he was a good egg."

Emma let out a hollow laugh before she could stop it. "You must have known a different Carlisle."

"No, I mean it. Owned that place out on the water at the end of Aurora Way. The one with the sea lions."

Emma pulled out a stool and sat down at the bar, facing him. "That would be the one, yes. Got any tips or life hacks for how to eradicate sea lions?"

Gary paused, drawing in a deep breath, waiting while the oxygen assisted him. "Tourists love 'em, especially when they pile on those buoys and whatnot. Be careful how you proceed."

"Good point." She tried for a smile. "Thank you."

Gary eyed her. "So how is your old man?"

Emma shifted, the stool creaking underneath her. "I don't really know. He's still in prison. We don't keep in touch."

Silence filled the kitchen.

Gary's expression softened. "Your dad was a good guy, Emma. A great friend to me. And a lot of fun."

Emma stifled an exasperated sigh. She'd heard this before. Always the same story. Her dad had been so charming. So kind. So fun. And yet, he was a fraud. A liar. A con artist who had ruined lives.

Gary hesitated, then added, "But sometimes there's more to a person than what meets the eye, you know?" He exhaled, glancing at Lainey. "Your mom though. Excuse me, but she was . . ."

Emma's stomach clenched. "She was what?"

Gary's gaze slid to Lainey. "Yeah, you know, I think I've said enough. Lainey, if we're done with our bonding session, I'd like to go now." Although his tone was less snide than before, his hand trembled as he reached for his oxygen tank.

Frowning, Lainey moved to help him. "Come on, then. I'll walk you out."

As they left the kitchen together, Emma sat still, watching them go. Whatever had happened with that oil spill had been before her time, but Gary's issues and Lainey's resentment were tangled and messy and raw. Sort of like her family drama. His disdain for her mother rattled her though. What did he mean?

He had to get this snowmobile fixed.

Luke's wrench slipped off the bolt. "Come on!" he grumbled.

He slid the wrench back into place, then tightened the last bolt on the engine panel and blew a slow breath. This thing had been giving him trouble for weeks. But with Hank out sick and unable to troubleshoot and six guests coming in two days for a long weekend's stay—praise God—he had to get this thing running. Because the last thing he wanted was unhappy clients.

He stepped back to assess his work and put the wrench back in the toolbox. When the crunch of tires on fresh snow caught his attention, he turned.

An SUV rolled to a stop, its doors caked with ice and road salt. The driver cut the engine, pushed open the door, and stepped out. When he slammed it shut, Luke gave him a quick once-over.

Early forties, maybe, with a long red beard that looked like it hadn't seen a razor in a long time. His Carhartt coat was thick, stained with grease, and his jeans had that quilted lining built for brutal cold. He rolled them up at the cuffs of his worn lace-up boots.

Luke met his gaze. Those eyes—somehow familiar—caught him. But he couldn't figure out why. The man had a quiet hesitance. He tugged his blue beanie farther down over his ears and approached slowly.

"Hi there. Can I help you?" Luke offered a polite smile.

The man shoved his hands into his coat pockets, shifting his weight from one foot to the other.

"I'm looking for Emma Carlisle. Somebody at the gas station said you might know where to find her."

Unease slid through Luke. People didn't just show up looking for Emma without a reason.

"She's not here right now. Who's asking?"

The man hesitated, his gaze dropping to the ground. "Gavin. Gavin Carlisle. I'm her cousin."

The eyes. He had Emma's eyes.

Luke gave a slow nod. "Yeah, she's been looking for you, Gavin. I'm glad you came to Redemption."

"I had a buddy running the Iditarod, so I helped out where I could. Otherwise, I would've tried to get in touch sooner."

Huh. Maybe the guy wasn't so bad. Still, Luke wasn't a hundred percent ready to trust him.

"I can text her," Luke said. "You wanna come in? Get some coffee? I'm sure she'll come right over when I tell her you're here."

Gavin's gaze drifted to the snowmobile. "You having trouble with that?"

Luke rubbed the back of his neck. "Yeah. Thought it was a hydraulic issue. Changed the filter. Hank is my usual ace-in-the-hole handyman, but he's not well right now, so I'm trying to get this thing going. It keeps stalling though. Or doesn't start at all." He gestured toward the sky. "More customers and more snow on the way, so I need to get it sorted."

"Maybe your fuel line's freezing up." Gavin moved closer. "These older models can be fussy. Mind if I take a look?"

Luke hesitated. He wasn't about to turn down capable help. He gestured toward the machine. "Go for it."

Gavin crouched down, pulled off one glove, and ran his fingers along the fuel line. His knuckles were caked with grease, and dirt was wedged under his nails.

"Got a wrench?"

"Yep." Luke handed him two options.

"Thanks."

Gavin worked in silence, loosening a small valve near the carburetor. After a few taps, a trickle of liquid seeped out.

"Vapor lock, maybe?" Gavin said. "Happens sometimes when the pressure builds up in cooler temperatures."

"Huh." Luke leaned in to watch. "Wish I'd thought of that. You work on snowmobiles a lot?"

"A few times." He glanced at Luke's toolbox. "Hand me that multi-tool there, please."

"You got it." Luke handed him the tool and watched in awe.

Gavin adjusted something Luke couldn't see.

"Worked in a few resorts over the years," Gavin added. "Had to run a trail groomer all winter once. Learned a few tricks." He grinned, his teeth yellowed, one even missing.

Luke packed that information away. The guy knew his way around machines, even if he looked like he'd been wandering off the grid for months.

A few minutes later, Gavin pushed to his feet and nodded toward the snowmobile. "See if it starts."

Luke climbed onto the bench seat and turned the key. The engine sputtered, caught, and rumbled alive with a deep, steady thrum. He grinned. "Gavin, my man! Not bad!"

Gavin just shrugged and put the tools back. "Sometimes all it takes is a little patience."

Luke turned off the engine, climbed off, and wiped his hands on a rag.

"I appreciate this so much. Thank you. And listen, Emma's going to be thrilled to hear from you. She's been searching high and low."

Gavin gave a tight nod. "Figured."

"I guess she—uh, I guess you know she's here to try to sell the house? The one she grew up in? The place is a mess, but she found something inside she thinks you might have a claim to."

Gavin's chin lifted. "That so, huh?"

"Yeah. Come on inside. You hungry?"

Gavin nodded. "I could eat."

Feeding the guy was the least Luke could do, given that he'd saved them a lot of time and maybe an expensive repair. As he led Gavin toward the resort, he pulled his phone from his pocket and sent Emma a quick text.

> Luke
> Hey, great news. Someone's here to see you.

The message sent, and Luke slid his phone back into his pocket.

He glanced at Gavin. The guy had fixed the snow machine quickly and hadn't asked for anything in return. Now he'd agreed to meet with a cousin he probably hadn't seen in years. Luke pulled open the resort's front door, then waited for Gavin to go inside first. He had no idea what Emma and Gavin's reunion might bring, but some small part of him hoped Gavin might convince her not to sell. Maybe then she'd choose to stay.

Fourteen

EMMA HURRIED ACROSS THE PARKING LOT toward the front door of the resort, a swarm of bees taking flight in her abdomen. Gavin? She couldn't believe it. And of all the places for him to turn up, he'd come here.

She spotted Luke standing just inside the front door. He grinned and pushed it open.

"Hey, come on in. Gavin's in the dining room. I fixed him some lunch."

"Oh, that was nice of you. Thanks for letting me know he's here. I can't believe it."

"Yeah, he even helped me figure out what was wrong with the snowmobile. He's a good guy."

She shrugged. "As far as we know, right?"

"You can go on in if you want. I'll sit here and watch the front desk. My parents are out."

"Got it. Thanks." She hesitated. Oh, the kindness in his eyes. His willingness to get involved in her mess and help her reconnect with her cousin. "I owe you, Luke. Big time."

He waved her off. "No, you don't. Go see your cousin."

She took a deep breath, then walked toward the dining room, her steps faltering when she spotted Gavin. He sat alone in the middle of a long table, finishing off a sandwich and drinking some pop.

She was stunned by the long red beard, faded flannel button-down, and how his broad shoulders held an unmistakable resemblance to her dad's.

"Gavin?" Her voice sounded softer than she'd intended. "Hi, I'm Emma."

"Emma." He wiped his mouth with his napkin, pushed his chair back and stood, then extended his hand, wincing a little. "Mostly clean. Sorry."

She shook his outstretched hand. "Thanks for coming to Redemption."

"Yeah, been a long time."

"Too long." She pulled out a chair and sat across from him. "I think it was the Fourth of July, and I was in middle school the last time I saw you."

"Wow." He sat back down. "Sorry, I didn't save any lunch."

"Don't worry. I'll get something later." She glanced over at Luke, visible through the doorway. He caught her eye and gave her a reassuring nod.

"It's taken me a little while to find you. I wasn't sure we'd connect."

"Me either," Gavin said, reaching for his drink. "I heard you were looking for me through your radio announcement on the Caribou Clatter. Then I was volunteering with the Iditarod and somebody near Skwentna mentioned that people in Redemption were looking for me."

"Wow. So where do you live most of the time?"

He stroked the end of his long red beard, and half of his mouth tipped up in a smile. "That's classified. I still run my dad's gold mine. Central Alaska."

"Got it." She picked at a hangnail on her thumb. "I guess you know I inherited the house."

His gaze sharpened. "Figured as much. Is that why you need to connect with me? Because you don't need my permission to sell it, if that's what you're worried about."

"I appreciate that. But in case you haven't seen the video, sea lions have overtaken the house. I don't know what's worse, those rascals or the fact that my mom hasn't paid the property taxes in years."

His bushy brow furrowed. "That sounds on brand for your mother."

She winced.

Gavin blushed. "Sorry, that was uncalled for."

"Maybe not." She hesitated. "Funny thing, you're not the first person to say that to me. Gavin, I don't really want the house. If you want it, we can work something out. But before you say yes or no, I want to tell you the whole truth."

He sipped his drink slowly, then set the can back down on the table. "All right, go on."

She leaned forward. "I found gold under the floorboards."

"Whoa, whoa." He held his hands up. "Keep that on the down-low, eh?"

She glanced around. "There's nobody here."

He craned his neck to see past her. "That guy's still sitting out at the desk."

Emma looked over her shoulder at Luke, then faced Gavin again. "That's Luke, and he already knows. We can trust him."

He didn't answer as he peeked inside his empty bag of chips.

"My dad has a reputation around here for being a swindler, and I'm not my father. I want to handle this fair and square, and I thought it was only right to let you know what I found."

"I thought my dad probably had some things stashed in the

house. That might not be the only surprise you find." He chuckled. "Just saying."

"What else could be hidden in the floors or the walls?"

Gavin shrugged. "Who knows? That's the thrill of the hunt."

"I'd still like to sell it. Unless you want it."

He leaned back, crossing his arms over his barrel chest. "Have you—did you ever hear from my dad before he passed?"

She shook her head. "And I'm so sorry for your loss."

"It's all right. Thank you. I appreciate that." He paused, a sad smile forming. "He was a real happy guy. He died doing what he loved—helping me mine for gold. We had a great day together. The weather was beautiful. Pulled in a great haul. He passed unexpectedly that night."

His voice turned thick. "I miss him. Every day."

"I'm sure you do. Even though mine wasn't a stellar human, he was a good dad. I miss him too."

Gavin cleared his throat. "My dad had a terrible speech impediment."

"Yeah, I remember."

"But he was a good man, and he loved the Lord. And more than anything, Emma, he wanted you to know how much you were loved too. He talked about you from time to time, and he always believed that someday you might want to come back here. And I didn't know about the gold, but I suspect he hid that, or maybe your dad did, hoping you'd find it and make a fresh start here. If you wanted to."

She nodded, her throat tight with emotion.

"I'd like to add that maybe this isn't just about the gold. Although there's likely a lot of value in what you discovered. Maybe this is really about what you'll do with the gift you've been given. Sure, you should pay the taxes owed. But what then?"

"I-I don't know," she whispered, swiping at the moisture on her cheeks.

Gavin's eyes filled with empathy. "God doesn't hide things from us. But sometimes I wonder if maybe He hides things for us. So what is He asking you to do with your story? Your life?"

"Wow, I had no idea you'd come in here and drop these truth bombs. Sure you're not a pastor?"

"Not a pastor." He grinned, then popped the last chip into his mouth. "Just had something on my heart that I wanted to share. Now . . . any gold you'd like me to assess?"

Emma let out a shaky breath. Nathan's photo with Courtney flashed in her mind. She sniffed, then blew her nose on a napkin. They'd probably danced and drunk champagne and mingled with generous philanthropists, while she sat here trying to figure out yet another way to evict sea lions.

Maybe Gavin was right. Maybe finding that gold under the floorboards had a bigger purpose. But how was she supposed to know what to do next when everything she thought she'd wanted felt like it belonged to someone else?

She stared at the napkin, crumpled and damp. Maybe going back to Boston wasn't what she wanted after all.

"Are you sure you want to do this now?"

Luke set the shoe box in the center of the kitchen table. Out at the front desk, conversation and muffled laughter filtered in as their six guests checked in.

Frowning, Emma tapped her fingernails nervously against the farmhouse table. The refrigerator hummed in the background. "Why did you hide it in a shoe box?"

"Because we left the metal container at your house. Remember?"

"Oh. Right." Emma glanced over her shoulder. "Gavin offered to look at it for me. I trust his assessment."

"Okay, sounds good." Luke smiled and turned toward the doorway as Gavin walked in, wiping his hands on a paper towel.

"Sorry, had to pop into the restroom." He tossed the paper towel into a trash can, then rubbed his palms together. "All right, let's see what we've got."

Luke stepped back. Emma hovered next to Gavin. Her shoulders looked tight, and she kept her arms crossed over her chest. Her cheeks were a little bit blotchy, a telltale sign that she'd cried. He hadn't wanted to press, but from where he'd sat, her conversation with Gavin hadn't been combative.

His chest pinched. So what was she upset about? Maybe everything that had brought her here—and everything waiting for her back in Boston—was colliding. He couldn't blame her for coming undone.

Gavin sat down, then slowly raised the lid. He gave a little whistle.

"Whoa, would you look at that?"

Emma shifted closer. "What do you think?"

"Oh, I think whoever hid this was incredibly generous." He sorted through a few nuggets with practiced hands, placing them gently in his broad palm. "Placer gold—that's nuggets like these—is solid. Heavy. Excellent quality, of course. Most gold found in Alaska is."

"Your dad, or maybe mine, or maybe it was a team effort, must have stashed this for a reason." He took one chunk and weighed it in his other palm. "This is probably five grand right here, give or take."

Emma sucked in a breath. "Five thousand dollars? In just one nugget?"

Gavin glanced at her, raising his eyebrows. "You've likely got somewhere between fifty and eighty thousand dollars' worth of gold here. Maybe more, depending on the market rate and its purity."

Emma clutched the back of the chair in front of her. Her gaze slid to Luke.

"Pretty cool, huh?" Luke said. He offered her a bottle of water from the basket Mom kept filled on the side table, but she declined.

"I can't believe this," she said, peering into the box. "That's enough to pay all the taxes and probably finance repairs."

Gavin patted her on the shoulder.

Was she relieved? Shocked? Did this churn up more grief over her father?

It seemed like she'd been wrestling with her family's legacy—and questioning her mother's role in her father's incarceration. Not to mention that he could tell she was conflicted about whether she should stay in Redemption or go back to Boston. And now she had enough gold to change her life.

"I do feel like it was left for me on purpose," she said, looking at Gavin. "You're right. This could be an invitation."

"Maybe," Gavin said. "I don't have all the answers, but I would challenge you to be intentional about what you do next."

"Do you want any of it? I feel like half of it could be yours."

Gavin shook his head. "I have more than enough. Besides, this was all meant for you."

Luke studied them. He should be happy for her. And he was—but his scalp prickled. She could do anything she wanted with her future. There was no reason for her to stay here. Boston was still out there, waiting. The fiancé. The fancy lifestyle.

She might be one step closer to walking away, and now she had the means to do it.

She glanced at him. "Luke."

He cleared his throat. "Yeah?"

"This wouldn't have been possible without you."

The words hit hard. He offered a smile. Rubbed at the tightness in his chest.

"You would have figured it out. You always do."

Gavin carefully placed the nuggets back in the box. "You'll want to get this appraised officially if you do plan to sell it. I've got a buddy in Fairbanks you can trust. He handles raw gold buys. He'll give you a better deal than hauling this out of state."

"Thank you," Emma said, smiling. "Really."

"It's no problem. Happy to help," Gavin said. "I've got to head out, but I'll send you his contact info."

Then he hugged her, shook Luke's hand, and left. But she didn't move.

"Can I ask you something?"

"Sure." Luke shrugged. "Anything."

"If it were you—if you found something like this and suddenly had options—what would you do?"

He hesitated, then circled around the table and came to stand beside her. "Depends. Are we running from something or toward something?"

Her gaze flicked away. "I don't know."

"Then I'd pray. And I'd wait until I had clarity."

For a beat, neither of them spoke. Then she nodded, slow and thoughtful, before closing the lid on the box and sliding it toward him.

"Safekeeping, please? And I need to grab those Easter eggs. I've got to take them back to the bed and breakfast so Lainey and I can finish stuffing them."

"Of course," Luke said. He put the gold back in the safe, then returned with a laundry basket full of plastic eggs.

She smiled. "Thanks."

His phone alarm rang, and he quickly silenced it. "I've got to run. Hanging out with Brody and Sadie tonight so Ethan and Tisha can go out for dinner. I'll see you at the Easter egg hunt on Saturday?"

"Absolutely. Thanks again."

Luke watched her walk out, the basket in her arms and her shoulders a little straighter than before.

The gold had given her options.

Now he just had to find a way to become one of them.

Fifteen

FIFTY TO EIGHTY GRAND IN GOLD?

Emma grinned, her whole body trembling. How was that even possible?

She slid behind the wheel of Abbie's borrowed Subaru and turned the key in the ignition. Beside her on the front seat, she'd wedged the laundry basket filled with plastic eggs, half a dozen bags of miniature candy, stickers, and temporary tattoos.

"Thank you, Lord," she whispered. "Please give me wisdom. I don't know what to do."

Then she drove away from the resort, one hand on the wheel and the other rummaging in the plastic bag inside the laundry basket for a peanut butter cup or three. The Easter egg hunt was only two days away and they still had more eggs to fill, so she couldn't eat more than a few pieces of candy. Otherwise there wouldn't be enough to finish filling the eggs. But sometimes sugar and chocolate hit the spot.

She unwrapped the pastel pink foil and popped the sweet treat into her mouth. Her thoughts kept circling back to Gavin's words and the gold and what that box meant, stashed back in the safe at the resort. So much potential. So much pressure.

This isn't just about the gold, he'd said. Maybe this is really about the gift you've been given.

That was the problem—she didn't know what to do with the gold. And she didn't know how to figure it out.

Yeah, okay, so she'd come to Redemption looking for answers and a way to pay off her mother's property-tax debt. She'd thought that would mean selling the house. But now, part of her questioned whether she even wanted the life she'd spent the last several years building.

Her phone buzzed against the console.

Nathan.

Her stomach flipped. Heat rushed to her face as she stared at the screen. She hadn't heard from him since she'd texted—no, confronted—him about the photo with Courtney. Not one word. She checked her mirror, eased to the side of the road, then turned on her hazard lights and swiped to answer.

"Emma," he said, calm and polished, like nothing had happened.

She bristled. "Oh, now you decide to call me back?"

"I've been busy."

"Convenient," she snapped. "Too busy to text or call, but not too busy to put your arm around Courtney LaSalle in front of a room full of donors."

He sighed the way he did when she was being—quote—emotional. "I gave you plenty of opportunity to show up at that gala. Everyone needs a date. It's optics, that's all."

"Oh, and your hand on her waist, pulling her close? That's for optics too, Nathan?"

"You're overreacting."

"I'm not stupid. I know what that photo looked like. And come to think of it, I've heard your mom say she'd prefer that you marry Courtney."

"Are you kidding me? Do you hear yourself right now?" His voice sharpened. "You're thousands of miles away. You ran off to chase sea lions off your old dock. And now you're mad that I took someone else to an event we'd planned to attend for months?"

"I didn't leave you," she said, her voice wobbling. "I asked for ten days."

"Which has now turned into two weeks."

"But you said you understood!"

"Well, that was before you went full-on frontier woman and dropped out of my life."

"Oh, please. I've been trying to talk to you. You've been busy." She emphasized the word, knowing as soon as she said it that he'd get angry.

There was a long pause.

"You know what? Maybe you're right. Maybe space is a good thing. It's showing us how different we are. I'm building something real, Emma. A life for us. The very future you said you wanted and needed."

Oh, he made her want to say bad words. "And I'm supposed to be grateful? Is that what you're saying?"

"I'm saying I'm making connections. Building my practice. Making sure I have a stellar reputation as a surgeon so you can live the lifestyle you're accustomed to—"

"—and stepping out on me in the process."

"I did not cheat," he said coldly. "But maybe I should have if this is how you're going to act."

She sucked in a breath. A hot tear slipped down her cheek. She swiped it away with the back of her hand, willing herself to keep calm.

"You know what? You have no right to say that to me. Don't bother calling. We're done."

"You're ending our engagement over the phone?" His voice

still held that maddening calm, but she could hear the current of fury beneath it.

"Sure am," she said. "And I'm ending this because I deserve better than someone who makes me feel small when I'm going through a crisis. I will not let you treat me this way."

He scoffed. "I do not make you feel small. That's ludicrous."

She swallowed back the lump in her throat. "Goodbye, Nathan."

She hung up before he could respond. The silence in the car swallowed her whole. Her breath came in shallow bursts. Her face still burned, her eyes stung. She grabbed another peanut butter cup and shoved it in her mouth. Then she shifted into Drive and headed for the bed and breakfast.

By the time she had driven up the hill and parked, her jaw ached from clenching it. The candy had done little to soothe the hurt in her chest. She slammed the door harder than necessary, marched around the car, gravel crunching beneath her feet, and grabbed the laundry basket full of Easter egg hunt supplies, wedging it against her hip.

Her vision blurred as she stormed toward the front door. Inside, she blinked back the tears that refused to stop. Angry crying. The worst kind. Her throat felt tight, like it might collapse in on itself. She couldn't breathe, couldn't think, couldn't even form a coherent sentence.

She rounded the corner toward the kitchen—and bumped straight into Mrs. O'Brien, who was carting a bag of flour from the pantry to the island.

The older woman glanced up. Her usual flat, stone-cold expression softened. "Uh-oh," she said. "You look like someone just kicked your puppy."

"I'm fine," Emma muttered.

Mrs. O'Brien raised one eyebrow. "You don't look fine."

Emma dropped the basket onto the table with a thud. "Thanks so much."

"Do you want to talk about it?"

"I'd rather scream into a pillow."

She crossed to the fridge, yanked open the door, and plucked out a can of sparkling water.

"I just dumped my fiancé. Over the phone. In Abbie's car. While shoving Easter candy into my face. Totally winning at life."

Mrs. O'Brien hummed—a low, oddly empathetic sound. "Men," she said, shaking her head. "They ruin everything."

Emma barked a laugh, but it caught and turned into a sob. She popped the tab on the can but didn't drink.

"I really thought he was the right choice," she said, leaning against the kitchen cabinet doors. "I thought if I just had it all together—neat and tidy—my job, my relationship, the wedding plans... then everything would gel and I'd have this perfect little life with my brilliant surgeon of a husband. But I think I've been lying to myself."

Mrs. O'Brien set her measuring cup aside. "Well, let me give you the advice no one gave me when I was your age."

"Can't wait."

"Marriage is a long time to deal with a bad choice."

Emma stared at her. "Um... that is not exactly comforting."

"It's not supposed to be," Mrs. O'Brien said. "It's true." She opened a drawer and pulled out a spoon. "It doesn't matter how good he looks in a tux, or how much your ring sparkles, or how many people tell you you're a lovely couple. If you marry someone who makes you feel like less than you are, you'll spend the next however-many years fighting—not just with each other, but with yourself. Trying to justify your decision."

Emma trudged over to the bar, pulled out a stool, and sat down. "I think I knew this," she whispered. "I think I've known for a while."

"Well," Mrs. O'Brien said, "be glad you figured it out before you walked down the aisle."

"I thought you didn't like me," Emma said, then took a sip of her drink.

"Poor assumption on your part," Mrs. O'Brien replied. "I didn't care much for how your parents behaved when they lived here, but I've been watching you. You've got grit. You showed up here and you're trying to make things right. That counts for something."

Emma set her can back down on the bar. "I appreciate that."

Mrs. O'Brien nodded toward the laundry basket. "Want some help finishing those?"

"Sure."

Mrs. O'Brien rolled up the sleeves of her sweater and moved to the table. "You stuff, I'll close the eggs. And when we're done, we'll split the bag of leftover candy."

Emma smiled. "That's the best offer I've had all week."

He would hide a thousand plastic eggs in eighteen-degree weather if it meant spending more time with Emma.

The sun had just climbed over the mountains across the bay, but its golden light added little warmth. Luke shivered, his breath leaving small white puffs in the crisp morning air. Not exactly ideal weather for the community Easter egg hunt, but he wasn't rooting for spring just yet. He still held out hope for an epic blizzard—the kind that dumped several feet of snow in less than twenty-four hours and kept their guests at the resort happy.

He plucked another plastic egg from his bucket and tucked it behind the wooden sign at Redemption Community Church, then looked around, searching for Emma.

She stood a few yards away, auburn curls catching the sunlight. Crouched near the propane tank, she stashed a few eggs underneath, moving quickly. Knowing her, she had some kind of strategy in mind. That was just like her. Always a little competitive. She probably wanted to empty her basket before he did, even with something as simple as hiding eggs for the kids.

The sight of her stirred something deep inside him. That same ache he'd thought he had buried alongside his teenage memories of her. Yeah, okay, so it had been years since they'd been a couple, but she still had that way of making his world brighter. Sharper. And now she'd extended her visit in a way that felt almost . . . permanent.

"Luke," she called out, breaking through his thoughts. She strode toward him, her basket nearly empty. Her smile was a little sad. Or maybe she was just exhausted.

"You're making this too easy," she teased, nodding toward the church sign. "This is supposed to be a challenge."

He nudged his beanie off his forehead and scratched his head. "What can I say? I've got a soft spot for these little tykes."

She rolled her eyes but couldn't hide the flicker of amusement there. That look had always been his weakness. Like muscle memory, it pulled him back to the days when he'd teased her just to see that exact expression.

"Well, don't make it too easy," she said. "Here, take these. I'm going to check in with Laincy and Chloe and make sure everything's ready inside."

She handed him her basket, their fingers brushing. The fleeting contact sent a jolt through him. A spark, electric and undeniable. He tightened his grip around the basket handle, but his mind stayed locked in on that brief touch.

Her lips parted slightly as if she'd felt it too.

He cleared his throat, forced himself to look away before his thoughts ran too far ahead—or before somebody caught him staring.

"You know," he said, crouching to carve out a basin in the snow to hide an egg. "I feel like something's different about you. Is it because you reconnected with Gavin?"

She paused, glancing over her shoulder at him. Her brow furrowed, but then her expression softened, and for just a second, she looked like the girl he remembered. The one who used to sit with him, talking about their dreams, their futures. Futures that had never quite turned out the way they'd planned.

Well, at least not for him.

"It's been a long week," she admitted, her voice quieter now. "But this helps. Being here, doing something for the kids reminds me that there's still good in the world. That I still have a purpose."

Luke straightened, both baskets of eggs in his arms. "There's always good, Emma," he said. "Even when it feels as though the bad guys are winning. And you absolutely have a purpose. God put you here for a reason."

Emma hesitated, then drew a breath. "Nathan and I... we ended things. It wasn't pretty."

His pulse kicked up. He wanted to shout "Hallelujah!" but that hardly seemed appropriate. "Ouch. That has to be hard."

She glanced down, fiddling with the zipper pull on her jacket. The silence stretched between them, thick and buzzing. Had he said the wrong thing? But then she smiled again. Softer this time. And a weight lifted from his chest.

"You've always had a way of making me feel better."

Oh, sweetheart, if you only knew.

Part of him wanted to tell her that he'd always be there to do just that. But he held back. This wasn't the right time. Instead, he returned her smile, easy and warm. "Anytime."

"I'll hide these on my way inside." She snagged two more eggs from the basket he held, then walked away, her curls bouncing against her puffy jacket, dark-wash jeans tucked into Sorel lace-up boots. Funny how quickly she'd ditched those Boston stilettos for something more practical. Every day, she looked a little less like the city girl who'd built a life in Boston and more like the Alaskan girl he'd never stopped loving.

And frankly that scared him.

He crossed the parking lot, tucking eggs into hiding spots, some clever, some downright obvious.

"Hey, Luke," Emma called. She crouched near the front steps of the church, holding up a bright green plastic egg. "Too easy if I leave it here?"

"Borderline, but I think it's passable. Just don't let Lainey see you. She'll accuse you of going soft."

Emma laughed, the sound light and musical and oh, so familiar. His heart twisted. He'd missed this. Missed her. And now, spending time with her day in and day out, it was all he could do to keep from confessing everything he'd held back for two decades.

He moved closer, standing under the portico as she studied him, her expression earnest. "You've been really great through all of this," she said, her voice soft. Almost shy. "I don't think I've thanked you enough, and honestly, I don't know what I would have done without you."

"You don't have to thank me," he said, his voice lower than he intended. "You've always been important to me. That's never changed."

Her gaze softened, and for a moment, the entire world narrowed down to just the two of them. He leaned in slightly, his heart thudding in his chest.

Then the church door opened, and Lainey popped her head out.

"Hey, you two!" Lainey waved them over. "Can you come in and help us with last-minute prep?"

"We still have eggs to hide." Luke lifted his basket in protest.

"We're going to have you hide some of those inside." Lainey leaned against the door, pushing it wider for them to pass through. "There are little ones who probably won't hunt outdoors."

"Got it," Luke said, following Emma into the church. The atrium had been transformed into a spring wonderland, complete with twinkle lights, succulents, and pastel-draped tables. He tried not to notice how effortlessly Emma fit into it all, like she belonged here, like they belonged here.

Off to the side, a photographer adjusted a camera on a tripod. A colorful Hoppy Spring balloon banner stretched across a floral backdrop with a faux grass mat below.

"Ta-da!" Lainey handed him a pair of oversize bunny ears. "Luke, these are for you."

He frowned. "Really?"

"Just try it," Lainey insisted, her grin mischievous.

"Fine." Luke reluctantly plopped the bunny ears on his head. He turned to Emma. "Go ahead. Say what you're thinking. I know you want to."

"Oh, I wouldn't dream of it," she teased, her voice sweet and her eyes sparkling.

"I don't believe you," he said, narrowing his eyes.

She shrugged, crouching to tuck a pink plastic egg into the base of a potted fiddle-leaf fig. "You look adorable. Like a rugged, reluctant bunny."

"Emma, put on the duck bill and you guys can pose together," Chloe said, holding up an oversized plastic orange prop with a rubber band.

"No, no photographic evidence of this," he groaned. "I knew I should've stayed in the parking lot."

"Adorable and grumpy." Emma nudged his shoulder with hers. "It's a good look for you."

The playful touch sent another jolt through him, one that zipped up his arm and spread warmth through his chest. He wanted to make her smile like this every day, to tease her and be teased right back. But now wasn't the moment to say anything. Timing had never been his strong suit, but he wasn't stupid. This was not the minute to make a move.

"How did you talk me into this, anyway?" Luke stepped carefully onto the faux green grass mat, then faced the camera.

"Because you're a nice guy," Lainey said, grinning.

"And because you were cornered by a volunteer with big sad eyes who told you half her help backed out." Chloe stood beside the photographer and feigned a pathetic face.

He shook his head. "I really am a sucker for someone lacking volunteers."

"The biggest," Emma agreed, taking her place beside him as she wrangled the band on the duck bill over her head. "But it's noble. Like a knight in slightly dusty Carhartts."

He smirked. "Knights don't wear bunny ears."

"You don't know that," she shot back, her voice muffled behind the ridiculous prop she'd slid onto her face.

He wanted to argue, but she was standing so close, smelling like vanilla and something floral as she slid her arm around his waist. For one reckless second, he considered planting a kiss on her cheek right there for the camera to capture.

"Look here and say, 'Hoppy spring,'" the photographer called out.

"Hoppy spring," Luke and Emma said, and he added a cheesy grin for full effect.

Lainey and Chloe burst into laughter nearby, and the moment slipped away.

His phone buzzed in his pocket, and he pulled it out, grateful for the distraction. A new text popped up from the owner of the lodge in Petersburg.

> Unknown number
> We've narrowed our list of applicants to the final three. Next interview on Tuesday, if you're still interested.

He stared at the message, his chest tightening. This was it. A solid step toward leaving Redemption. Toward a fresh start over a thousand miles away, on an island in southeastern Alaska. Away from his family's resort business and all the family baggage that came with it. It was everything he'd thought he wanted.

But now, the thought of leaving didn't sit right. Not when Emma was here.

"You okay?" Emma's voice broke through his thoughts, soft and full of concern. She tilted her head slightly, studying him with those green eyes that could see right through people if they let her.

"Yeah," he said, pulling off the bunny ears and tossing them back onto the prop pile. "Just wondering if this egg hunt is going to get super competitive. I hear five-year-olds take no prisoners."

She took off the duck bill, then smoothed down her curls with one hand. "What's your plan for the final egg? Rumor has it there's quite the prize inside."

He glanced at the oversize plastic purple egg sitting in the bottom of the basket nearby. "I'm taking the prize, giving it to one of Ethan's kids, and then I'll leave the empty egg on the pulpit in the sanctuary."

Emma feigned a dramatic gasp. "Luke McGuire, you're diabolical."

"I have to do what I can to maintain favorite-uncle status." He shrugged. "By the way, that wasn't a no."

"It was an 'I'm impressed but I'm also judging you,'" she said, her tone light but her eyes still searching his face.

"You've always had a great sense of humor, Emma. People still talk about the practical jokes you got away with in middle school."

She laughed then, warm and unguarded, and it was like a punch to his chest. He wanted to tell her she was the reason it was so hard to think about leaving. That the thought of walking away from Redemption had never felt more like a mistake than it did right now. But the words wouldn't come. They stuck in his throat, heavy and impossible.

"You ever think about staying?"

Her smile faltered, and something flashed across her face—equal parts fragile and hopeful. But then it was gone, replaced by the guarded look she always wore when he got too close.

She bent to pick up her basket, her fingers tightening around the handle. "I should probably finish hiding these eggs."

"Wait." He stepped closer. "You didn't answer my question."

She straightened slowly, her lips pressing into a thin line. "I don't know, Luke. My job, my friends, my whole life—it's in Boston." She hesitated, her gaze darting to the floor before meeting his again. "But things are super complicated now."

Complicated. He hated that word. It said everything and nothing all at once.

"Well," he said, forcing a casual tone he didn't feel, "you're pretty good at helping with community events. Maybe you should stick around. I hear it's standing room only at your water-aerobics class."

Her lips twitched, but the smile didn't quite reach her eyes. "Tempting."

He wanted to push, to ask her what was so complicated, to tell her that she was one of the reasons he didn't want to leave. But he couldn't. He wouldn't ask her to choose him—not when she wouldn't even commit to staying. So instead, he grabbed an egg from her basket and tossed it her way.

She caught it midair, her brows lifting. "What was that?"

"Just making sure you're ready for some competition," he said with a grin that felt hollow. "Not sure if you're aware, but there's a scavenger hunt for grown-ups too."

"Of course I'm aware. Don't be ridiculous. I fully intend to win the whole thing."

"Good luck, because I won't go down without a fight."

She held his gaze for a long moment, saying nothing. And for now, that silence was all he was going to get.

Luke's phone buzzed again in his pocket. Probably a follow-up to the other message, waiting for a reply. Waiting for him to make a decision.

He ignored the text, mostly because he needed time to think. Now that he knew Emma and Nathan had broken up, everything shifted. She might still leave Alaska. She might still leave him. But if he had a sliver of a chance, why walk away? Or would staying in Redemption be a mistake he'd regret? The questions gnawed at him, impossible to answer.

Sixteen

MAYBE IT WASN'T SO BAD BEING A LOSER. Emma sat at a high-top for two, tucked in the corner near the window at Dockside Pizza Company. She and Luke had scored the last empty table in the packed restaurant. Today's scavenger hunt for grown-ups hadn't gone her way. Not at all. But she kind of didn't care. Because as laughter and conversation swirled around her, warm and unrestrained, for the first time since she'd arrived in Alaska, it felt like she belonged. She didn't feel like an outsider anymore, the girl who left Redemption and came back with too much baggage in tow. Tonight, she felt like herself. Not the daughter of a swindler, not the girl whose fiancé cheated on her, and not the owner of a house that seemed almost uninhabitable. Just Emma.

Across the room, Chloe stood on a chair by the air hockey table and held up a gift basket filled with donated merchandise from local businesses. She grinned as the scavenger-hunt winner, some guy Emma didn't recognize, pretended to bow toward Chloe. The crowd erupted into cheers. Plastic drink cups clinked against each other, and Emma couldn't help but reach for her own diet pop.

Luke sat across from her, leaning back against the wall, arms crossed and a smile on his lips. He looked too good tonight—his dark hair tousled, his flannel rolled up at the elbows—comfortable and effortlessly handsome.

"The guy's only been here, like, two days," Luke said. "How'd he pull off a victory?"

"But he won fair and square," she teased, pinning him with a long look. "You're just bitter because you didn't win."

"Bitter?" He spread his palm across his chest, feigning offense. "Me? Never."

"Sure, that's why you've been pouting since they announced his name."

"I don't pout," he said, but the twitch in his mouth betrayed him.

"You are totally pouting," she said. "Admit it, Luke McGuire. You wanted to win that scavenger hunt just for the free mani-pedi."

"Maybe," he said, his voice dropping a little lower, just enough to send a tiny thrill dancing along her spine. "But I think I'm handling the crushing disappointment pretty well."

"Debatable," she said, but her heart wasn't really in the banter. How could it be when he looked at her like that? Like she was the only person in the room worth paying attention to? She glanced away, pretending to watch the winner pose for a photo, holding the basket. The truth was, Luke's gaze had her feeling too warm and too seen, and she wasn't sure what to do with these feelings.

"I'm glad you came tonight," Luke said. "You look happy. Even happier than today when you were hiding eggs from little kids."

Smiling, she swiveled in her chair. "It's nice, you know, not feeling like the town pariah for once."

"Pariah?" His brow furrowed. "That's a little harsh, don't you think?"

"Ha! Um, excuse me, but just two short weeks ago, I walked in here and I'm pretty sure I overheard some guy at the bar telling everyone I was just here to steal their money like my father did."

Luke winced and reached for his drink. "That was probably Joe, and he says a lot of things he shouldn't. I'm sorry that happened."

"It's fine. I'm over it." She sipped the last of her drink through the straw, then set her plastic cup down on the varnished table. "It's nice not having everyone whisper about me for a change."

"Trust me," Luke said. "The only thing anyone's whispering about tonight is how you completely crushed that egg toss earlier."

She laughed. "You're just jealous that I have better aim than you."

"Not jealous," he said, plating another slice of Canadian bacon and pineapple pizza, his mouth curving into a slow grin. "Simply impressed."

And there it was again, that look—that quiet, steady way he had of focusing on her. As if nothing else mattered. Her heart stuttered. Her engagement to Nathan ended less than three days ago, and she'd barely begun to untangle the mess of who she was and what she wanted. Jumping into something with Luke—someone who had once meant so much to her—felt reckless. But then he smiled at her, and all the reasons she should keep her distance faded. Vanished.

"So," he said, "are you going to make your big Redemption comeback? Eliminating sea lions, uncovering gold treasure—what's next? Headlining the egg-toss circuit?"

"I don't know. I'll have to see what fits into my busy schedule."

"Busy, huh?" He tipped his head to one side. "Too busy for a Ms. Pac-Man rematch?"

"Are you asking because you want to lose to me again?"

He laughed, and goosebumps skated across her skin.

"There you go, assuming that I'm gonna lose."

"Am I wrong?"

He shook his head, his grin widening, but he didn't answer. Instead, he held her gaze for longer than necessary.

The noise in the crowded restaurant faded into the background, and just like that, the playful energy between them shifted, became heavier. Charged. It was stupid how much she wanted him to kiss her, stupid how her heart raced just sitting this close to him.

Before she could think too hard about it, someone called Luke's name from across the room. He turned. His brother Tate. His expression pinched, and she blew out a breath.

"I should probably go," she said, feeling a bit unsteady.

"Emma—"

She didn't let him finish. Whatever he needed to say, she wasn't ready to hear it. "Thanks for the pizza." She flashed him a quick smile. "I'll see you around, okay?"

She didn't wait for his response. Instead, she yanked her coat off the back of her stool, grabbed her purse, and worked her way toward the door, her pulse pounding in her ears. She needed air and space to think. Because if she didn't leave now, she wasn't sure she'd be able to stop herself from making another reckless decision. And this time, she wasn't sure her heart would survive it.

"Emma, wait."

She had barely stepped onto the sidewalk outside when Luke's voice cut through the night, firm but quiet. She froze, then turned as she heard his footsteps behind her.

"I just need to pay," he said. "Wait for me?"

His eyes roamed her face. It wasn't a question—not really. He knew she'd wait. She swallowed hard, then nodded.

Minutes later, he was back, walking beside her. "Let me give you a ride."

"Okay."

"I'm parked over here." He pointed to his truck, sitting across the street, facing the harbor. He unlocked it and she climbed in, then buckled up for the short drive back to Lainey's bed and breakfast.

The air inside the truck was thick and charged, the space between them suddenly feeling way too small. The engine rumbled to life and neither of them spoke.

"I didn't expect to see you having so much fun today," Luke said, his voice quiet.

Emma turned her head, meeting his gaze in the dim glow from the dashboard.

"Yeah, I really just wanted to keep my word and help out."

His fingers flexed on the steering wheel. "It was good to see you smiling, laughing, hanging out."

Her chest squeezed. "I guess I had a good reason to."

"Yeah."

Something unreadable flickered in his expression. What was it? She forced herself to look away.

"Emma."

The way he said her name—low and rough—sent her heart into orbit. She didn't turn, didn't look at him, because if she did, she wasn't sure she'd be able to hold on to her resolve. Instead, she let out a nervous laugh.

"You're making it really hard not to think about the past, you know that?"

"I know."

Frustration twisted inside her. "And yet, you're still giving me all this space."

He shifted into Reverse, pulled out of the parking spot, and drove down the road, easing to a stop at the intersection.

"Giving you space because you need it."

She turned in her seat and faced him, her chest tight. "Do I?"

The question hung in the air between them. Luke's jaw clenched. Of course he didn't answer her. Because he was Luke—steady, careful, patient. The exact opposite of what she wanted right now.

They rode in silence up the hill to Lainey's house. He parked but left the engine running. Before she could say something she'd regret, she unbuckled her seat belt, pushed open the door, and stepped out into the cold night air.

His boots thumped against the steps as he followed her onto the porch. She turned to tell him good night. He was standing way too close. The space between them disappeared. Her pulse thundered. This was it. If he kissed her now, she wouldn't stop him. She wouldn't even try.

He lifted a hand, like he might cup his palm against her cheek. She leaned closer, stopped breathing just for a second.

Then he shoved his hand into his pocket.

The moment shattered. A sharp pang sliced through her.

"Good night," he said.

She swallowed past the ache in her throat and forced a smile. "Thanks for the ride. Good night."

Then she turned away and reached for the door. The porch light cast a warm glow across the faded welcome mat. But she didn't go inside. No, this wasn't how the night was going to end. Not with another almost. Her breath caught. Maybe she wasn't ready. But if she didn't take this opportunity now, she might regret it. And she was tired of living with regrets.

She whirled around, adrenaline pulsing through her veins. "Luke."

He was already halfway to his truck, broad shoulders hunched.

"Please stop."

He turned slowly. She launched herself off the porch, then raced toward him, clumps of snow spraying up from under her boots and spattering her jeans.

His brows knit together, his face half illuminated in the silver-blue glow from the security lights at the edge of Lainey's property. "What's go—"

She didn't let him finish. Didn't give herself time to overthink.

Instead, she reached up, clutched fistfuls of his jacket, and tugged him closer. Then she brushed her lips across his, tentative at first. The smell of his cologne enveloped her. Spicy. Outdoorsy. Familiar.

He pressed his hands into the small of her back and pulled her closer. Then he kissed her back. It wasn't wild or desperate. His touch was full of memories. And maybe a little bit of everything they'd both been too afraid to say.

She let her hands roam up the base of his neck and tunneled her fingers through his hair. Then he wrapped his arms around her as if he'd been waiting almost twenty years to hold her again.

Everything else fell away.

There under the stars, she finally stopped running from Redemption. From her past, and from him. He deepened the kiss, and she got lost in the warmth of his touch. For the first time in a very long time, she felt seen and known. Cherished.

Yeah, okay. It wasn't so bad being a loser. Not when it led her right here.

Right back to him.

—

He couldn't stop replaying that kiss.

Sunlight streamed in through the kitchen window, golden and warm—a welcome reprieve from the cold front that had just blown through. Maybe spring wasn't that far away after all.

Luke stretched his arms over his head, the click in his shoulder a reminder that he wasn't a young guy anymore. After the Easter egg hunt yesterday, he'd helped a buddy hang drywall in his house. Today his body protested.

Not that he cared. Not today. Not after that kiss.

Emma.

He smiled, then poured coffee into his mug and headed for the resort's front door. People were beginning to stir. A young couple in cabin three had already pulled their snowshoes from the back of their SUV and were heading for the trails, laughing. A family, dressed in their Easter finest, stood by the massive evergreen in the front yard, posing for pictures.

And the ruined cabin—the one that had gone up in flames weeks ago—was partially rebuilt. Tate must have figured out how to get things up to code because the framing was finished and new roofing materials sat in a neat stack off to the side. The local crew, friends or friends of friends, had agreed to work this week, and maybe they'd get the thing ready to rent by May.

But none of that good news compared to what had happened last night.

He stood at the porch railing and sipped his coffee, savoring each detail. The whisper of her lips against his. The way she'd raced toward him. The faint vanilla scent in her hair. Her fingers skimming his shoulders and then twining behind his neck.

His pulse sped.

He hadn't expected it—not really. Sure, they'd been sort of circling around each other during dinner. The banter. The flirting. The lengthy looks. But there'd been a hesitancy in her eyes, and he hadn't wanted to push her.

He hadn't felt like this in years. Not since before she left. Not since before his dad's injury and life got hard. But last night, with Emma in his arms—even for a few minutes—he'd felt weightless.

Not because all of his problems were solved. Far from it, really. His family was still going to struggle to make ends meet until the summer season came.

But somehow, today, he didn't feel like that was his burden to carry alone.

Birds flew overhead, and water dripped from a partially melted icicle still clinging to the roofline. He checked his watch. He still had a little bit of time before he needed to get ready for church.

Emma would be there. Hopefully.

He could picture her now, wearing something sweet and floral and understated, sitting in a pew in the sanctuary.

He couldn't wait to see her.

Not just because of the kiss.

Well—mostly because of the kiss.

He rubbed the back of his neck and grinned. He was acting like a teenager. Distracted. Downright useless, really. But he'd take it, because he deserved a little joy.

They both did.

Still, he wasn't going to rush this. She'd been through a lot. He respected that. But she wouldn't have kissed him like that if she wasn't ready to move forward. And when she'd pulled back, she hadn't looked scared.

She'd looked hopeful.

Grinning, he took a sip of his coffee and savored the taste of the rich warm liquid.

The door creaked open behind him. He turned. Megan stood in the doorway, her face blotchy as if she'd been crying. Her dark hair was twisted into a messy bun, and she wore a gray hoodie with a coffee stain down the front and jeans with two giant holes in the knees.

"What are you doing back in town?" He set his mug on the porch railing, then gave her a hug. "I thought you were in Fairbanks."

"I drove in late last night," she said, her voice muffled against his sweater. When she pulled back, her face crumpled. She covered her mouth with her hand, and her whole body trembled.

"Hey, hey," he said gently. "What's wrong, Meg?"

"He broke up with me," she sobbed. "Says he met someone else and he's moving in with her in her apartment in Germany."

The words tumbled out in a rush. Luke's stomach clenched. "Oh no."

Poor thing. He pulled her in for another hug. She clung to him, clamping her hands onto his arms. He rested his chin on the top of her head.

"Is this the guy with the dogs? The one who's deployed?"

She nodded, her shoulders still shaking.

He winced. "Yeah... I didn't like him very much."

Another sob wracked her. "Not helping."

"Okay, okay. You're right. I'm sorry." He patted her back. "It's... it's going to be all right."

Except it wasn't. Not really. She had the worst taste in guys, and every time they broke her heart, she came crawling home. Distraught.

"I feel so stupid," she choked out.

"No." He pulled back just enough to look her in the eye. "You are not stupid. He's the idiot. You hear me? You deserve so much better."

Drawing in a ragged breath, Megan swiped at her tears with the cuff of her sweatshirt. "I just... I couldn't stay there, you know? I had to come home."

"Of course," he said, brushing a strand of hair from her face. "You're always welcome here. You know that."

She gave him a watery smile. "Thanks. But Mom and Dad are going to have a cow."

"Yeah, probably."

She leaned against him again, her sobs quieting.

Then she pulled back, sniffling, and wiped her nose on her sleeve.

"You're gonna think I'm bonkers for saying this."

"Uh-oh. What now?"

She hesitated, then looked past him, out toward the snow-dusted yard and the half-rebuilt cabin.

"I stopped for gas in Glennallen on the way home. I also needed some coffee and to use the restroom. Anyway, I saw a guy I used to know."

"Meg." He fixed her with a warning glance. "I'm not sure now's the best time to—"

"Let me finish. He was standing by the register to pay, and I only saw him for a few seconds, but he reminded me of Trevor."

His scalp prickled. "Trevor? As in Trevor Kelly? The missing pilot from the plane crash?"

"I know. It's wild. But the way he carried himself. Something about him . . . very much reminded me of the Kelly brothers. And I can't shake it. I can't stop thinking about it."

A gust of wind picked up, blowing snow from a nearby tree branch.

Luke gripped the porch railing, then reached for his coffee cup and plucked it from its perch.

"I didn't get a chance to speak to him," she said. "When I came out of the restroom, he was gone. But I thought about him all the way here. Now I'm telling you. What if that was him? Or what if somebody out there knows what happened to Trevor and nobody's ever said anything? Can you imagine?"

"Typically it's Ethan that's obsessed with finding these answers. I didn't expect you to hop on board too." He checked the time on his phone. "I don't know what to say. Maybe mention it to Ethan later? Are you coming to church?"

She shook her head.

"All right." He leaned in and kissed the top of her forehead. "The plot thickens, huh?"

His thoughts turned back to Emma. Church started in thirty minutes, and he wanted to catch up with her. Sit beside her. Make sure she was coming to brunch at the café afterward.

Megan's words stuck with him as he went to finish getting ready for church.

Glennallen. Less than two hundred miles from here. Could Trevor really be alive?

Seventeen

THE MCGUIRES WERE RIGHT. PIE WAS THE PERfect way to celebrate. Anything, really. But especially Easter. And fresh starts. Emma scooped up every bit of flaky crust and smooth-as-silk chocolate filling left on her plate.

A hum of appreciation vibrated in her throat as she savored the last bite, then leaned back against the cushioned booth. "Tisha really outdid herself this time."

Luke smiled, his fork scraping his own plate as he chased a lingering crumb. "She'll be glad to hear that. She might start delivering whole pies to the bed and breakfast, though, if I tell her."

Emma dabbed her mouth with her napkin. "Lainey and I would not complain."

The café hummed with the chatter of other customers, thanks to the Binfords' decision to offer a buffet-style Easter brunch. The scent of freshly brewed coffee and maple syrup lingered in the air, mingling with the aroma of bacon and eggs. For the first time since she'd arrived back in Redemption, she truly felt at ease. The tension from the awful conversation that had her twisted in knots had ebbed. Kissing Luke probably had something to do with that.

Warmth blossomed in her chest as she reached for her coffee. Finally. She didn't feel trapped between a rock and a hard place. Or a sea-lion colony and a house in questionable shape.

Luke leaned forward, pushing his plate gently to the side and resting his forearms on the table. "I've enjoyed spending Easter with you, Emma. I'm glad you're here."

She grinned. "Same."

Luke's warm gaze settled on her. "I know you're worried about getting all these loose ends tied up, but you're not in this alone. I've told you that. You believe me, right?"

Her stomach fluttered, an all-too-familiar reaction when he looked at her like that. Like she wasn't just the girl who'd left all those years ago, but someone he believed in.

Before she could respond, the bell above the door jingled. She barely had time to register the sound before a clipped, unmistakable voice cut through the cozy atmosphere.

"There you are."

Emma stiffened. Luke's gaze flicked toward the entrance. A muscle in his jaw tightened.

Nathan.

Her heart sped.

Dressed in a tailored navy peacoat with a cashmere scarf perfectly knotted at his throat, Nathan strode toward her, scanning the café as if he expected a slew of people to greet him with applause.

"What are you doing here?"

Nathan stopped. His dark eyes pinged to Luke before settling back on Emma. "I had to drive five hours to get here. Five hours, Emma. Do you have any idea what that kind of drive does to a person?"

Luke made a quiet sound, something between amusement and disbelief, but he said nothing. Emma refused to budge, not after Nathan spoke to her like that.

"You didn't answer me. What are you doing here?"

Nathan's smile was tight, and a hint of surprise flashed in his eyes. "Frankly, I didn't like the way our conversation ended."

"So you flew all the way here to talk to me?"

His expression grew serious. "Of course. I'd do anything for you, you know that."

Luke's fingers curled into a fist, his posture shifting slightly, but he stayed quiet.

Nathan surveyed the table. "This looks cozy. Mind if I sit?"

Emma hesitated. "Actually, I do. I'm not interested in whatever pitch you're about to make. I told you—we're through."

"It's not a pitch. I just want to talk."

Luke's gaze toggled between them. But he said nothing.

Heat climbed Emma's neck. Suddenly, the café felt too warm and too full of curious glances. Her pulse drummed in her ears. She shot Luke a pleading look, hoping for backup. Why couldn't he echo her resolve? Step in. Remind her that she had every right to walk away.

Instead, his expression morphed into a guarded mask.

"Really?" she asked, her voice nearly breaking. "You don't have anything to say?"

He shrugged. "You've got to do what's best for you, Emma."

Her throat tightened. The confidence she'd felt just a minute ago melted like butter on a hot skillet.

"Right. Best for me, of course."

"Five minutes," Nathan said. "That's it."

"Fine." She set her napkin on the table and pushed back her chair, her stomach churning as she followed him outside.

The cool air hit her flushed cheeks. Spots peppered her vision. How could Luke just sit there?

Nathan led her to a silver Land Cruiser parked near the curb. He opened the passenger door, and she slid inside, arms folded tightly across her chest. He shut the door a little too hard behind her, then circled around and climbed behind the wheel. The engine rumbled to life.

"Wait. Where are we going?" she asked, reaching for her seat belt.

"You really want to have this conversation in the parking lot?" Nathan gripped the steering wheel with both hands. "Take me to where you're staying."

"Fine." She gestured toward the street behind them. "Take a right out of the parking lot, then the first left, and then right on Main."

Nathan shifted into Reverse. "Got it."

They rode in tense silence. The Copper Kettle, Dockside Pizza Company, and the community center all flashed by her window. Sunlight broke through the mottled clouds, and she squinted against the glare.

"You blindsided me, babe."

"What?" She turned toward him. "I blindsided you?"

"You got upset over one photo of Courtney and me, so I flew across the country to see you—to try to talk to you—and I find you giggling over pie with your ex-boyfriend."

She looked away. "I wasn't giggling."

"Hmm. Well, it looked like you were enjoying that pie."

"Turn here." She pointed toward the road leading to the bed and breakfast.

"I guess I just didn't realize you'd come here to get reacquainted," he said. "I thought you were trying to sell the house. Or get rid of the sea lions."

"I'm trying to do both."

"Then what's with this sentimental attachment to your past?"

"I've always been sentimental, Nathan. You just never noticed."

He shot her a disbelieving look. "You have maybe one photograph in your room of your childhood. Based on the things your mom has said, you all didn't have an easy time living here."

"Yeah, well, as it turns out, maybe we shouldn't believe everything my mother says," Emma said.

"What does that mean?"

Sighing, Emma shook her head. "That's a conversation for another day. All I'm saying is, I've buried a lot of my feelings and opinions, trying to be whatever version of myself I had to be to fit in with your world."

Silence stretched between them, taut and uncertain. He gunned the engine and steered the vehicle around the curve to the top of the hill.

"Whoa, this place is old."

"It's historic," she said. "One of my best friends owns the place, so keep your snide comments to yourself, please."

He eased to a stop in Lainey's driveway, then held up both palms. "Sorry. So . . . if you've been trying to fit into my world, do you even want that world anymore?"

"I'm not sure," she said, her voice barely above a whisper. "That's what scares me."

She stared out the window at the familiar front porch, her heart thudding painfully in her chest.

"I guess I just don't know this version of you. Sharp edges. Emotional. Unpredictable." He let the Land Cruiser idle in front of the B&B. Neither of them moved. "You're behaving so differently than you ever have before."

"That's the point," she finally said. "And I'm scared. Not of you. But I am scared that I've been chasing a life someone else curated for me. Starting with the way my mother rebuilt our lives when we moved east, which made it easy to say yes to everything you've offered me—because it's safe. All planned out. Controlled. Secure."

"And what's wrong with that?" he asked, blowing out a breath. "Feels pretty good to me."

"Yes, except I've been pretending. And I can't pretend anymore."

She gestured toward the windows, the trees, the hill behind them. "I'm not ready to walk away from all of this."

He scrubbed his hand down his face and looked out the windshield. "From snow? And trees? Suffocating small-town politics? And are you suggesting that I move my whole life here to be with you? How in the world would I do that? There's nothing for me here, Emma."

He reached across the console and brushed his fingers against hers.

"You think I don't get it," he said. "But I do. I spend my life trying to control what hurts, fix what's broken. And I think you're doing the same thing here—just in a different way."

She laced her fingers through his, grateful for the familiar warmth of his hand. "Then why does it seem like you're judging me?"

"I'm not judging you. I'm trying to understand you—because I love you. Look, I get it. This is your home. Or it was. But it doesn't have to be your home now. It seems like it's a place filled with pain. Let me help you sort through this mess. Carry your burdens. Babe," he said, squeezing her hand, "I want to save you from as much pain as I can. Come home with me. I'll help you solve this. Give me a second chance. Please."

The words lodged in her chest. She hadn't expected tenderness or grace. Not from him. Not today. So maybe he deserved a second chance. He'd come all this way. And been so kind. So gracious. Her kiss with Luke was probably just a flash in the pan anyway. It didn't matter.

"Okay," she whispered, brushing aside the doubt gnawing at the edges. Maybe Nathan was right.

Maybe it was time to put the pain of her past behind her and embrace the future.

Something wasn't right.

Luke parked in front of the resort, then climbed out of his truck and headed for the front door. A silver Land Cruiser sat double-parked near the porch. His gut tightened. That looked an awful lot like the vehicle Emma had climbed into outside the café over two hours ago.

Right after she said she'd give Nathan five minutes to talk.

He hadn't seen her since, which had set off plenty of alarm bells in his head. He'd hoped the guy had left town already.

Luke jogged up the steps, then pushed through the front door. The place smelled faintly of lemon-scented cleaner and the woodsmoke that lingered from the fire crackling in the hearth. He'd walked in here a million times. But tonight, the hair on the back of his neck stood on end.

His chest tightened as he spotted Nathan standing at the reception desk, leaning both elbows on the counter, chatting with Megan. His fancy wool knee-length coat fit like it had been made for him. The gray slacks and slick dress shoes probably cost more than Luke made in a week. Sure, with his dark hair styled in a fashionable swoop, he looked cool. Sort of approachable. But not at all trustworthy.

Megan stood on the other side of the check-in desk, her expression animated as she chatted.

Nathan's deep voice rumbled, and she leaned in, her lips parted in a little half smile.

No. He couldn't let this happen.

"Meg," he called out.

Megan flinched, and her wide eyes darted toward him.

Nathan turned around, offering a tight smile. "Hey. Perfect timing."

Um, not so much. Luke feigned an empathetic wince. "Sorry, man. We're full."

Nathan's dark brows sailed upward. "Is that so? Because that's not what your sister just said."

Luke looked at Megan.

She shrugged. "We have space."

"Don't worry about it," Nathan said, stepping away from the desk and facing Luke. "I don't need a place to stay."

"Oh?" Luke didn't even try to mask his relief. "Heading back? Already?"

"Yeah. If we hurry, we can catch the red-eye out of Anchorage."

Luke's stomach plummeted. "We?"

Before Nathan could answer, Emma came in from the kitchen. He surveyed her face—red-rimmed eyes, blotchy cheeks. Had she been crying? Or maybe trying hard not to?

His knees threatened to give way, but he locked them. She stopped when she saw him. Something like panic flashed in her eyes before she glanced at Megan. Then Nathan.

"Hey," he said gently. "You okay?"

She nodded quickly. "I just said goodbye to your parents. They've been so kind, and I didn't want to leave without thanking them. And you too, Luke. Thank you for everything you've done to help me."

"Wait." Megan's brows scrunched together. "You're leaving? Seriously?"

"I'm heading out." She looked at Nathan. "We're heading out."

"Where are you headed to?" Luke barely forced the words through his tight throat.

Emma's gaze slid to meet his. She blinked quickly, and her lip trembled. "Boston. I've made arrangements for Gavin to come and get the gold. Sorry for the inconvenience, but I'm going to need you to hold it a little longer. And then . . . I'll find someone online to list the house."

Her voice cracked on the word house, but she cleared her throat and tipped her chin up.

Luke's heart slammed against his ribs. Blood roared behind his ears. He shoved his hands into the pockets of his jacket so no one would see him shaking.

She was leaving. No warning. Not a word about that kiss. Just leaving. Like she had all those years ago.

Back then, he hadn't understood the ramifications of her parents' choices. Not until it was too late. Like a fool, he'd charged over to her place—full of accusations, frustration, and anger. Yeah, he'd thrown a punch at her dad and missed. Taken a hit to the face on the edge of the dock. Now he had the scar to prove it.

It had sort of healed, but he'd never forget the memory.

And now she was leaving him again.

He forced himself to suck in a breath, air scraping down his throat. Don't say something you'll regret. He jammed his fists deeper into his pockets.

"That's a hasty decision, don't you think?"

"I have to go," she said. "I can't stay here."

"Why not?"

Nathan stepped closer and slid his hand around her waist, pulling her close. "We're going to hit the road before another storm blows in. It's a long drive, and I don't want to miss that flight."

Luke glanced out the window. The skies were clear. The sun had dipped low behind the mountain, but there wasn't a single snowflake in the forecast.

Why argue though? What was the point?

Emma dragged her gaze to meet his one last time. "You've been so good to me, Luke. Better than I deserved. And I'll never forget it."

He clenched his jaw. Say something, his mind screamed. Tell her to stay. Tell her you love her. That you've never stopped.

But he didn't.

He couldn't.

His mouth ran dry. Because if he begged her to stay and she still left, he didn't know what he'd do.

He offered a curt nod. "Safe travels."

Her lips parted, then she turned toward the door.

Nathan reached back, twined his fingers through hers, and led the way.

Emma hesitated just for a second on the threshold and glanced back over her shoulder, eyes glossy. "Tell your mom and dad thank you again for everything."

He shrugged. Managed a nod. "Sure."

And just like that, she was gone. The door clicked shut behind them.

Megan skirted the edge of the desk and came to stand next to him. She clutched his arm, her grip tight.

"Are you seriously gonna let her leave?"

He didn't answer. Couldn't. His lungs felt like they'd forgotten how to function.

She nudged him gently. "Luke, you love her. Come on, anyone with eyes can see that."

He stared straight ahead, a crevasse of heartache cutting a jagged line through his chest. He swallowed hard, but the lump in his throat refused to budge. "It doesn't matter."

"Why not?"

"Because love doesn't keep her here. It didn't before, and it won't now."

"Oh, no." She shook her head, eyes shining. "That is not fair. People change. You've changed."

"Exactly," he said. "I've changed. And I'm not chasing somebody who doesn't want to choose me."

"I think she does want to stay," Megan said. "She's just scared. And Nathan sweet-talked her into leaving."

"That's a choice."

She shook her head, disappointment hovering in her eyes. "Well, you have a choice to stop her—and you're not taking it."

He looked away, out the window.

The silver Land Cruiser disappeared out of sight.

His legs itched to run. Go, go now. But he just stood there, rooted in place.

Megan let out a shaky breath. "You are going to regret this."

Yeah. Well. He already did.

But regret was safer than hope, wasn't it?

Safer than laying his heart on the line only to watch her stomp on it with her heel as she walked away. The last time he'd chased her, he'd ended up humiliated with a bleeding face and a shattered heart.

So why bother?

Somehow he'd figure out how to live with the ache of missing her. Again.

Eighteen

BLEARY-EYED, EMMA WALKED OUT OF THE airport in Boston, Massachusetts, squinting against the bright spring sunshine. Her eyes itched, her back ached from the red-eye flight, and uncertainty settled in her chest like a stone. The morning air was cool against her face, carrying the fragrance of blooming flowers. So different from the salt-tinged breeze she'd left behind in Redemption.

Nathan already stood waiting at the curb. He glanced back over his shoulder. "I've ordered a rideshare." His voice was threaded with fatigue. "Catch up later?"

She blinked up at him. "We landed less than thirty minutes ago. Where are you going?"

He stepped forward and gently cupped her cheek with his palm, then pressed a tender kiss to her forehead. "Something's come up. I've got to go, but your mom's here."

Oh no. Emma stifled a groan. "Why?"

"I asked her to come so you wouldn't have to worry about the logistics of getting back to your place," Nathan said as a Lincoln Town Car swooped in. The driver got out, put Nathan's bags in the trunk, and quickly returned to the driver's seat.

Nathan waved, then slid into the dark, cavernous back seat. He'd barely pulled the door closed before the vehicle eased away from the curb.

"Hello, darling. Over here!" Her mother stood beside a brand-new Audi SUV, waving. She wore wide beige linen pants and a crisp white button-down, her brown hair styled in a neat chignon at the base of her neck.

"Hi, Mom." Emma hugged her, then leaned back, scanning her face. "You look pretty. How was your trip to Egypt?"

"Splendid, of course. Richard is a dream to travel with." Her mother clicked a button on her key fob, and the hatch at the back of the silver SUV glided into the air. "Put your bag in here."

Emma hesitated. Was her mom not going to ask about Alaska at all?

There wasn't a hint of distress on her mother's face. Emma had spent the entire flight wrestling with gnawing doubt, drifting in and out of fitful sleep in her cramped coach seat. Had her mother been right? Maybe she didn't belong in Alaska. Maybe Luke deserved better. But was she really needed here?

She studied her mother's smooth, dewy complexion. Something was off.

"Oh, I'm so glad you're here." Mom's keys jangled as she tucked them into her bright yellow designer handbag.

I'm not. She swallowed back the snide words. "How's Richard?"

"At home, resting. He's much better now, really."

Emma's fingers tightened around the handle of her suitcase. "Much better? What happened?"

Her mother adjusted the strap on her designer handbag. "He was terribly sick after our trip to Egypt. Something dreadful he picked up. But he's made a remarkable recovery. Surely you're happy about that, aren't you?"

"Of course." Emma stowed her bag, distracted by fatigue and confusion over Nathan's quick departure from the airport.

They climbed into the car, the leather seats cold against her skin.

"Thank you for picking me up. Hope it wasn't an inconvenience."

"Are you kidding?" Mom patted her hand. "This is a delight. We get to catch up."

"Catch up. Right." Emma clicked her seat belt into place. "I'm sure you're dying to hear all about Redemption."

Her mother's smile faltered. "Sweetheart, we've talked about this. You were never meant for that rugged little town. That's why I made sure you got out before you ruined your life."

Emma refused to get into an argument. There was no point in telling her mother what these last two weeks in Redemption had meant to her.

Twenty minutes later, they pulled into the circular drive of a colonial-style mansion. The place looked as pristine as ever. She had been here only a handful of times since her mother married Richard. Flowers bloomed in massive terra-cotta planters, and gorgeous matching wreaths hung from the bright red double front doors.

"The place looks lovely."

"Thank you. There's a whole team of people keeping it spick and span. Grab your bag and come in. I'm sure you're starving. Would you like a mimosa? And Richard makes a mean omelet."

Emma frowned. "I'm sure he does, but I don't expect Richard to make me breakfast."

"It's no trouble. He loves to cook. He's phenomenal."

She grabbed her bag, then followed her mother inside and looked around. Gleaming hardwood floors. Expensive white furniture. Fresh flowers on every flat surface. Classical music wafting from a wireless speaker. Richard, a man in his early sixties with a Stanley Tucci-like vibe, sat in a recliner near a broad expanse of windows overlooking a pool and a lush garden. He glanced up and smiled, pulling off his reading glasses and setting them on a side table. Pushing aside a light blanket draped over his lap, he stood.

"Emma." He smiled, his ruddy cheeks creasing. "What a wonderful surprise."

Emma turned sharply toward her mother, her insides bubbling like a shaken pop can. "Why is he surprised?"

Her mother sighed, a weary, put-upon sound. "Don't be so quick to judge. I needed you home and you're here. Richard's happy to see you. Isn't that what matters?"

"No. It isn't." Emma's voice trembled. "Why did Nathan ask you to come pick me up?"

Richard's blue eyes slid from her mother to Emma, then back. "I'm not sure what's going on, but we're thrilled to have you, nonetheless."

"Honey, Emma's starving. She's flown all night. Would you whip up one of your egg-white omelets, please?"

"I'd be happy to, dear." Richard patted Emma's arm. "Lovely to see you again. Come into the kitchen in a few minutes. I want to hear all about Alaska."

Emma clenched her fists, her nails digging into her palms. "Mom, why am I here?"

Her mother's eyes flashed. "Because it is high time you start thinking about your future. I'm not going to stand back and let you sabotage your engagement. The Prescotts are one of Boston's finest families. Everyone knows that. How could you mess that up?"

Spots peppered her vision. "I didn't sabotage anything. Nathan's not the saint you think he is."

"I never said a word about saint." Her mother waved a dismissive hand. "We all make mistakes."

Emma's whole body trembled. "That may be the only thing you and I agree about today."

Her mother's expression hardened. "Whatever you left behind in Redemption, it's for the best. Now come into the kitchen. I'll fix you that mimosa, and since you're here, there's something important we should discuss. Something I've been meaning to speak with you about for a long time."

Sighing, Emma left her purse and suitcase in the hallway by the door, then trailed after her mother.

Mom took a seat at the kitchen table. Sunlight streamed through the windows behind her. Richard stood at the massive island, cracking eggs into a glass mixing bowl. He'd put an apron on that said Always kiss the chef. "Mimosa? Bloody Mary?"

"Just water, please," Emma said. "Thank you."

"Of course." Richard retrieved a glass bottle of sparkling water from the refrigerator, twisted off the cap, then brought it to her.

"I'm exhausted, Mom. What's so urgent that we need to talk about it right now?"

Her mother took a seat at the kitchen table, smoothing an invisible wrinkle from her linen pants. "It's your father."

Her stomach pitched. She slid the water closer but didn't take a sip. "What about him?"

"I've just been thinking how it's so unfortunate that his parole was denied." Her mother hesitated, scraping at a spot on the table with her red manicured nail. "It's really time he gets out."

"Agreed," Emma said. "But why the sudden change of heart?"

Her mother sighed, then glanced out the window. "Because I never expected him to go to jail, much less spend twenty years there."

"Mom, is there something you're not telling me?"

"It wasn't supposed to be this way," Mom whispered. "It should've been me."

The room tilted. "What did you say?"

Her mother's eyes filled with tears. "We needed the money, Emma. I didn't know everyone would react the way they did, and then things got out of hand."

A chill raked her spine. "I-I don't understand."

"I did it, Emma. I was the one behind the illegal transfer of funds and the wire fraud. Your father covered for me."

The air left the room. Richard cleared his throat. "I think I'll check the garage refrigerator for more spinach and cheese. Excuse me."

Emma's hands curled into fists. "You let him go to jail for you. You let him be cut off from the world for twenty years, and you let me believe—"

"I never meant for things to spiral out of control. He took the blame to protect me. Neither one of us thought he'd get more than a couple of years. Maybe five at the most, but then he got that massive sentence and everyone turned against us. I had no choice but to leave town. It was such a nightmare."

Emma leaned forward and fixed her mother with a fierce glare. "A nightmare that you could've prevented, Mom."

"Yes, I know." Mom swiped at the tears on her cheeks. "But it's too late now."

"It's never too late." Emma shot to her feet. "We have to fix this. There has to be a way to make this right."

"So you're saying you want me to go to jail?" Her mother scoffed. "That would make your father's time in prison pointless."

"This is horrifying."

The door to their garage swung open, and someone came in behind Richard.

"Kendall?" Emma faced Nathan's sister. "What are you doing here?"

Kendall strode toward her, wearing wide-legged denim trousers, high-heeled wedge sandals, and a silky orange blouse with puffed short sleeves. "I'm glad I caught up with you. Sorry to drop in unannounced, but this was the quickest way to get to you without Nathan."

"What are you talking about? We just got back from Alaska."

"So I heard." Kendall's gaze flitted between Emma and her mother. "There's something you should know."

Emma groaned. "Not you too."

"Kendall, do we have to do this right now?" Emma's mother pushed back her chair and stood. "Emma flew all night, and she's wiped out."

"It's absolutely necessary, Mrs. Wendel." Kendall tucked her hair behind her ears. Empathy filled her dark eyes as she turned toward Emma. "Because you deserve to know the truth."

"Is this about Nathan? Because he flew all the way to Alaska and asked me to come back to Boston and give him a second chance."

"And that's exactly why I'm here." Kendall drew in a deep breath. "Nathan and Courtney never broke up. They're still together. They've been seeing each other behind your back for months."

Emma's breath left her lungs in a single stunned exhale. "That can't be."

"I wouldn't lie to you. And I certainly wouldn't lie about this. I saw them myself. I can show you photos." She pulled her phone from her purse.

Emma sank into the nearest chair and held up her trembling palm. "That won't be . . . No. No, thank you."

"Well, they weren't exactly hiding," Kendall said.

Emma clutched the edge of the table. "How could he be so deceptive? I—"

"Kendall, you need to go," Emma's mother said. "You've caused enough damage for one day."

"No, please," Emma said. "Is there anything else you want to tell me, Kendall?"

"I just wanted you to hear the truth, because I hate that you've been dragged back here under false pretenses. My brother doesn't deserve you."

"You're right. He doesn't." Emma yanked the engagement ring

off her finger and pressed it into Kendall's hand. "Thank you for making the effort to find me. Please give this back to your brother."

Kendall closed her fist around the ring. "I will."

"And one more thing." Emma pointed toward Kendall's purse. "May I borrow your phone, please?"

"Of course."

Emma took the phone, scrolled through Kendall's contacts until she found Nathan, then typed out a message.

> Kendall
>
> It's Emma, borrowing your sister's phone. Just found out the truth about you and Courtney. I can't marry you. Kendall has the ring. Goodbye, Nathan.

"There." She sent the message, then handed the phone back to Kendall. "I let him know it's over. Thank you."

"Ending an engagement via a text is such poor form, Emma," her mother groaned. "He'll never forgive you."

Emma tipped her chin up. "You are the last person who should be handing out advice about choices, Mom."

"A text message and a returned ring are more than he deserves, to be honest," Kendall said. "I would've chucked that thing into the Charles River."

Emma couldn't help but smile. "The thought did cross my mind. No time for that though. I'm headed back to Alaska."

"Wait," Kendall said. "At least let me give you a ride."

"You don't have to do that," Emma said. "I can call a cab."

"Emma, sweetheart, don't be silly." Mom moved closer, arms outstretched. "Stay here. Let us help you sort this out."

Emma leaned in and kissed her mother's cheek. "Goodbye, Mom." Then she offered Richard a quick wave. "Take care, Richard."

Kendall's heels clicked on the hardwood as she followed Emma toward the front door. "You shouldn't be alone right now. Let me drive you home so you can shower and repack. Then we'll figure out the rest."

A knot rose in Emma's throat. She gave a small nod. "That's very kind of you."

"It's the least I can do." Kendall squeezed her arm. "Let's go."

Without another word to her mother or Richard, Emma grabbed her suitcase and her purse, then stepped out into the warm spring sunshine. As Kendall pulled the door shut behind them, Emma didn't look back.

He just wanted this family meeting to be over.

Luke eyed the platter of cookies his mom set in the middle of the table. Chocolate chip? Really? This hardly called for a fun treat. There wasn't anything to celebrate, was there?

He sat at the far end of the long wooden dining table—the one his grandfather had built decades ago—and slumped in his chair. Why bother trying to hide his heartache? Emma had been gone for two days, and he was miserable.

His family filled in around him. They didn't have any guests, so there was no point in pretending they needed to be attentive to anyone's needs. Conversation pinged around him as they waited for Caroline to join them on FaceTime.

"Hopefully this will be the last time we have to loop you in over the phone for a family meeting," Mom said.

Caroline waved. "Hey, everyone." Tate propped up his tablet at the far end of the table. "Eat a chocolate chip cookie for me? Pretty soon I'll be there to taste-test them myself."

Megan reached for one. Luke shot her a look. She shrugged and took a bite. "Mmm, so good."

He pressed his lips together and crossed his arms over his chest.

"Caroline, before we called you, I was just telling Luke that this is a solid offer," Ethan said, sitting across from him and leaning forward with both elbows on the table. "I'm sure you've seen the numbers. This developer isn't messing around. They've got cash, they're ready to move fast, and they're reputable."

Tate chimed in. "I talked to a friend in Anchorage who's thrilled with what these people are building downtown."

Dad caught his eye. "It's a fair offer, pal. Way more money than we ever expected." He smiled at Mom.

Luke shrugged, staring at the wood grain on the table, tracing his finger over a groove as their commentary blurred together.

He'd sat at this same table with Emma just a few short days ago. He'd cleaned up for the customers he was so certain would pour in, and she'd helped stuff Easter eggs like she belonged in Redemption. Man, he'd been an idiot for believing that was real.

"Isn't this what we've been waiting for?" Megan said. "I mean, I haven't been here very much, of course." She trailed off, two spots of color highlighting her cheekbones. "But it seems like this place hasn't really been profitable in years. So isn't this your chance to walk away?"

Luke barked out a laugh. All eyes turned to him.

"Is there something you'd like to say, Luke?" Tate reached for a cookie. "Not that you haven't made your feelings clear about this since day one."

Luke gritted his teeth, fighting to keep his emotions in check. A week ago, he would have argued, reminded them what this place meant to their family, to their town—that Redemption wasn't just a map dot at the end of the road slammed up against a mountain. It was home.

Not too long ago, he'd fought for their legacy, mediated their conflicts, tried to fix a broken snowmobile, and flown extreme skiers into the mountains. He prayed and fought for what he believed in, and look where it got him. Everything had been ripped out from under his feet. Even Emma had cut her losses and gone back to Boston.

He pinched the bridge of his nose, willing the ache in his chest to subside. He was not about to melt down. Not in front of his family.

Caroline's voice, tinny through the device's speaker, called to him. He glanced up. "What?"

They were all still staring at him.

"You haven't said much." Caroline's brow furrowed. "What do you think? Do you agree this is the right move?"

He leaned back in his chair. "It doesn't seem to matter what I think. You've already made up your minds."

"Oh. Well, Ethan said that he's been waiting for you to come around, that you were the lone holdout." Caroline wrinkled her nose. "So what happened?"

Luke glared at Ethan. "I was way too optimistic. That's what happened. How stupid of me for thinking this place was worth saving."

Silence settled over the room, punctuated by the faint hum of heat blowing through the vents nearby.

Mom cleared her throat. "Luke, sweetheart, we all know how much this place means to you. It means a lot to all of us, but sometimes it's okay to let go of what we love."

Ouch. "Too soon, Mom. Too soon."

Her eyes widened. "I didn't mean her—"

"Not everything has to be about Emma," Tate said. "Why don't we keep the focus on the main thing?"

Luke huffed out another sharp laugh. "How convenient for you that my heartbreak doesn't have to be a priority."

"Whoa." Dad held up both of his palms. "No one is saying that."

"Aren't you though?"

"Luke, we get it," Ethan said. "You love this place. But it's not just about you. The rest of us have lives too. Jobs. Tisha and I want to get married. Soon. We do have to think about what's best for everyone, as much as it hurts."

Luke clenched his fists in his lap. A small part of him still wanted to shove back his chair and stand up and yell that they were wrong. Selling this place would be a huge mistake.

But the words wouldn't come.

Deep down, he wondered if he even believed it anymore.

He stared at the table. "You're right. It's not worth it."

"So, are you saying you agree with us, then?" Caroline asked.

Luke shrugged. "Sure. Whatever. Sell it. Do what you want."

Mom leaned forward, concern etched in her features. "Luke? Are you—"

"I'm done," he said, cutting her off. "If you want to sell—fine. Sell. I'm tired of fighting."

Tate and Megan exchanged glances. Then Ethan leaned over. "Are you okay?"

"No. I'm not okay. But what does it matter?" Luke shook his head. "Tate just said that my feelings are irrelevant."

"Oh boy." Tate winced and dragged his hand over his face. "You're my brother. We all care about you. I'm just saying we're supposed to be coming to an agreement on this offer from the developer."

Luke shook his head, held up his palm. "Don't worry about me. I'll be fine."

"You don't sound fine," Megan said, wiping cookie crumbs off the table into her hand.

"You know what? The reason my opinion doesn't matter is because I'm not going to be here to deal with it."

He pushed back his chair and stood. "This has officially become someone else's problem."

Tate frowned. "What does that mean?"

"It means I'm leaving," Luke said, fighting to keep his voice even despite the storm raging in his gut. "There's a job open in Petersburg, and if I get an offer, I'm taking it."

Megan's jaw dropped. "What? Since when?"

"Since a couple of weeks ago," he said. "I wasn't going to interview, but ... plans change."

"Luke, honey." His mom's voice trembled. "You don't have to do this. We'll figure this out. You don't have to leave."

"Oh, but I do," he said. "There's nothing left for me here."

She sucked in a breath. Even Caroline gasped. But nobody argued.

He turned and headed for the door. The weight of their stares burned into him, but he didn't turn back.

"See you later. You can tell the developer I'll sign whatever they need me to sign."

He stepped out into the cold night air. Wind swirled around him, carrying hints of a snowstorm. He was too numb, too hollow to care. So what if it snowed? A late-spring storm was nothing new. If his family wanted to sell, then he didn't have to worry about how the weather impacted their guests' stay. Tonight, this felt like a place he no longer belonged in. The heavy front door groaned shut behind him. He paused on the porch, stared out into the nearly empty parking lot.

A distinct hum and creak behind him made him turn.

"Luke."

His father maneuvered his wheelchair through the doorway, one hand gripping the edge of the frame for leverage. He wore a plaid button-down layered over a T-shirt and black sweatpants.

"What are you doing?" Luke faced him. "It's cold. Let's go back in."

His dad didn't answer. Instead, he just reversed course, wheeled himself inside, and waited in the entryway.

"I can't let you leave like this," he said.

Luke followed him inside and closed the door. The great room sat empty, the leather couches facing each other in front of the massive hearth and the glow of embers in the fireplace tugging at his heart.

Yeah, okay, so he was angry and bitter, but he did still love this place. "I just—I don't know what else to say."

His dad looked up, eyes gentle, free of judgment. "Oh, I think there's quite a bit."

Luke blew out a long breath and jammed his hands into the back pockets of his jeans.

"Son, you've been carrying the weight of this place for years. I know what that does to a man. It twists your motivations, makes you think you have to earn love by performing or fixing all the broken things and being the duct tape that holds it all together." His lips formed a sad smile, and he scrubbed his fingertips along his stubbly jaw. "I know, because I used to think that too."

Luke shifted his weight from one foot to the other.

"It's no secret I nearly destroyed this family once." His dad paused, then cleared his throat.

"My pride, my temper, all the foolish ways I kept everything inside until I nearly exploded. That nearly cost me everything. Your mother, you kids, this resort."

"Dad—"

"Let me finish."

Luke shrugged. "All right."

"I didn't know how to sort through my feelings, so I just let my anger ooze out all over everything. And it nearly broke us. If it weren't for the Lord getting ahold of me—really getting ahold of my heart—I wouldn't be here. I wouldn't have your mom. I'm not sure you kids would have stuck around or come back. And I certainly wouldn't have had the wisdom or the insight to speak to you now."

He hesitated. "Please don't make the same mistakes I did."

Luke gritted his teeth.

His dad's eyes shone. "You don't have to be the strong one all the time. It's okay to hurt. And you're allowed to want more than just this resort. And you're allowed to love someone. Even if she wants to build a life far from here. I know you're hurting over Emma. I saw the way you looked at her when she was around. Feelings like that don't just disappear."

Luke dragged his hand down his face.

"I'm proud of you," Dad said. "You have made this a remarkable resort. You sacrificed so much. You could have had a much different life. But you don't owe us anything, Luke. You've done more than enough. And you have the right to go and be happy. Pursue those things that really make your heart soar."

Luke blinked back tears. "What if it's too late?"

"It's never too late. Go find her. Tell her how you feel. Let her decide what's next. But please, don't let your pride keep you here, planted in this place, if God's asking you to leave." His father extended a trembling hand. "You have my blessing. Your mother's too. Go."

The tears Luke had tried to keep tamped down pushed to the surface. He crossed the space between them in two strides, fell to his knees beside the wheelchair, then wrapped his arms around his father. "I love you, Dad," he choked out. "So much."

His dad patted his back. "I love you too, son."

They stayed that way. Two stubborn, wounded men. Both wrapped in God's grace.

Luke pulled back and swiped at his face with his sleeve. "I think I have a plane to catch."

Dad chuckled. "Well then, don't miss it."

Nineteen

EMMA SAT IN THE HARD PLASTIC CHAIR, GNAWing on her thumbnail. Fluorescent lights buzzed overhead, and the pungent scent of disinfectant drifted up from the surface of the hard table. She'd cleared three checkpoints, had her ID thoroughly analyzed, and then a female corrections officer had patted her down. Still, nothing had prepared her for this—waiting in the visitors' area of a federal prison in Oregon to see her dad for the first time in fifteen years.

The room could not have been more unappealing. Warm, dry air flowed from a vent overhead. A lifeless shade of olive green had been painted on the walls, and she felt like the security cameras were trained right on her. The vending machine glowed in the corner. Its bright, familiar light advertising a popular soft drink didn't bring her much comfort though. She rubbed her clammy palms on her jeans. A million questions scrolled through her head, tangled up with thoughts of Luke.

Oh, sweet Luke. What was she going to do? What was she going to say? Would he even talk to her?

A buzzer interrupted her thoughts, then a lock clanked, and the metal door swung open. Her pulse sped as a guard stepped through—a very large, broad-shouldered, muscular man with a buzz cut and piercing brown eyes. Then a man in a khaki uniform and prison-issued shoes came into the room. His red hair had faded to a straw color and thinned on top. He'd lost quite a bit of weight, but those eyes—hazel and bright, searching the room until they landed on her—hadn't changed.

"Dad," she whispered.

He stopped short. Something she couldn't quite identify flickered across his face. Disbelief? Joy?

"Emma," he said, then cleared his throat and glanced toward the guard.

"Fifteen minutes," the guard said. Then he hesitated, reached over, and undid the handcuffs. "Y'all can hug if you'd like."

Emma stood, hesitated, then darted around the end of the table and into her father's open arms. He smelled like soap and probably some kind of industrial laundry detergent. His hug was tight, and his body trembled. She couldn't erase the past with one hug, but she wasn't going to withhold affection. He certainly didn't deserve that.

"I didn't think you'd come," he said, his voice rough.

"I wish I'd come sooner," she said, pulling away. "I'm so sorry that I waited this long."

He tilted his head to one side. "You don't have anything to be sorry for." Then he motioned to the chairs and sat slowly, his joints cracking. "You look just like your mother."

"Oof." She claimed the chair across from his on the other side of the table. "That's not really a compliment, Dad."

His expression sobered. "No, I suppose not."

The guard lingered by the door, but he wasn't hovering. Emma leaned forward, clasped her hands in front of her.

"I need the truth—all of it. Mom always blamed you, said you were greedy. Said that's why we had to leave Redemption, and that you're the reason our lives fell apart. But lately I've heard a different story. Did she really do it—and you took the blame?"

Her father sighed. "I wondered when this day would come."

"I'm thirty-three years old, Dad. Not a kid. I need to know."

He looked down, rubbing the pad of one thumb over the knuckle of the other. "It's true. Your mother transferred the funds. She rerouted all the money we'd collected in donations for the cannery. I found out about it by accident really, but by then it was too late. People were suspicious—especially when she convinced me to take that anniversary trip to the Cayman Islands."

Emma nodded. "I remember."

"Yeah. Well, that's kind of like . . . not okay."

"Sort of like a Kickstarter gone wrong."

Dad grimaced. "Pretty much. Then she said she couldn't go to prison and insisted you needed her."

Emma gritted her teeth. "But I needed you."

"I know." He nodded. "And I really thought I'd be back sooner. My lawyer was supposed to get me a reduced sentence if I pled guilty, but wire fraud's a federal crime. I got slammed. Twenty years minimum."

"And parole denied." She blinked back tears. "Why haven't you fought back?"

"Against your mother?" He lifted one shoulder. "With what resources? Besides, I thought I was protecting you. I'm already here. I didn't want you to lose a second parent. Your mother . . . what she did was wrong, but I hoped somehow she would give you a normal life. Besides, you were so angry with me, and so if I disappeared, I thought you'd be better off."

"No." She swiped at the moisture on her cheeks. "I was never better off."

He reached across the table, tentative, and clasped her hand between both of his.

"Emma, believe me, I've been over every decision, every detail for the last eighteen years. But I loved her, and I loved you too. We made mistakes—big ones—but I never meant to destroy your life."

"No, I think that's on her," Emma whispered.

He shook his head. "Don't let the bitterness take root, sweetheart. That's what the enemy wants. To plant that doubt, to use your hurt and twist it till it spreads. Chokes out everything good. Believe me, I've seen plenty of men pass through here who are so full of hate and bitterness and resentment."

She drew a wobbly breath. "I wanted to believe you weren't guilty. The man who taught me how to catch a fish, fillet it, but also held my hand and sat in the front row at my first piano recital . . . I didn't want to believe that you could have been that selfish."

"I'm not selfish. At least I don't think I am. To be honest, I wanted to help the people of Redemption. I believed in that cannery. We were going to change lives—create jobs, put food on the table for a lot of families. It never occurred to me to check up on what your mom was doing. I trusted her more than I should have, but I had no reason to suspect she was up to no good."

Emma nodded. "Relatable."

His brows arched. "Say more."

"Well, I was engaged to a man who . . . he wasn't who I thought. He lied, cheated, begged me to come back, and so I did. But it's not going to work out."

His expression softened. "What next?"

"You might not be thrilled to hear this, but . . . Luke McGuire. From Redemption. He's a good man, Dad. One of the best I've ever known. But I pushed him away because I chose the cheater. And now I'm so ashamed. I don't know how to make it right."

"Maybe now is an opportunity to take a step toward healing. Start with the truth."

She looked down. "I just want to stop running, you know? Some part of me has been bracing for impact ever since our family unraveled, and I just have this constant fear. I'm always looking over my shoulder."

"Well, I'd say you're normal. Can I tell you what the Bible says?"

She nodded.

"The truth will set you free."

She gave him a look, then gestured around the room. "Really?"

"Maybe not in a literal sense. I'm talking about your heart. I've clung to that verse all these years. And even though I'm not free yet . . . you have come to see me. You're speaking to me. And that's an answered prayer, Emma. Can you forgive me? For not being the dad you needed me to be?"

She blinked back a fresh wave of tears. "Yes. Of course. You're easy to forgive, Dad. It's Mom that I have trouble with."

"I understand. Your quick response is more than I deserve. Thank you."

"You're welcome." She squeezed his hand. "I want to stop being afraid of being hurt. I want to be someone who loves freely and trusts."

"Then don't let fear have the wheel. Rest in God's love and His promises. I know it sounds cheesy, but it's the only thing that's true."

"Do you think it's too late with Luke?"

"Do you love him?"

She nodded.

"Then go tell him. Hang on to the ones who love you. That's the whole point, Emma." He grinned. "So tell me about him. This is the same Luke that was crazy about you back in the day, right?"

She laughed. "Yes. He's still just as stubborn. Loyal too. He's helping his family run the resort. He's good, Dad. He takes care of people. Always trying to fix things, even when they're not his to fix."

"Sounds like he's turned into a pretty incredible guy."

"I think you'd like him. He believed in me—even in us. I wish I'd seen what he saw."

"Go make it right. And don't wait eighteen more years."

She stood slowly, came around the table, and wrapped her arms around him again.

"I've missed you."

"Oh, you have no idea how much I've missed you, sweetheart. Every single day."

The guard cleared his throat. "Time's up, folks."

Emma pulled back slowly. "I'll come again. I promise."

"That's all I needed to hear." He squeezed her arm. "I love you, Emma."

"I love you too, Dad."

She turned and walked from the room, her steps a little lighter. She still had miles to go, but this time she knew exactly where she was headed and who she needed to see.

That was the most miserable flight of his life.

Luke stepped out of the airport in Boston and nearly turned around to go right back in. A cold rain fell from a drab gray sky, landing like BBs and bouncing off vehicles, the pavement, and the sea of umbrellas shielding the pedestrians streaming into the terminal.

He squinted in the mist, trying to get his bearings. The cab line snaked around the corner, and people barked into their phones as they hurried past him.

"What in the world? Slow down, people," he grumbled, pulling his phone from his pocket. He backed inside the double doors and set his duffel at his feet. At least this space offered protection from the rain. Fatigue made his brain foggy. He scrolled through the apps on his phone, then opened Uber to request a ride.

"Sheesh, these rates are ridiculous." He closed out of the app, then shoved his phone back inside his parka. "Cab it is."

He joined the line, and by the time he reached the front, he was soaked.

The driver grunted at him. "Where to?"

He hesitated. He only had one address—Emma's apartment. The address she'd given to Lainey when she paid for her stay at the bed and breakfast. He rattled it off from a note in his phone.

The cab lunged into traffic, horns blaring. He grabbed the handle near the window, watching vehicles dart in and out of lanes like salmon headed to their spawning grounds. Except, unlike salmon, these drivers were angry. And maybe a little unhinged.

Every time his phone buzzed with an incoming alert, hope sparked to life. At least he had service now, but when he glanced at the screen, it was just one of his siblings checking in. Even Justin must've gotten word of this adventure because he'd sent a text:

> Justin
> Praying for you, man. Hope this goes well.

Luke gave the message a thumbs-up, then scrolled through the last three notifications.

Nothing from Emma.

Over an hour later, the cab eased to a stop in front of a tall, narrow house with flower boxes in the windows and six buzzers mounted by the door. The bricks looked ancient, and the steps had seen better days. Luke stared up at the building.

Wow. He felt out of place here. Everything felt too tall, too old, and moved too fast.

He paid the driver, grabbed his duffel from the trunk, and headed up the steps. He pressed every button until finally someone answered.

"Who is it?" asked a tired female voice through the grungy intercom speaker.

"I'm looking for Emma. Emma Carlisle."

There was a pause. "Hang on."

Then the door unlocked, and Luke stepped into a poorly lit foyer. The place smelled like pizza. Or maybe cats.

A woman with curly hair and a sleep line embedded on her cheek poked her head out of a door. "You're the guy looking for Emma?"

"Yeah. I'm a friend. From Alaska."

Her eyes grew wide. "Wow. That's a long way."

He forced a tight smile. "You have no idea."

"I haven't seen Emma. She was here briefly the other day, but then left again. You should talk to Brittney, her friend on the third floor. I happen to know she just left for the coffee place around the corner. The Wicked Bean. Can't miss it. One block up, on your right."

"Perfect. Thanks so much."

He turned and hurried out of the house and down the steps. The rain had eased to a light drizzle. His duffel bag bounced against his shoulder as he strode down the sidewalk. The woman's directions were spot on.

He found the coffee place, and after dodging a guy on a bike and a man jogging like he planned to win a 5K, Luke stepped through the doors.

The scent of espresso wrapped around him, and the croissants in the glass bakery case made his mouth water. When had he eaten last, anyway?

"Welcome in!" the barista called out.

He offered a tentative wave.

A woman sat at a tall two-top near the windows facing the street, staring at her phone. She looked up. "Are you by any chance Luke?"

He hesitated. "I am. But how did you know?"

"I'm Brittney, one of Emma's housemates." Brittney smiled. "She told me about you. And also Petra, the woman who buzzed you in at the house, texted me to let me know you were coming." Brittney's gaze slid from his parka to his soaked duffel. "Did you come all the way here from Alaska?"

"I had to," he said. "She left Redemption, and I didn't stop her when I should have. Now she won't answer her phone. And I thought maybe she didn't want to see me. But I had to come here and know for sure."

"Wow. You really care about her, huh?"

"I do."

She patted the stool beside her. "Have a seat. I'm afraid I have a bit of a downer to share."

Oh no. His stomach clenched. "What?"

"She's not here. Left two days ago. Said she was going to see her dad and then heading back to Alaska."

He left his duffel on the floor beside his stool, then raked his fingers through his wet hair. "Unbelievable."

"I'll let you get the whole story from her," Brittney said. "I don't think she'd mind me telling you that she's on her way to find you."

He sat in stunned silence. The rumble of the milk frother, the whir of the coffee-bean grinder, and the hum of pop music from the overhead speakers swirled around him. This didn't make sense.

"So she went back to Redemption."

"She might be there by now, actually. I'm not sure how long she stayed in Oregon, but she didn't want to wait."

He blew out a laugh, a short, disbelieving sound. "And I flew all the way here. What a mess."

Brittney grimaced. "You two are either the most romantic people I've ever met or the worst communicators on the planet."

"Maybe some of both," he said.

She pulled out her phone. "Want me to try her? Maybe she's landed somewhere and has Wi-Fi."

"No," he said. "I think I've got my answer. Thanks though."

She paused, then grabbed a brown paper napkin from the table. "Before you go, let me give you some directions to the airport. It's easy to get there on the train."

"All right."

Brittney pulled a pen from her purse. "Okay, you'll want to take the Orange Line from Green Street Station. It's about a five-minute walk from here."

Luke leaned in, trying to follow along, even though she'd already confused him with the green and orange-lines part.

"Get on the train heading inbound—toward Oak Grove." She scribbled as she spoke. "Ride it to Downtown Crossing. Then transfer to the Red Line, just one stop to South Station."

She underlined something and added a few arrows. "Once you're at South Station, follow the signs for the Silver Line—SL1. That's in the bus terminal upstairs. It goes straight to Logan, all terminals."

She handed him the napkin, her brown eyes gleaming. "You'll be at the airport in under an hour, depending on the transfers. It's honestly your fastest option."

Luke stared at the napkin, the ink still fresh and a little smudged. He paused as he saw the small, hurried scrawl at the very bottom.

P.S. She still loves you.

He folded it carefully and tucked it into his jacket pocket. "Nice to meet you, Brittney." He smiled. "Thanks for everything."

"Go get your girl, Alaska."

Twenty

WHY HADN'T HIS FLIGHT LANDED YET?
Emma paced back and forth on the other side of the security checkpoint at Redemption's airport, then craned her neck to see through the wall of windows to the runway outside. Still no sign of an airplane taxiing in.

A chime echoed over the loudspeaker. She stopped and listened. "Attention passengers: Flight 221 from Anchorage is experiencing a slight delay due to weather and traffic congestion on the runway. We appreciate your patience and expect arrival shortly."

"Oh, c'mon." Emma shook her head and resumed pacing, her sneakers squeaking against the worn linoleum. She paused, then glanced out the tall windows facing the tarmac again. Still nothing. No blinking lights in the distance, no rumble of engines, no plane taxiing toward the gate.

"Please hurry," she whispered. Luke's mom had said he was on this flight, so she'd staked out the airport almost an hour ago. Just in case he was early.

Around her, a crowd had started to form. Locals, mostly. An older couple holding hands and murmuring about their granddaughter's graduation. Two teenage boys discussing summer fishing plans with exaggerated gestures. A mom juggling a toddler and a diaper bag. The airport, usually a sleepy stopover, buzzed with small-town chatter.

But all Emma could think about was him.

The baggage carousel sat silent, awaiting the incoming flight. Six or seven tourists stood in line at the ticket counter, a mountain of luggage at their feet. Two couples funneled through the only security checkpoint, probably headed for the gate nearby and the only remaining outbound flight left on today's schedule. A teenage girl perched on a stool at the cash register, keeping watch over the snack kiosk. Emma had bought a granola bar there earlier but hadn't taken a bite. Her stomach was a churning mess.

The delay was only making it worse.

Then outside the window, a white plane with navy-blue letters cruised into view and stopped on the tarmac. An airport employee rolled the stairs out, and a few minutes later, passengers descended and strode toward the glass double doors. One by one, they trickled past the rope barrier and a bored-looking TSA agent with a clipboard.

And then she saw him.

Luke.

He trudged forward, head down, hat pulled low, his flannel shirt rumpled, jeans stiff from long hours of travel. A duffel bag hung from one shoulder. His movements were slow. Heavy. He wore his hat shoved low, but not enough to hide the circles under his eyes.

Her body moved before she could stop it, one foot in front of the other, stepping into his path. She didn't care about the stares or the low murmurs around her.

When he saw her, he stopped short.

Everything in the tiny airport faded away. Conversations paused. She moved closer, her heart pounding.

"Luke."

He didn't respond, just stared, eyes guarded.

She drew in a shaky breath. "I was wrong. About leaving, and about Nathan. I shouldn't have let him convince me he deserved a second chance."

She paused, then swallowed hard. Wow, this wasn't coming out right. "I thought I was doing the right thing, but really I just messed it all up."

"One hundred percent," someone in the crowd said.

"Shh, that's not nice," a woman hissed.

Heat singed her cheeks, but she plowed on. "I feel like all I've done is hurt you, and I'm so sorry."

His duffel bag slid from his fingers and dropped at his feet. A muscle in his jaw tensed. His eyes roamed her face, but still he said nothing.

"When Brittney texted me that you had gone all the way to Boston, I couldn't believe it." She blinked back tears. "I stopped in Oregon to visit my dad, and I was thinking you never wanted to see me again, but there you were—chasing after me. After everything I've done. After I've left you twice."

A muscle in his arm flexed, and he scrubbed his fingers across his stubbly jaw.

"I don't expect you to forgive me. Not right away, maybe not ever." Her voice trembled. "But I have to tell you face-to-face—I'm sorry. I love you, Luke. A part of me always has, I think. Even when I was too stubborn or scared to admit it. Even when I trusted the wrong people instead of the one who has always been there for me." Her voice cracked.

"I'm done running—from this town, from my past, from us. I'm here, if you'll still have me. If there's even the smallest chance that we could find our way back."

She stopped, rubbed at the tightness in her chest, and glanced around. No one moved. She dragged her gaze back to meet his.

Still, he stood there. He opened his mouth, then closed it. He turned and looked around.

She took a step forward and stopped. "Say something, please."

"I flew across the country for you, Emma. Crisscrossed half of Boston, it seems like. I've barely slept this week. Can't remember the last time I ate anything good. I just kept thinking I needed to find you, that somehow I could fix this. But when I couldn't get ahold of you, I was pretty sure we were done."

Her stomach lurched. "No," she whispered. "We can't give up."

She swallowed hard against the rising tears. Trembling, she cast a quick glance at the people who fanned out around her. It felt like everyone in the place had paused to watch the spectacle unfold. Yet she barely cared. Because she'd poured out her heart for the man she loved. What did it matter if she drew a crowd?

She searched his face. But his expression remained a mask of indifference, those blue eyes cool and unyielding, like a frozen lake in the middle of winter.

His Adam's apple bobbed as he swallowed, but still he didn't move. Instead, he looked away.

What if he walked right past her and never said a word? The thought sent white-hot pain coursing through her. Why had she been so foolish to think that he would forgive so easily?

She'd found him. But maybe it was too late.

≈

She looked as if she might fall apart right there in front of him. "Oh, Emma."

He'd loved her for so long—first as a headstrong, impulsive teenager, now again. Still, really, because he'd never stopped. She might have left twice, but she still somehow managed to hold every single piece of his wounded heart.

Bleary-eyed, he blinked. He still couldn't believe she'd come.

Not after everything they'd been through. Not after the silence. But there she stood, trembling, her eyes filling with tears, and she'd bared her soul to him in the middle of the airport, like it was the most natural thing in the world.

And frankly, it wrecked him.

He swallowed hard, his chest aching. Her words echoed in his head, every syllable soothing the jagged edges of his wounds. Oh, she loved him—she still did. He used to dream about this. Over the years, he'd thought of what he'd say if she ever came back. He'd rehearsed a few angry words, and some bitter ones too. But after his dad's pep talk, and the way she stood here now, confessing all of her fears and telling him how much she loved him, all the anger and regret melted away.

She was here. She had come back for him. And that was really all that mattered.

He stepped forward slowly, watching as her shoulders rose with another ragged breath.

"I really wanted to be angry with you. After you left with him, I told myself I should try to forget you, that I deserved better."

Her face crimped, and he reached for her hand, gently threading his fingers through hers.

"But the truth is, Emma, I never stopped loving you."

A soft gasp slipped past her lips.

"Believe me, I tried." He brushed his thumb over her knuckles. "But I couldn't. I love you with every part of who I am. I love the girl who left because she was scared to challenge her mother and had just lost her father. I love the woman who came back because she wanted to pay a debt she didn't really owe. I love your courage and your fight." His throat clogged with emotion. "I love your heart."

A tear slipped down her cheek, and he reached up and caught it with the edge of his thumb.

"I have spent my whole life waiting. Like I needed to prove

something or make some huge change in the world or rescue lost souls. Instead, I'm just an ordinary guy getting up every day and trying to do what's best for the people I love. And then you came back, and somehow, staying here and waiting here—it all made sense." He smiled softly. "You feel like home, Emma Carlisle."

She made a sound—a mix between a sob and a laugh—and then stepped closer until there was only a sliver of space between them.

"I want a life with you. All of it. The hard times, the silly stuff, the shoveling snow and sickness and bills and binge-watching shows on Netflix. I want to argue about which movies we're going to watch and hold your hand in church and build a future with you in the only town that's really ever mattered."

Her lips trembled. "Do you mean it?"

"Of course," he said. "You are it for me."

And then he kissed her. Slow and reverent, like a man grateful for a gift he didn't deserve.

Her hands framed his face as she pulled him closer.

No more leaving. Only fresh starts.

Epilogue

THE SUN DIPPED TOWARD THE JAGGED MOUNtains rimming the bay, casting the hillside in a rich, velvety purple. Overhead, wispy clouds stretched across the pale blue sky, streaked with hues of pink and orange. Below, the bay around Redemption shimmered, rippling as a cruise ship pulled away from the port, bound for the Pacific. A cool breeze lifted Emma's curls, carrying the briny scent of the ocean.

Perfect. Alaska in May was hard to beat.

Footsteps crunched over gravel behind her. She turned just as Luke crested the trail, his hands tucked into his shorts pockets, his cheeks ruddy. That boyish charm—the charm that had stolen her heart when they were teenagers—still lingered in his smile, but time had sculpted something more in him. Confidence. Strength. The kind of presence that had made her fall even harder for him over the last two months.

"Hey," she said as he stopped in front of her. His blue T-shirt hugged his muscular torso and drew out the deeper shades of indigo around his irises. She hooked a finger in the waistband of his shorts, tugging him closer. His eyes flared as he leaned in, brushing his lips over hers.

"I missed you." She thumbed away a streak of dust on his cheek. "Long day?"

"Took longer than I thought, wrangling yoga mats and folding chairs for fifty guests."

Emma laughed. "Beats repairing a broken snowmobile."

"True." His familiar woodsy cologne drifted between them. "You should've seen the spreadsheet with the registration info. We're booked solid, babe. And people are already asking about next year."

"That's amazing."

"For the first time in a long time, I think we all feel hopeful. Like we're not just surviving, you know? Like we're actually building something we can sustain."

Her heart swelled. The resort meant everything to him. He had been the glue holding it all together. Holding his family together.

"I'm so proud of you," she whispered.

His smile softened, and he cupped her cheeks, his palms warm against her skin. She leaned into his touch, savoring the moment, the certainty in his gaze.

"I'm exactly where I'm supposed to be," he said.

Her breath hitched. It was hard to believe how much had changed—how they had found their way back to each other.

"The last sea lion finally swam away," she said.

"Really?" Luke looped his arm around her waist, turning them toward the water. "Guess they figured out they'd worn out their welcome."

She wrinkled her nose. "Now I miss them."

"Seriously? After all that? The noise? The smell?"

"They kept me company. The house felt less empty with them around."

He studied her for a long moment, then asked quietly, "You're not going to leave again, are you?"

Her heart clenched. She nudged his hip with hers. "Ouch."

"Sorry." He grimaced, and uncertainty lingered in his gaze.

She swallowed hard. "I'm not leaving."

His shoulders eased. "Good. Because I don't think I could handle that again."

She opened her mouth, but before she could respond, he reached for her hand. "Come on. I want to show you something."

She laced her fingers through his, relishing the steady warmth of his grip as they followed the narrow trail toward the overlook. Wildflowers lined the path, their vibrant petals swaying in the breeze.

At the clearing, Emma stopped short. She'd never get over this view. The cliffs tumbling down into rocky outcroppings, waves lapping against the shore.

"Look," Luke said, pointing.

A pod of orcas surfaced, their sleek black-and-white bodies arcing gracefully above the waves before disappearing beneath the water. Mist spouted, glistening in the golden light.

Her breath caught. "That's incredible."

Luke's voice softened. "You know, this is where we had our first kiss."

She turned to him, cheeks warming. "You remember that?"

"How could I forget?" His lips twitched. "Best moment of my teenage life."

She laughed. "You've had better kisses since then. Admit it."

"Maybe." He traced the line of her jaw with his fingertip. "But I've thought about that moment a lot over the years. About you. About us."

Her heart pounded. "Luke, what's going on?"

"Hey." He tipped her chin up with his finger, forcing her to meet his gaze. "Let me finish." He took both of her hands in his.

"I've loved you for as long as I can remember, Emma. Even when you left, even when I thought I'd never see you again, I couldn't stop loving you. And then you came back, and everything in my life turned upside down."

Tears stung her eyes. "I'm so sorry—"

"No." He pressed a finger to her lips. "I waited for you for years. And I know we still have things to figure out. I was going to wait until Christmas to do this, but I just . . . I can't."

He reached into his pocket, pulled out a small velvet box, and dropped to one knee.

She gasped, splaying her palm across her chest.

"Emma," he said, his voice shaking. He held the box open, revealing the ring. "Will you marry me?"

For a moment, she couldn't speak. Couldn't breathe. The edges of her world blurred until the only thing in focus was this man in front of her—the man she loved with every fiber of her being.

"Yes," she whispered. "Yes, Luke, I'll marry you."

Relief and joy flashed across his face as he stood, slipping the ring onto her finger before pulling her into his arms. She laughed through her tears.

"I love you," he murmured against her hair.

"I love you too."

And then he kissed her—not like that first kiss, hesitant and unsure, but deep and certain, filled with the unspoken promise that whatever came next, they would face it together.

Forever.

Thank You!

Thank you so much for reading *The Long Way Back to You*. We hope you enjoyed the story. If you did, would you be willing to do us a favor and leave a review? It doesn't have to be long—just a few words to help other readers know what they're getting. (But no spoilers! We don't want to wreck the fun!) Thank you again for reading!

We'd love to hear from you—not only about this story, but about any characters or stories you'd like to read in the future. Contact us at www.sunrisepublishing.com/contact.

Read on for more of the

WELCOME TO
REDEMPTION, ALASKA

series

Return to Redemption for Jude and Caroline's story in *The Last Mile Between Us.*

Where broken hearts come to heal.

Some hearts are worth the risk of breaking twice.

Caroline McGuire returns to Redemption, Alaska to prove herself as the town's new physician assistant. Haunted by a teenage mistake, she's determined to rebuild her reputation and keep her heart safely guarded.

Then Jude Mercer shows up injured at her family's resort.

Six months ago in Colorado, they shared an incredible night—and a kiss that made Caroline believe in possibilities. Then he ghosted her without explanation. Now the suspended biathlete needs her medical expertise, and Caroline must treat the man who already broke her trust once.

Jude came to Redemption to rehabilitate his scandal-wrecked career and avoid emotional complications. But facing Caroline again forces him to confront his pattern of running when things get real. This time, the stakes are higher—her professional reputation hangs in the balance, and his athletic future is slipping away.

When a medical crisis threatens everything they've both worked for, Caroline and Jude must decide: Is protecting yourself worth losing the person who could heal all your wounds?

A story about second chances, professional redemption, and finding the courage to trust again.

 One

JUDE MERCER HADN'T PLANNED TO TORCH HIS career in front of the television cameras, a panel of veteran judges, and bleachers packed with devoted fans. Cheating had always gotten under his skin though. And this time had been no different. Yeah, okay, maybe he shouldn't have confronted Myles Griffin at the finish line. But what was he supposed to do? Let him leave the venue and destroy the tiny device tucked in his ear? Jude was ninety-nine percent certain Myles had used it to communicate with his coach during the biathlon. He hadn't been about to overlook the blatant illegal activity.

But somehow in his quest to make things right, their interaction had gone horribly wrong. Myles had walked away unscathed. Well, mostly. And Jude had gotten suspended. Unsportsmanlike conduct, making allegations without proof, and creating a disturbance detrimental to the competitive environment.

A week had gone by, and the whole mess still made his blood boil.

And a trip to Alaska to film a commercial hadn't eased his frustration one bit. He stood inside the doorway of his rental cabin in Redemption, Alaska, and stared through the screen door. A monarch butterfly dipped and bobbed over the freshly mowed lawn. Four little kids played a game of tag under a trio of spruce trees. May sunshine glinted off the metal roof of Redemption Resort's main building.

Turning away, he pawed through his duffel bag until he found bug spray, sunglasses, and his trail runners. The single-story log cabin smelled like cedar and laundry soap. He hadn't asked for much detail when he'd booked the reservation. Mainly because he didn't have the luxury of being fussy. The huge bathtub made up for the bare-bones kitchenette, but the place was rather basic. Not that he was here for the amenities. This trip was more about exile.

He grabbed his CamelBak, along with his shoes, and stepped outside. The screen door creaked and slammed behind him with a hollow *whack*.

His phone buzzed. Of course it did. He groaned. "Not now."

He fished the phone out of his vest pocket, half tempted to leave it on the cabin steps when he saw the name on the screen.

Braxton Dale.

Agent. Babysitter. Voice of reason.

Sighing, Jude thumbed the green icon, then pressed the phone to his ear. "Well? What's the latest?"

"Hello to you too," Braxton's deep baritone rumbled. "I wish I had good news."

Jude rubbed his forehead with his fingertips. "Lay it on me. Not like things can get any worse."

But the silence on the line said otherwise.

He sat on the green plastic Adirondack chair on the porch, then shoved his feet into his trail runners. He needed to move. He needed to *run*.

"The energy-drink people just bailed," Braxton said.

"High Voltage? Why?" Jude sat up straight. "I'm *exactly* the kind of guy they need representing their brand. Bold. Fresh. Not afraid to say what I think."

Braxton cleared his throat. "Right. Except a guy who knocks over a camera and nearly takes out a camera operator isn't quite the on-brand message they're looking for."

"He was in my way."

"In your way to *what*?"

"I had to get to Myles before he got to the locker room and tampered with the evidence."

Braxton sighed, a long exhale that said he'd had this conversation far too many times. "Listen. At some point we're going to have to address your unconventional conflict-resolution strategy. It's—"

"What about it?" Jude pinched the phone between his ear and his shoulder, then tied a double knot in his shoelace. "Somebody had to call Myles out."

"As the ruling body tried to point out, there's a time and a place and proper channels established to voice allegations," Braxton said.

"Whatever," Jude scoffed. "They're ignoring the cheating that's going on right under their noses. I can't pretend I didn't see that earpiece."

"At what cost, Jude? You've lost almost all your endorsement deals, and you're suspended from competition."

"Thanks for the reminder." Jude stared up at the sky and let the silence stretch. "Everybody needs to calm down. They overreacted."

"Regardless of what you think you saw, this community doesn't respond well to unsubstantiated allegations." Braxton's tone turned flat. "Myles's coach is pushing for a stiffer punishment."

Jude's stomach pitched. "Such as?"

Braxton hesitated. "I'll keep you updated if anything substantive develops."

"Okay, fine. What's next? Who else? Forget High Voltage. How about those meal-kit people? The ones that deliver straight to your door? I'd be perfect for that."

"Uh-huh." Braxton didn't sound convinced. "How about you

focus on working out, blowing off some steam, and filming that commercial."

"Braxton, wait—"

"I gotta be honest, my guy. If you don't pull it together—"

"Whoa." Jude pushed to his feet, adrenaline spiking in his veins. "Whose side are you on?"

"Yours, of course. But I'm also not kidding. You're not getting any younger. You need to behave. Get your head right."

Jude kicked a pine cone across the grass. "What's that supposed to mean? There's nothing wrong with my head."

"Really? Then how about running a race without accusing people of cheating? And what if you competed and you didn't care what other people did? You just focused on winning?"

"It's tough to ignore the competition when they're cheating."

But the line went dead. Braxton was already gone.

"And I'm always focused on winning." Jude stared at the screen, then squeezed the phone until his knuckles turned white. His hand ached, but it wasn't enough to distract him from the pressure mounting in his chest.

He wanted to hurl the phone into the woods. Instead, he popped back inside the cabin and tossed the thing onto the blue upholstered love seat. Then he unzipped his fleece vest, shrugged it off, and left it beside his phone.

Get your head right.

Braxton's horrible advice echoed in his head.

Jude might be frustrated. Misunderstood. Ridiculed.

But calling out that cheater Myles wasn't wrong.

For now, he'd focus on filming the commercial and getting back in the good graces of the public. He double-knotted the laces in his other shoe, adjusted the mouthpiece on his CamelBak, and took off down the trail the front-desk clerk had said made a five-mile loop. Perfect. He'd redirect all of his aggravation toward Myles into gutting out the next five miles.

As he jogged into the woods, a raven cawed from a tree branch overhead. The breeze picked up. Moss squished beneath his feet. Pine needles whispered with every step. The rhythm of running was familiar—like the start gate at a biathlon course, the moment before the gun went off and everything faded except his breathing and getting to the targets.

A memory stabbed through him. His dad giving him a lecture after a bad race. The same lines. The same tone. Always circling back to *You let us down, Jude.*

But what about when people let him down?

How could he win and perform at the highest level if the other competitors cheated? Between doping, cheating via earpieces, smart contact lenses, and hidden devices or using drone surveillance to spy, some days he wondered if any biathletes weren't sidestepping the rules to gain an advantage.

Some days he wondered if he should join them.

No.

He banished the thought. Biathletes were wired different. *Built different.* He didn't need to cheat to win.

He'd prove to Braxton, to Myles—to the entire competitive community if he had to—that following rules mattered. This most definitely *was not* the beginning of the end.

The trail forked. He stopped, took a sip from the tubing, then stretched his quads again. The left fork led deeper into the trees. That's what the woman at the desk said—*hill at the far end.*

Excellent.

He turned left, picked up speed. Every pump of his arms, every crunch of gravel underfoot was a push against the voice in his head: *You're not getting any younger.*

His knee twinged. Back muscles ached. More of Braxton's words looped like a bad playlist.

Behave.

He hit the base of the hill and charged ahead. Legs burning.

Lungs tightening. Sweat dripping down his back. The trail narrowed. He reached the top but barely noticed the view. Someone had built a crude bench overlooking a small pond. Wildflowers bloomed in the tall grass.

He didn't stop.

Instead, he took another quick sip, wiped the sweat from his brow, then headed down the hill.

Pebbles skidded under his shoes. He stumbled, and his stomach lurched. Arms flailing, he lost his balance. Then his body pitched forward, and he hit the ground on his left side. His hip and shoulder protested. Grunting, he clawed at the hard ground. But there wasn't a single blessed thing in sight to grab onto. He rolled like a log down the embankment.

A guttural sound ripped from his throat as white-hot pain exploded in his left quad. The world tilted, blurred, and then he stopped with a sickening thud.

He lay there gasping, limbs sprawled in the dirt, pulse thundering in his ears.

No. No. No.

He didn't move.

His leg—

Lord, please. I know we're not speaking right now, but a little help here?

Spots danced across his vision. His breath came in short, ragged bursts. The pain felt sharp and unrelenting. Different from anything he'd fought through before.

He'd faced down world champions. Outskied a herd of caribou. Come back from a compound fracture that nearly ended his career the first time.

But this?

This felt like something else.

This felt like his leg had ripped open.

There wasn't one single mention of moving back home anywhere on her vision board. Because accepting a job in Redemption wasn't even plan B.

Caroline McGuire balanced a small cardboard box on her hip and shoved the brand-new key into the lock. The deadbolt clicked. She turned the knob and pushed the door open. The hinges creaked and the smell of fresh paint and new drywall greeted her.

Moving into a small apartment above a sporting-goods store and working in the same clinic where she'd had all her well-child checkups, sports physicals, and X-rays sounded like her worst nightmare.

But she'd taken the job because it was her only offer. So now she'd smile through the pain. Pretend this was exactly what she wanted. Because there was no way she'd admit to her family that she didn't want to be here.

Her mom stopped behind her in the hallway, carrying a plastic bin filled with cleaning supplies. "Oh, look at those windows," her mom said, squeezing her shoulder. "You are going to be so happy here."

"Yeah, so happy." Caroline stepped inside, letting the box drop to the floor with a soft thud. She pulled her phone from the back pocket of her denim shorts and opened the notes app where she kept her never-ending to-do list.

"Are you taking a picture of your empty apartment?" Mom scooted past her and crossed to the windows. "Come check out this view, hon."

"I'm adding 'measure for curtains' to my list of things to do."

"Oh, don't buy any," Mom said. "We have five bins of fabric in storage. I'll make you some."

Caroline hesitated. Homemade curtains were not exactly what she had in mind.

Bright sunlight poured through four huge windows overlooking Redemption's Main Street. Outside, baskets of petunias hung from the new lampposts, their purple, pink, and white blooms spilling over the sides. People wandered along the sidewalks, stopping to chat in front of the Copper Kettle coffee shop, where the doors stood propped open. A sandwich board near the entrance advertised Mocha Moose Tracks in chalky blue letters.

Caroline's chest tightened. It was a perfect May Saturday, but the unease twisting in her stomach wouldn't let her enjoy it.

Her sneakers squeaked against the ash-gray luxury vinyl plank flooring as she crossed the room to survey the rest of the space. A granite-topped counter with space for two stools—maybe three if she bought basic ones—separated the kitchen from the living area. She peeked inside the stainless-steel fridge to make sure it had been turned on. Cool air soothed her flushed face. Exposed wooden beams stretched across the ceiling, and the gas fireplace tucked into the far wall added a cozy touch. It was a great apartment. A great opportunity.

So why did it feel like a consolation prize?

Her mom set down the cleaning supplies in the middle of the empty room and crossed to the half bath situated just off the kitchen. "I doubt the people working in the store downstairs will get too rowdy, so it should be nice and peaceful for you."

"Yeah, and Redemption Outfitters isn't opening for another couple of weeks, so I've got plenty of time to get settled." Caroline forced a smile when her mother came out of the bathroom. "Come on, let's go help the guys with those boxes."

They headed down the stairs, the echo of their footsteps bouncing off the narrow walls, and pushed through the heavy door at the bottom. Out on the sidewalk, her dad sat in his wheelchair, offering tips as her brothers Ethan and Luke unloaded the pod that contained all of her belongings and furniture from Colorado.

They wore jeans, T-shirts, and work gloves, sweat gleaming on their foreheads under the midday sun.

"Wow, look at you," a woman's voice chirped.

Caroline froze mid-step. Slowly, she turned. "Hi, Mrs. Dawkins."

The older woman stood on the sidewalk in a leopard-print cardigan that hung to her knees, a beige T-shirt, and faded black jeans. Her black slip-on shoes were scuffed, and her curls—springy and almost entirely white—framed her face like a halo.

"Did you just come from the salon?" Caroline grabbed a box from the neat stack Ethan had created beside Dad's chair.

Mrs. Dawkins patted her hair and grinned, revealing a smudge of lipstick on her teeth. "I sure did! How could you tell?"

Caroline forced herself to keep her voice light. "Oh, just a feeling. It looks good. How are you?"

Mrs. Dawkins's smile faded, her expression shifting to something sharper. "Well . . . I'm a wee bit concerned."

Caroline's pulse quickened. She braced herself.

"You've got big shoes to fill," Mrs. Dawkins said, her tone dripping with faux sympathy. "If Dr. Wallace is really retiring, are you sure you're up for it? Lots of folks think you're a little . . . well, a little too new, sweetie."

A hot flush climbed Caroline's neck, burning her ears. She could feel her family watching, their silence amplifying her humiliation. Her dad's disapproval radiated toward Mrs. Dawkins like heat off asphalt.

Caroline cleared her throat, forcing herself to meet the woman's hawkish gaze. "I graduated near the top of my class. I'm board-certified. I've done all my clinicals and gained a ton of experience. Everybody has to start somewhere, right? But I think I'll manage."

Mrs. Dawkins scraped at a pebble on the sidewalk with the toe of her shoe, her mouth pinching into a tight line. "I guess we'll see. Have a great day."

Caroline exhaled as Mrs. Dawkins turned and shuffled away.

Her mom leaned in and whispered, "It would've been nice if she'd offered to carry a box or three."

"Actually," Caroline said, "I don't want that woman inside my apartment. Ever."

Her mom gave her an encouraging pat on the back. "You handled that well, dear."

Oh, she wasn't so sure. The words clung to her, heavy and sticky. There would always be skeptics here. People who doubted her. And she certainly didn't need anyone to point out that it had taken her three attempts to get into PA school. Redemption loved its second chances, but it loved its judgment even more.

She drew a deep breath, shook off the awkward encounter, then carted her box toward the stairs.

She was halfway up when her phone buzzed in the back pocket of her shorts. Setting the box down at her feet, she swiped to answer. "Hey, Tate. What's up?"

"We've got a problem," her brother said.

"Uh-oh. What happened?"

"One of our guests fell on the trail, and he's hurt pretty bad. I tried calling Doc Wallace, but he's not answering. I'll call 911 if you want me to, but . . . do you think you could come take a look first?"

"Of course." She didn't hesitate. "I'm on my way."

She ended the call, put the box inside, then hurried back down to the sidewalk. "Bad news. I need to run over to the resort. Can you carry on here without me?"

"What's wrong?" Ethan asked, his brow furrowed.

"Someone's injured. Tate asked me to check it out."

"What about Doc Wallace?" Dad rolled his chair closer. "He's good about coming by whenever we need him."

Ouch. Thanks for the vote of confidence. Caroline swallowed back the terse words. "He didn't answer his phone. When I saw his wife at the post office yesterday, she said he was going fishing today."

Mom took a bottle of water from the portable cooler she'd brought along. "But I thought you didn't start until Monday?"

"You're right, my official start date is Monday, but that doesn't matter. If someone needs help, I'm not going to blow off Tate's request."

Luke tossed her his keys. "Take my truck. Your medical bag is still in back."

"Thanks." She caught them, then jogged down the street to where he'd parked.

Caroline climbed into the driver's seat of Luke's truck, double-checked that her bag was still wedged behind the passenger seat, then started the engine. She adjusted the rearview mirror, checked for traffic, and pulled out onto Main Street.

Redemption unfolded around her like a postcard, picturesque and vibrant. Sunlight shimmered off the bay to her right. Emerald-green water rippled in the breeze. Two kids stood on the sidewalk in front of the bank, licking ice cream cones that were already melting. One of them tilted his cone too far, and a chocolate scoop plopped onto the pavement. He froze, staring at it for a moment before bursting into laughter, his friend joining in.

On the bike path that ran parallel to the road, a couple pedaled bicycles. A golden retriever on a leash trotted beside them, its pink tongue lolling. The scent of fresh-cut grass drifted through the open window as she passed a roadside park where a man walked with a tiny, energetic dog on a neon-green leash. The dog barked at a flock of seagulls that had gathered near a picnic table, scattering them into the air.

Wildflowers bloomed along the edges of the road, splashes of yellow, purple, and white standing out against the deep green underbrush. In the distance, mountains rose up from the sea, their peaks capped with patches of snow that hadn't yet melted.

She tightened her grip on the steering wheel, her thoughts spinning as she turned onto the gravel road that led to the resort.

The crunch of the tires on the loose stones was a familiar sound, one that tugged at memories of growing up here—lazy summer afternoons exploring the trails, bonfires in the field, and the way the air always smelled like pine and saltwater.

But today, none of that offered comfort. Her stomach churned as she replayed Tate's words in her mind. Someone was hurt. Badly. Sure, she'd trained for emergencies. But this wasn't a clinical rotation under a mentor's watchful eye. This was real. And it was on her to help.

As she approached the resort's main building, she spotted clusters of guests outside. A family gathered at one of the picnic tables on the lawn. Three kids played with a Frisbee while the adults unpacked a cooler. Two young couples unloaded luggage from the back of an SUV, their friendly banter filtering toward her.

Caroline parked the truck in the closest open spot and grabbed her bag. Slinging it over her shoulder, she hurried toward Tate, waiting for her with an ATV parked near the end of the building.

"He's on the trail by the ridge. Something's stuck in his leg."

Caroline's chest tightened as she climbed onto the ATV behind him. "Who is he? Do we know?"

"Elite athlete. He's here filming a commercial. Guess he decided to go for a run."

When they reached the ridge, Caroline grabbed her bag and rushed toward the injured man. He lay sprawled in the dirt at the base of the embankment, his body twisted at an awkward angle. A jagged stick jutted from his thigh. Blood trickled from the wound and soaked the fabric of his shorts. Dust clung to his skin, and bits of grass and dirt marred a scrape along his left arm.

His CamelBak lay on the ground beside him, and the drinking tube rested on his shoulder. His T-shirt was damp, and his shoes, which looked expensive, were scuffed. His chest rose and fell rapidly. Grunting, he flung his arm across his forehead. Was he in shock or just agony?

Then her eyes locked onto his, and everything inside her froze. No, it couldn't be. The last time she'd seen him, he'd made a hasty exit out of her life in Colorado.

Well, he wasn't running today.

"Jude," she whispered.

His stormy hazel eyes flicked up to meet hers, pain darkening their depths.

"You're the last person I expected to see," he said, his voice tight. Chagrin rippled across his pinched features.

Her resolve faltered, her memory replaying a montage of how he'd looked at her that night in Colorado. And the way his lips had brushed against hers, slow and deliberate. She also remembered the silence that had followed. For days, weeks, and months.

"Yeah, well—" She hesitated. "I'm your best hope right now."

His eyes lingered on hers. Something unspoken flickered behind them. An apology, maybe? Or regret?

It didn't matter. Her hands shook as she tugged on her disposable gloves. She'd already learned the hard way that Jude was lousy at apologizing.

Acknowledgments

I'm so grateful for the many people in my life who make this writing journey possible. I spend a lot of time working at home by myself, writing day after day one word at a time. But the production of a book requires a team effort so this novel wouldn't exist without the following:

To my husband Steve I couldn't write a single word without your unconditional love and support. For years, you have graciously shared me with a lot of fictional friends and never complained. And you've cheered me on when I was certain I couldn't keep going. Thank you. I'm blessed to call you mine.

To our three boys, thank you for the laughter, the hugs and most of all your love. I hope watching your mom chase her big dreams inspires you to chase your own.

To my mom, Nancy, I'm certain you're my biggest fan. Thank you for always being in my corner, helping me find new readers and praying without ceasing. Your faith journey and commitment to the Lord is my inspiration. Thanks for the many memories made in Alaska. I wouldn't trade my childhood for anything.

To my sister, Heather, and her family, thank you for being a loyal reader and telling your friends about my books. I know how much Alaska means to you and I hope you love this story as well.

To Lisa, Wendy, and Linda Jo, our chats are the best! Thank you for the laughter and the prayers. I'm so glad we've been able to encourage each other week after week and month after month. You are a blessing.

A big thank you to my awesome extended family for supporting my writing dreams and celebrating my successes.

Steve Laube, you're an extraordinary human and an awesome literary agent. Thank you for your tireless efforts, encouraging words and your sense of humor. Your professionalism is unmatched and I'm proud to be a part of your agency.

Susan May Warren, a thank you hardly seems adequate for all you do. You've invested tirelessly in the lives of other writers, set an incredible example for us to follow, and challenged us to put forth our best effort every time we write a book. Thank you for helping me make this story shine!

To everyone at Sunrise Publishing, thank you for your phenomenal efforts to get our books out into the world. You rock!

About the Author

Heidi McCahan writes uplifting inspirational romance novels set in small towns. She is the bestselling author of sixteen books, including *Her Alaskan Family* and *A Baby in Alaska*. A perfect day for Heidi includes a cup of good coffee, dark chocolate, and reading stories with happy endings. She makes her home in North Carolina with her handsome husband, three amazing boys, and the world's greatest Goldendoodle.

Heidi enjoys connecting with writers and readers, so please visit her website at HeidiMcCahan.com.

PUBLISHERS WEEKLY BESTSELLING AUTHOR

Heidi McCahan

Welcome to Redemption, Alaska
WHERE BROKEN HEARTS COME TO HEAL

Stories of loss, healing, and the courage to embrace life's messiest and most beautiful second chances.

We solve the problem of what to read next.

It's time to come Home to Heritage

"*A heartwarming and inspiring story of second chances, renewed faith, and the enduring power of love.*"

—SUSAN MAY WARREN
USA Today bestselling author

We solve the problem of what to read next.

Created by New York Times bestselling author

RACHEL HAUCK

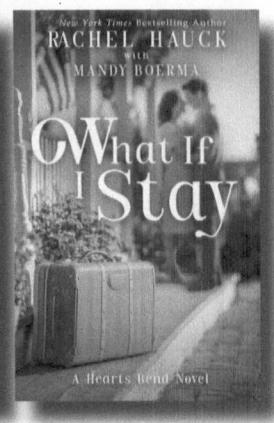

Welcome

Home to Hearts Bend

for sweet stories of romance,
faith, and happy endings.

We solve the problem of what to read next.

YOU MAY ALSO LIKE...

When Noah Hebert inherits the struggling Blue Pirogue Inn, he must solve a puzzle left by his grandfather to save it from his family's nemesis, Isaac Bergeron. Teaming up with Elisa Bergeron, the café manager and his rival, they must navigate family feuds—and unexpected sparks—while racing against time.

Where I Found You **by Besty St. Amant**

Working together to keep Fox Bakery from going under, Robin and Sammy find that something more than friendship is simmering between them. But will Robin follow her old dreams back to the glamor of Paris, or will she discover how sweet it is to be loved in Deep Haven?

How Sweet It Is **by Andrea Christenson**

Dani Sullivan is determined to revive Jonathon Island's fading charm and reunite her fractured family. Her plan? Reopen the Grand Sullivan Hotel. But without the funds to restore the hotel, Dani's forced to accept help from Liam Stone—a big-city hotel developer whose sleek, modern vision is everything she's trying to avoid.

Meet Me at the Grand **by Lindsay Harrel**

We solve the problem of what to read next.

WHERE EVERY STORY IS A FRIEND, AND EVERY CHAPTER IS A NEW JOURNEY...

 Subscribe to our newsletter for a free book, the latest news, weekly giveaways, exclusive author interviews, and more!

---

follow us on social media!

 @sunrisemediagroup

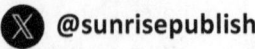 @sunrisepublish

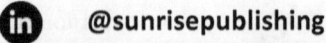 @sunrisepublishing

Shop paperbacks, ebooks, audiobooks, and more at
SUNRISEPUBLISHING.MYSHOPIFY.COM

www.ingramcontent.com/pod-product-compliance
Lightning Source LLC
LaVergne TN
LVHW040044080526
838202LV00045B/3481